The Waterfront Way

SWEET ROMANCE & WOMEN'S FRIENDSHIP
FICTION

HILTON HEAD ISLAND ROMANCE
BOOK SIX

ELANA JOHNSON

feel good fiction

ELANA JOHNSON

ISBN-13: 978-1-63876-276-8

Chapter One

S age Grady finished with her last appointment of the day and spent a half-hour cleaning up after herself. With the floor at her station pristine, and her tools sanitized and ready for tomorrow's haircuts, Sage left the upscale salon and sank into the driver's seat of her car.

A sigh likewise sank through her, and Sage started the car to get some air moving. It wasn't really too hot yet, as it was still February in Hilton Head, but it wasn't cold either. She just liked having some movement, so she didn't have to inhale the stale, stiff air that had been trapped in the car for the past eight hours.

She wasn't heading back to the apartment tonight, because her Supper Club was meeting to work out their schedule for the rest of the year. With holidays and vacations and people moving in and out, their schedule had been up, down, and around too. Most of them had switched months for one reason or another, and therefore, Cass had texted last

1

week to say they'd just be meeting at a restaurant to go over their schedule for the rest of the year.

It, of course, could still change, and they'd all go with it. Sage felt like she was the one who could step in and accommodate anyone else's changes, for she didn't do anything.

She walked her dog in the morning. She cut hair all day. She went home. Sometimes, when she was feeling particularly rowdy, she'd then change into a swimming suit and go down to the beach or lounge by the pool.

Yeah, Sage was a real party animal.

Her life felt as stale and stiff as the air she wanted to move around, and not for the first time, she missed her hobby farm in Texas. No two days were the same on a farm, and at least she'd had some variety in her life.

She couldn't even imagine life without her five best friends in it, but they'd all moved on without her. Even Bessie was engaged now, and that left Sage as the eleventh wheel whenever they all wanted to get together for a party, a beach day, or a holiday meal.

She'd been told to bring Thelma, her sister, over and over, and that was fine. Of course she'd bring Thelma as her "date," but while she loved and lived with her sister, she was a poor substitute for a man.

Sage finally put the car in reverse and backed out of the spot where she'd parked behind the salon that morning. She had a few minutes to run into the grocery store and get a few things she and Thelma needed, but she drove on by. "Can't leave milk in the car during dinner," she reasoned.

She arrived at Bakersfield, the chosen restaurant for that

evening, with twenty minutes to spare. After she'd parked in the shade several rows away from the entrance, she pulled out her phone to check it.

Nothing exciting, as usual. A couple of texts from her sister was all, and even her Supper Club thread had been quiet all day. Cass or Bea would probably make them all say something they didn't want to say, and Sage ended up leaning her head back against the rest and closing her eyes.

In quiet moments like these, she let her thoughts roam freely, go wherever they wanted to go. She often thought about starting her own salon, though that idea never stuck around for long. She had a good setup at The Salon Mionic, and she made good money there. Enough to get her and Thelma out of the apartment they rented, but neither of them had wanted to pack up everything they owned very badly.

They were oceanside, and they had all the amenities of great apartment living. True, the space was small. She had to go down several doors to get to the laundromat, which she shared with everyone on her side of the building. But they had sand volleyball courts—not that she played. A pool— which she sat beside but had never been in. A game room she'd walked through once.

She and Thelma mostly worked, then came home. One of them made dinner, and they watched TV at night. Thelma liked to take her walk in the evening, though Sage really didn't know how she could breathe such hot air in the summer. She got up at five-thirty to take Gypsy out, and after the short rough patch with

Ed had been smoothed, she'd resumed walking with him.

His dog never tripped her again, and Sage's thoughts moved to the most taboo of topics—Tyler Parker.

She'd been out with Ty exactly once. She'd cut his hair a few times too, but after the concert in the park during Heritage Days, she hadn't seen him again. Here and there, briefly, if their friend groups happened to overlap. He was friends with all of the men that had captured the hearts of her Supper Club friends, but he claimed to be too busy for holiday parties or sit-down meals for twelve.

She honestly wasn't sure if they would've been good together or not. One date certainly wasn't long enough to know that, especially as they hadn't been able to talk for a large percentage of it. Still, she remembered the awkwardness and second-guessing that had happened for her, because it sure hadn't seemed like they had much in common.

She thought of Bea and Grant, and they didn't love all of the same things either. Heck, Oliver and Bessie were like night and day, and they'd figured things out. Perhaps Sage just needed to get together with Ty again and see if that fizzing, boiling chemistry between them still existed.

She opened her eyes to check the time, and she realized she was almost late. She grabbed her purse and headed for the entrance of the restaurant.

Inside, she found everyone except Bessie had arrived, and the power blonde who'd opened her own bakery for the first time last year entered only a half-minute later.

"We're all here," Bea said as she stepped over to the hostess station.

The woman there nodded, collected six menus, and said, "Follow me."

Sage generally hung back in times like these. She didn't want to be the first at the table, because then she'd have to make a decision about where to sit. Number two, in a booth situation—which Bakersfield had—she'd have to climb in and slide all the way over, never to get out again. She'd much rather be on the end.

Her wishes came true, and she sat on the end of the horseshoe-shaped booth as she took her menu. "I've never been here before," she said, taking in the appetizers and salads first. The conversation went round about who had, and it turned out only Cass had been here before.

Of course. The prices on this menu weren't cheap, and Cass seemed to have more money than any of them. Whether that was true or not, Sage didn't know. She didn't keep books for her friends.

"The burrata is amazing," Cass said. "So is the calamari."

"Look at that salad," Bea said, leaning closer to Sage. "It has balsamic *and* ranch dressing." Her blue eyes rounded with wonder. "I think I'm going to get that."

"It looks like a souped-up wedge," Sage said, reading the menu. Candied pecans, bacon, avocado, blue cheese, craisins. "I'm getting that too." Her mouth watered, and anything she ate here would be a far cry better than the granola bar she'd eaten between clients at mid-day.

A waitress arrived, and they put in their drink and appetizer orders. She'd only taken two steps away from the table when Cass said, "All right, ladies. Let's get the hard stuff out of the way."

"We're all really boring now," Lauren said from the middle of the booth. She'd recently cut her dark hair, but it still fell to her shoulders. Sage smiled at the new do, because she'd done it, and she thought it fit Lauren's face so well. She had delicate bone structure and pure beauty in her high cheekbones.

Sage had thinned her hair too, and she looked much more glamorous now—in Sage's opinion.

Lauren caught her looking and said, "Unless Sage has something to tell us," with her eyebrows raised.

Sage laughed and waved her off. "Sage does not."

Bessie's engagement was about a week old, and the whole story had been told over an app that recorded video instead of text. They'd been using that a lot more lately, and while Sage didn't entirely dislike it, she didn't like it either. She couldn't check a quick text at work if it was a thirty-second video others might be able to hear.

And she could face the music, even if none of her friends could. None of them talked for only thirty seconds. Bessie's engagement story had taken about thirty *minutes* to get through from beginning to end.

Then all the reactions...

Sage usually played the videos in her car on the way home from work, or around the apartment if it was her turn to put together dinner. She and Thelma were simple eaters, and neither liked spending too much time in the kitchen, so eating out somewhere fancy like Bakersfield had perks.

"I know it's okay if we swap Supper Club," Cass said. "But I would like to get a schedule ironed out. I feel like if we don't." She paused and looked around the table at the rest of them. "It'll be too easy not to do it."

"I agree," Joy said. "And I want to keep doing it. It's way easier if I have it on my calendar, so other things don't get scheduled over it."

"Mm him," Bea said. "So where are we?"

"February was supposed to be mine," Cass said. "But I swapped with Lauren in November. Things have sort of been off since then."

Sage didn't argue, though she'd been assigned December last year, and she'd fulfilled her commitment just fine, busy holiday season and all.

"Joy, you're usually after me," Cass said. "Can you do next month?"

"Yep." Joy had her phone out, and she started tapping with her thumbs. She looked up. "Do we need to revisit the date?"

"Third Thursday?" Bea asked. "That's always what we've done."

"Yes, but we don't operate under the community center guidelines anymore," Cass said. She looked around again, and Sage didn't care what day of the week Supper Club fell on. Her life could be completely molded around it, even if they decided to make it a lunch club instead of dinner.

"I'm fine with whatever," she said. Bessie and Joy nodded, and Lauren said, "Me too."

"Let's leave it there," Joy said. "I'm in March."

"That puts Bessie in April," Cass said, actually reading from a small piece of paper that looked like it had come from a child's notepad. "Lauren in May, Sage in June, Bea in July, and I'm in August." She looked up, but Bea was already shaking her head.

"Grant and I are going on our National Park road trip all of July," she said. "I won't even be here for Supper Club that month, and I can't host it."

"August?" Cass asked, her lips only pursing for a moment.

"Yeah, I can do August."

Cass made the note on her slip of paper and looked up again. "Everyone else good?"

"Yeah," and "Yes," and "Sure," came from the others. Sage simply nodded, and since she'd already chosen what she wanted for dinner, her gaze wandered out into the restaurant. Everything gleamed in the evening light, and Sage sure did like the upscale atmosphere here.

The chatter at the table turned to less serious things than their Supper Club schedule, and to her surprise, no one called for them all to share something that month.

The drinks came; orders got put in; appetizers arrived. Sage laughed with Bea, asked about Shelby, her step-daughter, and listened as Lauren talked about a surgery her cat had to have.

She loved these ladies, and she'd been supping with them

for so long, she couldn't imagine not having this monthly occurrence in her life. That was why she'd moved here. It was why she'd given up the variety of the hobby farm and left it all behind.

"Oh, boy," Joy said, and that drew Sage's attention across the table to her. She sat on the end on the other side of the horseshoe, and she met Sage's eye before nodding out into the restaurant.

Sage followed her gaze, wondering what she was looking for. It became obvious when she spotted the deliciously good-looking man in a full suit—slacks, jacket, white shirt, tie, and shiny wingtips.

He smiled at a woman who had dark hair—like Sage— and placed his hand on the small of her back as he pulled out the second chair at a table for two. Then Tyler Parker rounded it and sat across from her, in plain sight of Sage. If he'd look up and to his left the teensiest bit, their eyes would meet.

Her gaze flew back to Joy's. "What's 'oh, boy' about that?"

"It's Ty," Joy hissed, and hissing was never good. It drew the attention of Bessie at Joy's side. And Bea at Sage's.

"What?" they both asked.

"Ty's here," Joy said loudly, practically bellowing the man's name. *That* was "oh, boy."

Sage leaned forward, her eyes narrowing. "Joy."

"Oh, it's Ty," Bea said. "Were you...? Didn't you guys go out?"

"Once," Sage said. "And it's fine. It's not like I never see him." But the truth was, she hadn't seen him again. Not really. Here in there across a crowded room or beach full of people didn't count.

Her heart pumped out extra beats as she looked over to him again. He was too handsome for his own good, especially when he smiled and tipped his chin toward the ceiling as he laughed.

As he brought his head level again, he looked past his date, and his eyes landed on hers. Instant heat roared through Sage as the smile slipped from his face. He was the picture of calm, cool, and collected, as he leaned in and said something to his date.

"Stars in heaven," Joy breathed. "He's getting up."

"He's seen us," Bea whispered.

"Why are you whispering?" Lauren asked. "What's going on?"

Ty indeed had risen to his feet. He buttoned his jacket as the dark-haired woman turned their way. Sage didn't know her, but Bessie said, "Sugar and salt, that's Katherine Tallison."

"Who's Katherine Tallison?" Sage asked, wondering why she'd decided to whisper too. Probably because all six feet of the sandy blond god name Tyler Parker was walking her way, his eyes fastened to hers and no one else's.

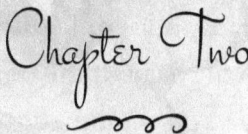

Chapter Two

Tyler Parker wasn't sure why he'd just abandoned Katherine. Maybe because it felt like his body was made of steel and Sage Grady's a very powerful magnet. He was simply drawn to her, and he couldn't resist the pull between them.

Her hair looked like she'd washed it and let it air dry, as it curled softly over her shoulders, and on the one date they'd been on, she said it did that if she let it do whatever it wanted.

Their drinks hadn't come yet, and his mouth felt like he'd been chewing on cotton since he'd picked up Katherine. He glanced around at the drinks and appetizers on the table where Sage sat with her friends, finally able to take his eyes off her.

"Hello, ladies," he said pleasantly. He tucked his hands in his pants pockets, his eyes going right back to where Sage sat on the end. "Sage. It's great to see you again."

All six pairs of eyes focused on him, and Ty felt them weighing him down. Oh, and another female pair behind him. He had no idea what he was thinking, coming over here. He should've ducked his head and texted Sage later.

He missed her, plain and simple, and he recognized those feelings as he stood at the head of the table.

"You too, Ty," she said diplomatically. Her eyes traveled up to his hair. "I see you've found someone else to cut your hair."

That was the worst thing she could've said to him, because then he wanted to tell her why he'd stopped coming to her for a trim. The words sat right there in his throat, but he couldn't get them out. Just like the text inviting her out to dinner again had sat on his phone, unsent for weeks before he'd finally deleted it.

Something foamed between them, and it wasn't until Bea asked, "Are you seeing Katherine?" that Ty could pry his eyes away from Sage's.

His first inclination was to laugh, but he merely let a smile grace his face. "No," he said. "Sage, could I speak to you for a minute?"

She blinked rapidly, and Ty could understand why. He'd taken her to a concert in the park. Held her hand. On his side of the equation, he'd had a great time. Something wasn't exactly right, but he couldn't pinpoint what that night, and in the months since, he hadn't been able to either.

She hadn't texted him much afterward, and to be honest, he figured she wasn't interested. Fine, if he was being totally honest, he hadn't wanted to press the issue, because he knew he wasn't ready to be dating again.

But it had been a little over six months since the Heritage Festival and their first and only date, and his heart and mind were in a much better place now.

"Go on," Bea hissed at Sage, practically pushing her out of the booth. She stumbled right in front of him, and Ty reached out to steady her. Even at fifty-three years old, he felt like someone had poured popping candy into his bloodstream.

Everything fizzed, and white noise buzzed in his ears. Sage smelled sharp, like her salon, and soft, like the perfume he fantasized about her dabbing behind her ears. He kept his hand on her elbow as he turned his back on Katherine even more.

They walked away from the booth of her friends, and Sage moved her arm enough for Ty to get the hint that he better drop his hand. He did, and when they'd moved away from everyone and stood in front of an empty table, he said, "I'm sorry I never called you after the concert."

Regret pulled through his very core, and now that he wasn't constantly thinking about Gloria and if he'd made the right decision in finally ending things with her, he definitely felt more ready to open the door to another woman.

"I...I wasn't in a good place." He cleared his throat, the sparks racing through him like a meteor shower. He really wanted to try again with Sage, but he wasn't sure he'd get another opportunity with her.

"I appreciate you saying so," she said. "I don't want to keep you from your date."

Ty gaped at her, then let a bit of light laughter come out of his mouth. "Sage," he said. "I'm not on a date with Katherine."

"No?" Her eyebrows went up. "It sure looked like it."

"She's a client." He shifted his feet, suddenly too hot. "Well, a potential client. With a lot of money." He raised his eyebrows too, hoping to get across his point without having to say it.

Sage's face melted into a smile, and she nodded slightly. "Ah, I see. You're wining and dining."

"Something like that," he said.

She reached out and brushed something from his tie. "I didn't get a dinner at a fancy spot when I needed help finding somewhere to live." She smiled and ducked her head at the same time, and Ty wasn't too old to recognize flirting when it came his way.

"I can fix that if you're not seeing anyone."

Sage looked straight at him now, and she simply gazed at him. "Are you in a better place?"

"Yes," he said. "I think I can probably tell you about where I was." He swallowed, though he hoped she hadn't noticed the slight hitch in his voice. "If you'd like to know."

"Ty," a woman said, and he didn't have time to turn fully before Katherine eased into his side. "She's asking for our order." Her eyes landed on Sage too, and Ty suddenly wanted to shield her from the eyes of Katherine Tallison.

"Yes," he said, ducking his head as Katherine slipped her

arm through his. "I'll call you, Sage." He held her eyes for another moment, clearly asking for her permission.

She gave the slightest nod of her head, and that allowed Ty to turn and go back to his table with Katherine. He settled into his seat as he unbuttoned his jacket. "I'm sorry," he said to the waiting waitress. "I'd love the surf and turf, medium rare." His eyes wandered just over Katherine's right shoulder, where he saw Sage settle back onto the end of the bench seat in the booth.

Immediately, her friends leaned in, and she began talking to them. He didn't particularly like that, but he'd been the one to walk over there and interrupt their dinner. He'd stolen her away for a few minutes.

He couldn't even remember what he'd said to her, and as Katherine cleared her throat, Ty focused on his task for tonight: get her to sign a contract of intent.

"Sorry about that," he said. "She's a friend I haven't seen in a while."

"A friend, hmm?" Katherine wore a look of supreme interest, her right eyebrow higher than her left.

Ty gazed evenly back at her. "Yes, she cuts my hair."

Katherine's eyebrows settled down, and she placed both arms on the table. "Tell me about her."

He shook his head and gave a light laugh. "She's just a friend."

Katherine checked behind her, and Ty took the opportunity to glance over to the table of Sage's Supper Club ladies. "She seems like she has good friends." He hurried to pull his gaze back to his own table as Katherine faced him again. "I'd love my daughter to have friends like that."

"There are a lot of good men and women who live on this island full-time," he said.

"How long have you been here?"

"Over twenty years," he said easily. "I like it in the summer too, when all the tourists are here."

Katherine gave a laugh that screamed false in Ty's ears. He'd worked with a lot of people over the years, and he could read them pretty well. He himself had fake-laughed and falsely smiled through plenty of conversations and situations.

He was honestly tired of it.

Thankfully, the fried calamari Katherine had ordered arrived, and that provided enough of a distraction for her to allow the conversation to die for a moment. It wouldn't matter, because he'd have to come up with the next small-talk topic anyway.

Another glance over to Sage found her looking at him, and when his phone chimed, he plucked it out of his breast pocket. "Oh, this is my mother," he said. "Give me five minutes?"

"Of course, dear," Katherine said.

Ty didn't need to step away from the table for the second time to text his mother back. But he took his phone and turned away from the table, away from the booth where Sage sat, and went back toward the waiting area in the restaurant.

Your daddy got a new dog, she'd said. As Ty tried to formulate a response, a picture of the puppy came in. The tan fluffball seemed to be smiling at him, and Ty grinned back at this phone.

Wow, he typed out. *I thought he said he was too old to get another puppy.* As he waited for his momma to text him back, he quickly started another text string to Sage.

What's your schedule like this weekend? Are you still walking on the beach in the morning? Would you have time for dinner?

"Can't send her three questions," he told himself. He jammed his thumb on the delete key and watched the words disappear from his screen. He also didn't need to hover in the lobby to text Sage. It wasn't now or never.

So why did it feel like it?

LATER THAT NIGHT, TY STOOD ON THE BALCONY that extended his bedroom closer to the sea and let the night air brush his face. He loved the sound of the waves in the dark, because they roared on whether there was sunlight or not. He couldn't see them, but he sure could hear them just fine.

A feeling of contentment warred with the slip of unrest in his soul. "You got Katherine to sign the letter of intent," he told himself. He should be happy.

He *was* happy.

But at the same time, he was utterly lonely. Sage had not texted him, and in the end, he'd messaged with his mom for a few minutes about his father's dog, and then he'd returned to the table just before dinner had arrived.

He'd managed to charm Katherine enough with stories of the dog, his parents, and the upcoming beach volleyball tournament out on Carter's Cove, a sister island to Hilton Head. Ty did sell some properties there. Not many, as there were no cars allowed on the island. Only golf carts, scooters, or small motorcycles. Everyone had to take a ferry to get there, and most homes stayed in families for generations.

Still, Blake Williams, one of his good friends here on Hilton Head, had asked him to help his ex-wife sell her tiny, two-bedroom home on Carter's Cove last winter, and Ty had done it gladly. She'd relocated to Hilton Head, and Ty had gotten her into a small beach cottage that would serve her needs.

He knew Sage got up early, but he wasn't sure he could go to sleep without following up with their conversation. "You get one question," he muttered to himself. He stayed on the deck and thought through his options.

He could simply invite Sage to dinner. Or ask if he could go walking with her in the morning. He'd kept running with his dogs, but he'd never seen her again.

Outside, his dog nosed his hand, startling him enough to yank it away. "Hey, bud," he said to the golden retriever. "What should I ask her, huh?"

A simple dinner request felt stupid to him. He couldn't take her back to Bakersfield, not right now at least. He couldn't just show up and get a haircut. Could he?

He moaned and leaned against the railing, straining to

see the tips of the waves in the dark. Without a moon, though, such a feat was impossible. "I'm too old for this to be so hard," he muttered to himself. "Come on, Brother."

After the dog trotted back into his bedroom, Ty followed him. He reached for his phone, ready to ask Sage the one question he had for her. His thumbs flew over the screen, and he practically punched send so he wouldn't second- and third-guess himself.

A sigh moved through his whole body as he sank onto the bed. Brother jumped up and joined him and Sherman, the black lab who'd already leaned up against the pillows next to where Ty slept.

"All right," he said as he lay down and reached over to turn off the lamp. "I guess we'll see what she says in the morning."

Chapter Three

～⚬～

S age had entered the tossing and turning stage of her sleep cycle. It seemed like she could get four or five good hours of sleep. Dead-to-the-world sleep. Then, she had to get up to go to the bathroom, and once she came back to bed, she got very little true rest after that.

Sure, she'd doze off here and there, only to wake when her arm had fallen asleep or her back hurt. Sometimes, she got up and slept on the couch for an hour or two, and that allowed her to get more rest.

Tonight, or rather, this early morning, she reached over and picked up her phone. She silenced it when she went to bed, because sometimes Kayla texted, and her daughter lived in a time zone three hours behind Sage's.

She didn't have any messages from her daughter, but she did have one from Ty. She could see the first four or five words without opening it, and she read, *I had just gotten out* before she tapped to see the whole thing.

Squinting, she tilted the phone away from her, the brightness of revealing the whole text a little too much for her. She eased the phone back into her field of vision and blinked rapidly, hoping to get her retinas to adjust faster.

I had just gotten out of a long-term relationship, he said. *I wasn't really sure if I was ready to date again, and I apologize that our first date suffered because of that.*

Part of her expected another message to come in. Right now, as if he'd just sent this and would be typing more. But he'd sent it only a few minutes after ten p.m., which was five hours ago now.

She let the phone fall to her chest, and she closed her eyes as darkness enveloped her again. He hadn't asked her out again. He hadn't mentioned running on the beach. He'd said he'd call, and then he hadn't. He'd texted.

Now confused and tired, Sage turned onto her side and put her phone back on the nightstand. Ty was a problem to be dealt with in the daylight.

By the time dawn rolled around, Sage had a bunch too, and she'd managed to sleep a little more. She dressed and leashed Gypsy, then went to meet Ed for their morning beach walk. She wouldn't tell him about Ty. She couldn't imagine what she'd even say.

She could tell Thelma later that day, or put it on the Supper Club string and see what everyone else thought. As Sage walked, ate breakfast, and drove to the salon for a full day of clients, she didn't do any of those things. She simply kept Ty in her thoughts as she cut, colored, and blow dried.

Once she got off at the salon, she once again found

herself in her car, switching up the AC so it would blow harder. She stared straight ahead, looking at the trees beyond her windshield.

Everything in her life was so boring. She needed to stuff sticks of dynamite into the cracks and then blow everything up. "You could do that with Ty," she whispered to herself.

It would take a few texts, and she felt certain she could have another date with him. As the blessed AC finally cooled and started to waft across her face, she realized she didn't want a date.

She wanted to start as friends. She needed a friend to do things with—wild and crazy things. Scuba diving. Whale watching. Sneaking onto a private yacht for a wealthy person's wedding she didn't know.

Smiling at her imagined reckless behavior, she picked up her phone from the cupholder. *It was a little awkward,* she typed out. *I'm not sure why, but maybe because of that. I'm sorry it didn't work out with whoever you were seeing before.*

Statements. Facts. No questions.

She'd thought they had nothing in common, but maybe he had been more reserved than usual. Sage had lived in Hilton Head for almost a year now, and she'd barely done any of the touristy things she and Thelma had joked about.

She'd be fifty next week, and perhaps she and Ty could... hang out. A semi-scoff burned in her throat. "Fifty-year-olds don't hang out," she muttered to herself.

Still, her thumbs seemed to have a mind of their own as she typed out another message to Ty. *Once upon a time, you said you wanted to be around for my fiftieth birthday. If that's still true, I've had my eye on this whale watching tour, but I've never done it. I need a friend to go with me. Could you possibly clear your schedule next Thursday and come with me?*

She'd been planning to take the tour with Thelma, but her sister didn't particularly like boats. She'd be fine if Sage said she had someone else to go with. Thelma probably wouldn't even ask any questions.

Sage thought she better at least check with her first, so she quickly sent a text to her sister while she waited for Ty to respond. He did own and operate a very busy real estate firm here on the island, but she knew his phone operated like a third hand.

I found someone else to go on the whale watching tour, she sent to Thelma. *So you're off the hook! Is that okay?*

Oh my goodness, I was just going to text you! Thelma said. *You know that medical supply guy I've told you about? Reid? He just asked me out!*

For next Thursday, so I was going to try to beg out of it. I can tell him no. It's your birthday.

Relief sang through Sage, her fingers flying now. *That's great, Thelma! And remember, we're having the birthday party on Friday, at Bea's new place.*

She and Grant had wanted—and needed—a bigger place to host all of her kids when they came to visit. So they'd just bought a bigger house on the island, and it would fit the twelve of them for dinner easily.

Right, Thelma said. *So I'll go with him. Who did you get to go with you?*

Ah, the question of the hour. Sage didn't want to answer

it, because she didn't really have anyone confirmed yet, as Ty hadn't answered her. Just then, his reply came in, and he said, *Sure, that sounds fun.*

She couldn't really read the emotions behind that text. It could be nothing, like, *Sure, I'll go.* Or it could be something more like, *Sure! I'm so glad you asked, and I can't wait to see you again.*

Sage really should write romance novels for how romantic she wanted things to be in her real life. She wanted fun, flippant, quick-fire, back and forth texting sessions that made her heart pound and her smile fill her whole face.

She wanted someone to see her, pay attention to her, and be absolutely thrilled to see her. Her first husband had been the opposite of that, and since Sage wasn't a fussy woman, it had taken her decades to realize she was living with a room-mate, not a soulmate.

Have you been on the whale watching tours before? Ty asked.

Nope.

Which one did you book?

"Uh..." Sage couldn't remember, and she told him as much.

I'm sure it'll be great, he said. *Do you still walk on the beach in the morning?*

Yep.

Great. He added a smiley face emoji. *Maybe I'll run into you again sometime.*

He wasn't pressing for a date or the beginning of a relationship either, and Sage smiled and sighed back into her seat as she said, *Well, I hope not really run into me. But I haven't fallen again since that day.*

Good news, he said. *You know what I can't stand? When a restaurant puts tomatoes in the fridge. Don't they know—they're chefs!—that it makes them all mealy?*

Sage grinned at her phone, that flirty warmth she craved blanketing her.

And I hate biting into one. Makes my teeth hurt.

Oh, someone has old teeth, Sage teased. *Where are you eating?*

Old teeth? Someone's turning FIFTY next week.

Someone is ALREADY fifty.

I'm at RK. Have you eaten? Want to come join me? I just got a salad and sandwich, and I'm on the boardwalk. It's not too birdy, even.

"RK," Sage mused. She hadn't been there, but her GPS could get her anywhere on the island. Anywhere in the world.

And an unplanned dinner with Ty? On a night where it was her turn to feed her sister and herself?

Sounded like the complete opposite of what Sage would ever do.

Sure, she typed out. *I'm on the way.*

He was a risk she wanted to take, and Sage set her phone aside, realizing she'd have questions to answer later. That was okay. Right now, she wanted to take a step into the unknown and see if Ty Parker could save her before she plummeted to her certain death.

Chapter Four

Ty knew he was eating astronomically slow. He didn't want Sage to show up and have him be done with his food and her just starting. She hadn't said where she was, but he assumed she'd just finished at the salon. He'd texted her to get her order, and she'd texted back two terrible words.

Surprise me.

Ty had a pretty good memory, and he remembered her getting a turkey sandwich from the deli food truck at the concert, months ago. So he'd ordered her something similar to that here—with turkey, Swiss, bacon, and all the usual sandwich toppings—as well as a bowl of chili. He distinctly remembered her saying she liked that, and she'd always make a big pot when the thunderstorms rolled through Texas.

He feared it would be cold by the time she arrived, or that the sandwich would be too moist. Sitting at a tiny table with the ocean only a few feet away, the humidity had to be off the charts today.

"Hey," Sage said as Ty leaned over and took another painfully slow bite of his sandwich. In the four seconds he'd stopped scanning for her, she'd shown up. Of course.

And now his mouth was full of food. "Hey," he said anyway, but it sounded like a grunt or a belch. She smiled as she sat down, but embarrassment flowed into every nook and cranny of his soul.

He couldn't chew fast enough, and by the time he got all his roast beef, provolone, and green peppers swallowed, she'd opened the chili. "It's chili," he practically yelled at her.

She looked up, surprise in those pretty brown eyes. "I see that."

"Turkey sandwich," he said. "It's Swiss, and that's kind of a strong cheese. Wasn't sure how you'd feel about it."

"It's not my favorite," she admitted. "But it's okay." Another smile, and she tucked her hair behind her ear. "Thanks, Ty." She dug her plastic spoon into the chili first, and Ty simply watched her.

"You aren't having a big fiftieth celebration with your friends?" he asked.

She nodded, her mouth now full of food. "Mm, I am." She licked her lips, which distracted him so completely, the world around her went white for a moment. As the blue bled back into the sky, Ty blinked. "It's on Friday. You could come if you wanted."

"I'll look at my schedule," he said. "But the whale watching sounds good to me too." He wasn't sure what this was, if it was anything. Sage didn't seem like the type of woman to want to play games, or keep things too casual, or be afraid of jumping into something real. But then again, he wasn't sure what he wanted either. He was drawn to her, that was undeniable. There was something about her spirit, her kindness, and her openness that made him want to be around her, to know her better.

She was so different than Gloria, and that intrigued him.

"Yeah," she said, glancing away as she picked up the first half of her sandwich. "I'm excited for the whales."

"You've never been whale watching before?" The wind practically blew his question away, but Ty simply turned his face into it. He loved the beach breeze with his whole heart, and he couldn't imagine a better place to live, to breathe, to work, to eat.

"Nope," she said, taking the first bite of her sandwich. She didn't seem to mind the Swiss cheese—and he happened to love it. "I've lived by the ocean for years and never gone."

"Well, I'm glad I get to be your first-time experience," Ty said with a grin. Sage smiled back, and he swore it got brighter, like the sun coming out from behind a cloud. Warmth rushed through him, and it wasn't from the humidity.

Something existed between them, and he had to know if it only came from him or not. At the same time, her text had been very clear—she wanted a friend. As he watched her, he couldn't help wondering if he could be her friend for a day or two, and then quickly ease into being her *boy*friend.

As she finished her sandwich, Ty tossed his napkin into his empty basket. "So, what do you do for fun when you're not at the salon? When you're not walking on the beach or hanging out with your Supper Club?"

Sage leaned back in her chair, a smile playing at her lips. Those eyes sparkled like fool's gold, and oh, Ty could certainly be fooled into falling for her. "Well, I like to read. And I enjoy spending time with my sister. We watch movies, TV shows, crochet."

"Cooking?"

Sage laughed lightly, and Ty couldn't tell if it was the sound a friend would make when laughing, or if it held certain...flirtier qualities. "I leave the baking to Bessie," she said. "Thelma and I trade nights for dinner, but it's easy stuff."

"Define 'easy stuff.'" Ty didn't do much cooking either, and he felt like this might be a tile they could stand on together.

"All right." She settled back in her chair, the wind toying with the longer locks of her hair, and folded her arms. "I cooked a couple of nights ago, and it constituted me opening a couple of cans of beef stew that I'd put up a year or two ago —before moving here—and then making mashed potatoes. That all went in the oven until the stew was hot, and *voilà*. Shepherd's pie."

He grinned, because something about Sage required it of him. "Wow." He chuckled. "I'm not sure where I should go with that. The fact that you 'put up' cans of beef stew—I'm not even sure what that means—or that I should tease you about calling that easy."

"It didn't take too long," she said with a mini-frown

forming between her eyes. "Half-hour maybe, plus the baking."

"Mm, the baking," he said, feeling flirty inside himself. "Can't do that for too much longer. You'll sweat yourselves out of that apartment."

She laughed, but she didn't argue with him.

"I can't remember the last time I peeled a potato," Ty admitted as she quieted. "Or made mashed potatoes. That's why it sounds like a lot of work to me."

"Peeling potatoes is one of my most dreaded tasks," she said. "But we were out of the freeze-dried ones, and." She shrugged one shoulder and reached for the iced tea he'd bought for her. She took a drink, her eyes widening. "Mm, this is great."

"Best sweet tea on the island," he said proudly, as if he'd made it himself. "That's why I come here."

She glanced back toward the shack where their food had come from. "It's kind of off the beaten path."

"Just my kind of place."

Their eyes met, and Ty wasn't sure what chemical reactions had started, only that they had. He leaned toward her, but cut off his voice at the last minute, her text burning through his whole body.

I need a friend to go with me.

"Really?" she asked in the interim. "You seem like the Total Beaten Path type of guy."

He grinned at her as a round of squawking seagulls tried to drown him out as he said, "I don't know what that means."

She smiled back as she gathered her hair, which had really started to tangle, into one hand. "It means you're The Guy. The guy who knows all the best places on the island. The best biking paths, the best restaurants, the best whale watching tours." Her eyebrows went up, clearly challenging him. "Tell me I'm wrong."

He chuckled and shook his head, all she was going to get. "It's getting windy and dark." He stood and gathered their dishes and trash. She helped, picking up his drink for him when he ran out of hands to carry it with.

"Thanks," he said.

She simply smiled and nodded at him, but the attraction between them bubbled. Surely she didn't feel that with all of her *friends. Maybe she doesn't feel it at all,* he told himself as he shoved everything into a big, metal trashcan next to the main RK building.

He glanced over to Sage and took his own iced tea from her, and they started up the boardwalk toward the parking lot. His time with her streamed away from him, and he couldn't grab onto the grains of sand for anything.

"So, you'll text me the details of the whale watching?" he asked when his feet hit pavement instead of landing on wood.

"Yes," she said. "You're sure you can go? I know you're really busy."

"It's February," he said by way of explanation. "I can go." He'd do anything to clear his schedule, but he didn't need to say that out loud. He wondered what he did need to say out loud, and as Sage came to his side in the parking lot,

Ty relied on his fifty-three years of life experience to guide him.

He slipped his hand along her waist and leaned into her. He breathed, because that was a non-voluntary thing to do, right? He murmured, "It was great to see you, Sage."

Then he pulled everything back to himself, because he wasn't sure where she stood, or where she wanted him. For him, right now, that was okay.

She smiled at him and said, "Your hair is looking scruffy, Mister Big Shot Real Estate Agent." She reached up and brushed her fingers through it, the heat of her touch practically causing an inferno to blaze through him.

"Yeah?" He could throw her flirt right back at her. "I guess I better stop by and get it cut."

Sage pulled her phone from her front pocket. "I have..." She scanned and swiped. "A twelve-fifteen." She looked up. "Maybe you could come in on your lunch hour."

Once again, Ty found himself willing to cancel anything, chance anything, move anything, to see her tomorrow at twelve-fifteen. So he said, "Sure, I'll be there."

She nodded, typed into her phone, and ducked away from him. "Good to see you too, Ty." He watched her walk back to her car, nothing really moving through his head. When her door slammed, he startled and turned to get into his luxury SUV.

He practically followed her home, but that couldn't be helped, as they lived only a mile apart. By the time he walked in, the sun had started to paint rose and gold in the sky—and

Brother and Sherman were none too happy about his late arrival.

Sherman, ever the black lab drama-king, actually nosed his empty food bowl off the plastic mat where Ty put it and barked.

"Yeah, all right," Ty said as he bent to get the bowl. "Sorry, guys. It's just…" Sage had texted. She'd come. They'd been together for less than an hour, but it had been time well spent.

So well spent.

He opened the back door for Brother, then got out the raw food he fed his dogs. After mixing it with some of their dry food, he put down Sherman's bowl and kept Brother's back. His mind seemed to be like a butterfly, flitting and flying wherever it wanted—but it always came back to Sage.

She hadn't asked him about Gloria; he hadn't volunteered any more information. She hadn't said she wanted to go out with him; the meetings they were setting up couldn't really be considered dates.

So he just need to be there, be present with her, and maybe he could find himself in a more serious boyfriend role. That thought made him smile, and Ty went through his evening paperwork the happiest he'd been in months.

All because of Sage.

Chapter Five

S age waved good-bye to Ed and made the turn to go
down the sidewalk to her apartment. The sun had
come up, and it blazed over the concrete already. A sigh
pulled through Sage as she stepped inside, despite the
blasting air conditioning.

"Morning," Thelma said, and Sage gave her a quick
smile. Yes, it was morning. And the fact that Thelma was up,
dressed, and ready for work already told Sage she wasn't
getting out of talking about Ty.

She'd put her sister off last night, claiming to be tired
and unsure of what had happened. Of course, Thelma had
found something to eat on her own, and there'd be no
lasting damage to Sage's impromptu pseudo-dinner date
with Ty Parker.

Unless she considered her heart. If she truly allowed the
door to open to him again, she felt strongly that he could
take her heart into his palm and crush it.

She pushed those thoughts away, because they led down dangerous paths. As she laid in bed last night, she'd actually been excited about getting her heart broken. It sounded like a thrill she hadn't experienced yet.

And what kind of sick woman wanted to get their heart broken?

But to Sage, that meant that she'd have truly loved someone deeply, passionately, authentically. And they'd have loved her like that too, and all the angst and chaos of a breaking heart would mean she'd *lived*. She'd *finally* lived.

She felt like she'd been merely existing on this planet for almost fifty years.

She bent to release Gypsy from his leash, and he trotted over to the big, green water bowl she and Thelma kept by the pantry door.

"You're ready early," Sage said when she couldn't put it aside any longer.

Thelma patted the only other barstool at the tiny peninsula in their kitchen. "Come tell me a story." A cup of coffee sat there too, still steaming, as if Thelma had been spying through the blinds to know when Sage would arrive home.

Like that was hard. Sage did everything the same, every day. She loved and thrived on her routines—and that was exactly why she wanted to blow them all up and do everything the opposite of how she'd always done it.

She sighed as she sank onto the stool, and she took a half a minute to put sugar and cream in her coffee and stir it. Thelma said nothing, which was a feat of pure willpower, Sage knew. She'd been raising her sister for thirty years, and that fact alone had her opening her mouth.

"Ty Parker texted," she said. "We're...well, we're not seeing each other. We're not dating. I don't even know if I want to date."

"Him, or just in general?"

Sage could still feel the buzz in her fingertips from where she'd brushed his hair off his forehead last night. "I don't know." She lifted her mug to her lips and took a sip of the hot liquid that always seemed to soothe her.

"I need a change," Sage said, and truer words couldn't have been spoken. A flare of light, of life, filled her, and she looked over to her sister. "Yeah, I like Ty Parker, but I'm not sure he's the change I need. But I need something."

Thelma looked at her with worried eyes. They'd been through a lot together in the past year, and Sage had worked hard for her whole life to erase the look on her younger sister's face. "Maybe we should look for a house," she said.

The light within Sage grew, and she nodded. "Yeah, I think that's a good idea." She took another sip of her coffee. "I won't be able to walk Gypsy on the beach in the morning if we move."

"So you'll find a group of grandmothers to go with," Thelma teased, nudging Sage with her elbow. Sage smiled, but the gesture didn't sit long on her face. Their eyes met, and Thelma added, "Sage, I'll be okay on my own again. Really."

Sage brought back the smile, and it felt very much like one her mother would've worn once-upon-a-time. "I know you will be, baby. I know that." She brushed Thelma's bangs to the side, but her sister turned away, her eyes dropping to her nearly empty coffee cup.

She got to her feet and went into the kitchen. "Should I make eggs for breakfast?"

Gypsy heaved himself up from where he'd been lying in the living room and came over, clearly understanding the word "eggs."

"I think someone wants you to," Sage said dryly. She let Thelma get away from the conversation about her abusive past by cracking eggs and scrambling them up for the three of them. But when she returned to the barstool with breakfast, Sage looked at her. Really looked.

"So we'll both look for a place. I don't want somewhere small. I want—I want—" She wasn't sure what she wanted.

"Paint the picture, Sage," Thelma said, which was an echo of what Sage used to say to her growing up. She'd dropped out of college to finish raising her siblings after her mother's death, and Sage hadn't had any idea what she was doing. Whenever one of them had a hard time talking, she'd simply tell them to paint her a picture.

She closed her eyes and saw her hobby farm in Texas. "I want chickens," she said. "And a big yard for Gypsy to run around in, and of course, I'll have to teach him not to chase or eat the chickens." She smiled, because she could just see her big, black dog galloping around an acre of green grass.

"I want the quaintness of a well, but I don't really want a well."

"Too much work," Thelma murmured, and Sage

nodded. She wanted to open her eyes, but then the picture would disintegrate, and she wasn't finished yet.

"I want a little barn, where I can do refurbishing projects, and I want a big long driveway, so I can hear someone's tires crunching over the gravel before they get there. I don't need a lot of animals like I had in Texas, because I don't want to go back to Texas. I want to be able to get to the beach and go walking there, or sit with my friends, or hear the ocean. But I want...*space* to grow into who I'm supposed to be."

Thelma's hand curled around Sage's, and she took a breath and opened her eyes. She picked up her fork and took a bite of her eggs. "Really good," she told her sister.

"Garlic salt," Thelma said back.

They smiled at the routine conversation, and Sage realized she didn't want that to change. She just needed to have more room to find her own brand of happiness. "It seems like I'm going to have to talk to Ty again," she said. "Professionally, of course."

"Of course," Thelma said with another ducked-head smile. "I don't know how you talk to him at all."

"What do you mean?" Sage knew some of the injustices Thelma had suffered, but not everything. She'd gotten her into a therapist for that, and her sister shared what she felt comfortable sharing.

"I don't know how to talk to men," Thelma said. A bitter laugh followed, and she shook her head. "Who's forty years old, never been married before, and scared of the male species?"

Thelma was.

"Hey, honey, you have good reasons," Sage said. "And you can live with me in the new house. It just needs to be bigger."

Thelma shook her head. "No, Sage. I love you; heaven knows you're the only reason I'm alive right now, but I don't want—I don't *need*—to live with you past this." She flashed Sage a watery smile that shook her lips. "I'll find the right place for me. I know that now."

Sage couldn't get more words out past the lump in her throat, so she just nodded. A man had asked Thelma to dinner, and she'd originally said yes. But before Sage had gotten home last night, she'd canceled already with Reid.

We'll both find a new place, she thought, and yes, she'd have to call Ty. He was the best real estate agent on the island, after all.

A few minutes later, Thelma got to her feet. "I have therapy after work tonight," she said. "I'll be home a little later, okay?"

"Okay," Sage said, and she fork-waved her sister out of the apartment. She didn't have to be to work for another couple of hours, but Thelma was obviously opening the drugstore today. She'd been hired as the assistant manager, and she did have money coming in from her ex. Enough that she could potentially find something small here in Hilton Head.

"Or she can keep this apartment," Sage said. Thelma could afford the rent here already.

When she couldn't carry her thoughts, worries, and

burdens alone any longer, she did what she'd always done: She got out her phone and texted her Supper Club friends.

Bea, Cass, Joy, Lauren, and Bessie had been there for her when no one else was. Sage could tell them anything, and they'd either come back with advice, or simply express their love.

I'd like to request some extra prayers if y'all have them, she typed out, really letting her Texas roots show. *Thelma and I have decided we're going to find our own places to live...and I want to find something with a little more land.*

She sent the message, already feeling lighter. Her friends knew a couple of the least heinous things that had happened with Thelma, and she expected to get plenty of affirming messages while she went to get dressed.

They did not disappoint, and Sage smiled at all of their love and support.

Prayers incoming! Joy had said. She was probably rushing off to school this morning, and Sage would likely get a longer message that night.

Wow, your own place again, Bea had said. *Let me guess. You want chickens.* She'd included an emoji of the bird. Bea usually kept things light on the text string, but she felt things deeply and had opinions if Sage sat down with her in person.

I'll pray for you and Thelma, Cass had said. *How's she doing?* Leave it to Cass to always ask about someone, as she'd suffered her own heavy losses when her husband had died a few years back. Looking at her now, in a big, beautiful, beachside home, with a handsome husband, Sage would never guess the path she'd once trod.

She tried hard not to judge someone from the outside in, because she never knew where they'd been before. It was a strategy she'd actually learned in her stylist trainings, because she talked with a lot of people. People from all walks of life, and she'd found herself in a situation or two where she'd had to bite her tongue, hitch a smile in place, and try to finish the job quickly.

But she knew that people didn't normally say hateful things. They didn't want to be rude or disrespectful— usually. If they were acting that way in her eyes, it was usually because she didn't understand something funda- mental about them. She didn't know their past. She hadn't suffered in the same ways they had.

Her friends called her the most laid-back of them all, and she supposed she was. But that hadn't come naturally to her; she'd worked at it. She'd learned to let go of what she couldn't control.

Sort of.

"Yeah." She scoffed as she picked up her keys and put them in her purse. "This thing with Ty...you didn't even let that get off the ground, because you couldn't control it."

She had a reason for that, though, and Sage wasn't going to apologize for wanting a fairy tale love story. She'd never had one, and fifty wasn't too late to hope for one.

Oh, no, it was not.

Chapter Six

S age put her client under the dryer and said, "Let me know if it gets too hot. You'll be here about twenty minutes."

"Thanks, Sage." Debra looked up at her and took the comb from her. She had a scalp that sometimes didn't like the bleach Sage had just carefully put all over it, and she'd use the comb to scratch when it started to burn a little too much.

Sage went to clean up her station, because while Debra sat under the hot air, she had a gentleman waiting for a haircut. She'd squeezed Ty into a slot like this today, and her heartbeat leapfrogged itself at the thought of him.

She tried to deny it, but it got tiresome lying to oneself at her age. So she was excited to see Ty again. That probably had more to do with talking to him about finding somewhere else for her to live than it did actually seeing him.

Oh, and there was the liar inside her again.

"Come on over, Dave," she said to the man, and he put aside the magazine he'd been flipping through. "Something interesting in there?"

He laughed heartily, the only male in the salon today. "Right, Sage. I think I took a quiz on what type of shorts I should wear."

"Hopefully the Bermudas," she joked back.

Dave had to be close to her age, and he'd first come in with his wife. Now, he came when he could, as Martha's appointments took about five times as long as his, and no one could read teen fashion magazines for that long.

"How's Gypsy?" Dave asked, and Sage talked about her dog all day long. All of her clients knew about the black behemoth, as Sage had a picture of him and Thelma on her workstation.

"He's amazing," she said. "We're going to the bark park tonight. There's a Furry Friends meet-and-greet, and I'm trying to get him to be more social around other dogs."

"Oh, where's that?"

Sage got out the clippers and started shaving up the sides of Dave's head. They continued to talk about their pets, and within twenty minutes, his hair was fresh and ready for another month. She walked him up front, and the two girls there got him rescheduled for another appointment and checked out.

Sage went to clean up her station, her thoughts now on Gypsy. He wasn't a problem with other dogs at all; he simply had no interest in them. That seemed a little strange to her, so she had been trying to socialize him more. He didn't seem unhappy about his apartment life, but Sage still sometimes felt guilty.

By the time Ty sat in her chair, Sage had done another haircut and had her second color of the day under the dryer. "Hey," she said. Once she finished with him and the soon-to-be-cornsilk-blonde in the chair, she could get off her feet and have something to eat for lunch.

"You look busy today," he said as he leaned in and brushed his lips along her cheek.

"Seems like we're always busy when you come by," she said with a smile. He smelled like sunshine and subtle cologne, and Sage sure did like standing beside him. Without thinking too hard about it, she said, "I'm taking Gypsy to the Furry Friends thing tonight at Beach Bell Park. Do you want to bring Sherman and Brother and meet me there?"

He sat in the chair and Sage put the drape around his neck, pulling it tight enough to choke before she snapped it in place. "Oh, and Thelma and I would like your real estate prowess to help us each find somewhere new to live."

Ty had started to open his mouth, but as their eyes met in the mirror, it snapped closed. Sage grinned at him and ran her fingers through his hair. She normally only did it a couple of times for her male clients, but she couldn't stop herself with him.

He had hair the color of golden sunshine, with a hint of beachy sand thrown in. It ran like silk through her fingers, and he'd definitely let it grow a little long this time. "Going for the surfer boy look?"

"No," he said quickly. "Take me back to something

respectable, would you?" His eyes cut over to Melinda, the stylist who worked next to Sage. "I can help you with a house. You two aren't going to be living together?"

Sage pressed her lips together and shook her head. She mentally commanded herself to stop fondling his hair, and she reached for her scissors first. He did keep the top a bit longer, and she wouldn't use her clippers on it. "Do you want me to style it like I did last time? A little cream and that swoop?"

She thought he looked like a non-silver George Clooney, with a little curl in his hair that barely showed when she swept it to the right. She met his eyes in the mirror again, and she could see her delight on her own face.

"Sure," he said. He pushed himself upright and cleared his throat. "That sounds good."

She started snipping, and Sage had cut so much hair in her life, she didn't even really have to look. "Thelma and I are ready for a change," she said. "Maybe me more than her, but it's time."

"Did you live together before you moved here?"

"Nope."

"When's the Furry Friends thing?"

"It's at six," Sage said. "They're doing low-or-no-cost vaccinations and setting up appointments for spays, neutering, and microchipping. It's just for fun for us, and I thought..." She trailed off, because she wasn't sure what she thought.

"Gypsy needs to get out and see more dogs," she said. "I thought it would be good for that." That was why she and her dog would be going. She had no idea why Ty would bring his pair of canines. Just to see her?

The thought was scoffable.

But Ty did not scoff. "What time are you done here?"

She took a big breath and moved around to the right side. "Oh, probably three-thirty or so. Why?"

He sat in the chair, his eyes closed perfectly, no twitch in his eyelids at all. With the drape, she couldn't tell if he fidgeted or moved, and he sure seemed to be the picture of calm and collected. "At the risk of sounding like I'm asking you out, because I know you just want to be friends, I was thinking maybe we could take the dogs to dinner before Furry Friends."

Sage smiled, glad for once that her client couldn't seem to keep his eyes open as she cut his hair. Not all of her clients did it, but Ty certainly did, and the ones who normally wore glasses did as well.

"Sure," she said as nonchalantly as she could. "Thelma has an appointment tonight, and there's a French dip place on the way to the park that had plenty of outdoor seating. Maybe there?"

"I was going to suggest Nightingale's," he said, his eyes fluttering open. "It's amazing. Have you been?"

"Not yet," she said. "Bessie told me about it, but I can't keep the names of every restaurant in my head the way you can." She gave him a flirty smile as his eyes closed again, and Sage honestly didn't know what she was doing.

She had told him she wanted a friend to go whale watching with her. He had not been overly physical last night or today, for that matter. His words—*At the risk of sounding like I'm asking you out, because I know you just want to be friends*—moved through her mind as she finished up the top of his hair.

"All right," she said, and she stepped by him to get her clippers. As she moved back, she decided not to hold her tongue the way she might have in the past. "And Ty, it's not that I *only* want us to be friends. But I would like to *start* there, because honestly?"

She waited for him to open his eyes and focus on her. "It feels like a lot of pressure to me to jump right into dating. That's all."

He didn't grin like he'd known it all along. He didn't dismiss what she'd said. He looked at her, and after a few seconds, he nodded. "All right," he drawled out in that South Carolina way he had. Sometimes he hid the twang, but she'd heard it a few times, like right now. "Then I'll come pick up you and Gypsy, and we'll go to Nightingale's on the way to the park."

"Five then?" she asked. "It's a fast-casual place. I don't think they'll be busy that early."

"Not in February," he said, and she wondered what it would be like to live so much of her life by what month it was. She sort of did, because she saw clients on a really regular basis, but she hadn't considered the month in her prediction that the French dip restaurant wouldn't be busy tonight. Just the fact that most people didn't eat dinner at five p.m.

"Maybe we'll get the early-bird discount," she joked. "Or a senior deal."

He grinned and made a small shake with his head. "Come on. We'll not that old yet."

"Not yet," she agreed, and then she finished up his hair. She couldn't sit with him for longer than normal, because she had dye to wash out and then another cut and style to do before she could sit down.

She did walk him up front like she'd done for Dave, and she had Morgan rebook him for a few weeks. Then she waved to him and went back to work. By the time she got a half-hour to sit and eat, she had a dozen more texts from her friends.

A new place to live is just what you need, Bessie said, and Sage smiled softly at her phone. Out of all of them, she was probably the closest to Bessie. She also didn't speak up at everything, and they'd made the decision to leave the Coastal Bend of Texas in their rearview mirrors and move here after Joy had started dating her now-husband, Scott.

I'd love to come look at places with you, Bessie had texted privately. *Wyn and I obviously need a different situation as well.*

You won't move in with Oliver? Sage surprise carried her through the next message. *I thought he had a nice place.*

Yeah, but Wyn can't really afford this house.

Maybe Thelma could take it... Sage just let the words flow from her fingers.

Oh, that's a great idea! Bessie said. *Let's get together and talk through some things.*

Anytime but tonight, Sage said, feeling brave and scared all at the same time. *I'm taking Gypsy to that Furry Friends event, and Ty and I are trying that French dip place you told me about.*

Her phone rang, and Sage laughed as she answered it. "You're going out with Ty?" Bessie asked.

"Sort of," Sage said as she lifted her package of trail mix to her mouth. "It's a doggy awareness thing, and we're stopping for food on the way." Bessie might lose her mind if she knew about last night's chili and sandwich on the boardwalk. "I've told him I don't want the pressure of diving right into like, a relationship."

Bessie sat there for a moment, and Sage could admit she didn't make sense. "I said I wanted to be friends."

"You told him that?" Bessie didn't have to sound like she'd seen a three-legged hippo.

"I want my partner to be my friend," Sage said.

"Yeah, but, Sage, you want so much more than that." Bessie had erased all the shock from her voice now. She spoke with a quiet reverence, in fact, and Sage couldn't—wouldn't even try to—argue with her.

"Yes," Sage said matter-of-factly. "So we'll see where this goes. Right now, I don't have to feel so much pressure that —that we have to have everything in common, and that we have to see each other every single day, and that—I don't even know what else."

"That you have to put on makeup," Bessie said with plenty of teasing in her voice.

"Yes, that," Sage said, seizing onto it. "Or that I need to

model five different outfits for Thelma before I can leave the house." She waved her hand as another stylist came back into the break room. "I'm done with all that pressure. I just want to see if this fizzy, foamy feeling inside me when I see him can become something electric and passionate, and maybe a little naughty."

Bessie burst out laughing, and Sage's face heated as her co-worker turned toward her. Deanna couldn't be older than thirty, and she surely wouldn't understand that Sage had lived twenty-six years with a man who didn't love her.

Still, she ducked her head and lowered her voice. "So it's not really a date. We're getting some food and taking our dogs to the park. Gypsy is ambivalent about other canines, and I'd like him to be more social. The end."

If she happened to get a delicious free meal out of it, wonderful. If she happened to show up with the hottest man on the island, also fantastic.

But Sage didn't want to carry the pressure of either of those things, and this way, she didn't have to.

"So will you kiss him tonight?" Bessie asked. "I mean, if we're going all the way to naughty."

Sage smiled, but she kept her face turned away from Deanna, using her long hair to shield her from the other woman. "I don't know," she said. "I'm done making plans about this kind of stuff."

"You're done making plans?" Bessie pulled in another stunned breath. "Sage, I don't even know who you are anymore."

"Join the club," she muttered. Taking a deep breath, she

added, "This is why I'm here. This is why I'm finding my own place. This is why Ty and I are starting slow. So I can figure out what I want and who I am."

"Sage, you know who you are."

"Yeah, but...I feel like there's more for me to discover, and I'm excited to meet her."

Bessie let a beat of silence go by. "Then I am too."

Relief sang through Sage for a reason she couldn't name.

"And don't think I didn't hear you say you and Ty are starting something," Bessie said. "Because I totally did." They laughed together, and that cleansed Sage's soul more than anything else could've.

"Thanks, Bess. See you soon." The call ended, and Sage finished up her trail mix while she read the rest of her texts.

Lauren had said, *There's the cutest little house over by me, Sage. I'll have Blake tell Ty about it.*

Funny how she'd just assumed that Sage would hire Ty to find her a house. Of course she was, and not only because then she'd get to see him more often. But because he was the best real estate agent in Hilton Head, and Sage needed the very best property available so she could start her life makeover.

Chapter Seven

T y's nerves fluttered through him like a flag at the lifeguard station on a breezy day. He wasn't sure why, other than he'd never been to Sage's apartment to pick her up for a date before. He'd seen her earlier that day. Yesterday. The day before even. They'd been out before, and he'd held her hand.

Maybe it was because he wanted to get back to that hand-holding status, and he didn't know how. He did know how to knock, so he did that, and only a few seconds later, Sage opened the door with Gypsy already leashed and ready to go.

"Hello," she said brightly, and she wore a pair of shorts that went a respectable way down her leg, a striped black-and-white T-shirt, and a pouch cross-wise across her chest. "You look nice."

"I traded my white shirt and tie for a polo," he said, looking down at himself. "I didn't have much time at home." He started walking down her sidewalk, glad she and Gypsy came with. "The dogs barely had time to wolf anything down for dinner, and let me tell you, Sherman gave me a glare for that."

She laughed with him, adding, "He must be the one you were complaining about last night."

"That's him," he said. "He looks at me like I've done him a personal wrong about ninety percent of the time. The rest of his life is spent sleeping. On *my* bed." He shook his head, starting to settle into the evening.

He'd said he'd drive, and he'd parked in a visitor space just around to the front of her building. He'd put the seats down in his SUV, but even so, getting Gypsy in would be a tight fit.

"He's just bushy," Sage said as Ty raised the liftgate. "He'll fit."

"Stay in, boys," he said to Brother and Sherman, who already had their noses going. Sure enough, Gypsy jumped in just fine, seemingly unbothered about the other two dogs with their noses glued to him.

Once he and Sage had taken their seats, Gypsy put his face right over the netting keeping the dogs in the back. Brother would do that once he recognized where they were, but for the most part, he looked out one of the side windows.

"Stay back there, bud," Sage said as she buckled. "I like the net. I need to get something like that."

"Do you take him in the car often?" She drove a sedan, and Ty couldn't even picture the huge black dog in the backseat.

"Only to the vet," she said.

"Do you groom him yourself?"

"And the groomer." She rolled down her window as he got moving, because the AC hadn't started to blow very hard yet. He touched the button to turn it up, and she rolled up her window a moment later. "I'm super-hungry and hope these French dips live up to the hype."

"Super-hungry, huh? I think I remember you telling me once that you don't eat lunch at work."

"I have a snack," she said.

"What was it today?"

"Trail mix."

He made a face. "Yeah, no wonder you're hungry."

She smiled at him, something he caught out of the corner of his eye. "You don't like trail mix?"

"No, ma'am," he drawled out. "I do not. I've actually spent quite a bit of time wondering how those companies stay in business."

"Maybe like those popcorn chips you like," she said dryly, but Ty practically preened that she'd remembered a conversation from six months ago.

"Yeah," he said with a chuckle. "But those are actually good."

"We'll agree to disagree." Sage flipped her hair over her shoulder, and Ty noticed she'd braided it back on the sides a little bit. She had a *lot* of hair, and he couldn't even imagine what it would be like to wash that and then dry it.

It was pretty, with a slight wave in it, and several streaks of gray. She'd told him once that she saw no need to dye her hair, though some of her Supper Club friends had teased her about doing so.

They arrived at Nightingale's, and they met at the back to get down their dogs. Ty leashed his and said, "Brother first," to let the golden retriever down. If Sherman led, everything about tonight would be more frenzied.

Once the golden got out, he tugged on the leash and said, "All right, Sherman."

"Do you know why he was named Sherman?" Sage asked as she reined in Gypsy at her side.

"I don't," he said. "But Brother came from a little of only two—one boy and one girl. One was named Brother and one Sister."

"That's kind of cute." She smiled at him, and Ty's natural rhythm with women would be to take her hand in his. However, they had to wrangle three dogs—at least two of whom smelled some meat—and he tugged against the straining of both of his dogs.

So instead of holding her hand, he went with her to the hostess stand and said, "Evening, Glenda. Two humans, and we want to sit outside with the dogs."

"You got it, Ty."

He didn't dare look over to Sage, but he also wasn't going to apologize for knowing Glenda. Maybe he'd eaten here a time or two. They had amazing sandwiches, and the service couldn't be beat.

He finally did look over to her. "I practically live out of my car, so I know all the fastest, best places to get lunch."

"Ah, I see. I thought maybe you'd sold her a cute little bungalow on the north side of the island."

Ty paused for a beat, because that sounded exactly like something he would've done. "No," he said, the word almost shooting out of his mouth before he could curve up his lips. "But that does sound like something I would do."

Glenda finished looking at her table map, grabbed a couple of menus, and led them to a table with plenty of shade. Thankfully. Ty had lived in the South his whole life, but that didn't mean he loved sitting in direct sunlight at dinnertime.

They settled with the dogs and their menus, and Ty had only started to look for the Thanksgiving feast when Sage said, "I did want to talk to you about finding me a house." She picked up her napkin and laid it in her lap. "Should I come in and you can go over your questionnaire with me?"

Ty shifted in his seat, because he normally signed anyone he could. "Here's the thing."

"There's a thing?" Her eyebrows went up, and she leaned a little bit into the table. "Do tell."

"I've...I don't usually sell houses to someone I'm dating. It's messy, and complicated, and..." He didn't know how to finish. Saying he had a personal rule not to date clients sounded stupid. Buying and selling real estate was a temporary thing; relationships could be permanent.

"Good thing we're not dating, then," Sage said as a waitress arrived. She wasted no time putting down lukewarm glasses of water, and Sage looked up at her. "I'd like the classic French dip, and unsweetened iced tea, please."

Ty also knew what he wanted, and he put in his order of the Thanksgiving feast sandwich, and, "Diet Coke, please. Lots of ice."

The waitress—yes, Ty knew her—walked away, and he nudged Brother back a little, so he had room for his foot under the table. He looked at her, unsure how to pick up the conversation.

"Did you buy or sell for your last girlfriend?" Sage made a huge mistake by reaching for her water glass.

Ty reached out to stop her. "I wouldn't. It's not...good. Just wait for the tea."

Sage looked at his hand blocking her path to the glass, then the water, and she pulled her hand back. "Fair enough." She gazed at him, and it took him an extra moment to remember she'd asked him a question.

"No," he blurted out again. "No, I didn't buy or sell anything for Gloria."

"Ah, Gloria." She smiled at him in a pleasant way, clearly expecting him to say more about his relationship with her.

He supposed he hadn't said anything more than what he'd put in a text a couple of nights ago. "We were together for a long time," he said, a sigh pulling through his chest with the words. "Probably a year and a half? Something like that." He shifted in his chair again, these wrought-iron things not that comfortable. "I asked her to marry me. Twice." Notwithstanding the terribleness of the water, he reached for his and took a big gulp of it. A horrible moan came out of his mouth, and his face contorted in disgust. "Ugh, big mistake."

Sage didn't laugh, but her eyes crinkled as she smiled. "You were trying to hide behind that."

Ty couldn't deny it. "A little." He wiped his mouth with his napkin, which only made his lips drier. "She didn't wear either ring," he said. "Told me no twice, but she wouldn't break-up with me. I ended things with her last summer, about oh, a couple of months before the Heritage Festival."

Sage nodded, her expression softening. She finally reached over and covered his hand with hers. Finally, that skin-to-skin contact he'd been craving. He expected flashing lights and sirens and an electric kick—and he got all of that and more.

"I was married for twenty-six years to a man who never loved me." Sage pulled her hand back, and Ty wasn't fast enough to turn his and grab on to stop her. "I didn't think —I'm ready to meet someone new," she said. She went to tuck her hair behind her ears and realized she'd braided it out of the way.

"But I don't think I knew what I wanted, and when our first date was...sort of dry, I maybe wrote you off when I shouldn't have."

Ty didn't like hearing that the date was dry, but they'd gone to a concert in the park. It had felt safe to him at the time. He'd met her there, bought her dinner from a food truck, and enjoyed the band.

But she was right, there hadn't been much time for talking or getting to know each other.

"Fair enough," he said.

"I just have to say," Sage said. "I want the whole shebang."

Ty grinned at her, hearing the Texan in her. "The whole shebang? Care to elaborate a little more? Are we talking about the house?"

She shook her head, her eyes sparkling, but her expression somehow also remaining serious. "Not the house. The romance. I want a man to sweep me off my feet. Take me on grand adventures. Kiss me like I've never been kissed. I've never had the fairy-tale romance, and I want it." She tried to tuck her hair again, failed again, and finally put her hands in her lap. "It might sound silly. I'm almost fifty, but...I want it."

"Ah, down here in these parts, we call that 'everything and a side of grits.'" He grinned at her, and she beamed back at him for a moment, filling his world with her sunshine. When she laughed, it sounded carefree and so, so happy.

Ty realized then that he himself could use some romance. Some grand adventures. Some kissing like he'd never kissed before. He could use some of her laughter, some of her happiness.

He'd dedicated his whole life to work, and what had it yielded him?

Certainly not the kind of carefree joy currently pouring from Sage.

Brother sat up as the food arrived, and Sherman joined him. Gypsy raised his head, but otherwise, he didn't seem to notice a very big plate of delicious meat had just arrived.

"You feed your dogs from your plate," Sage said.

"Judge away," he said good-naturedly.

"I would never." She acted like he'd insulted her in the worst way possible, and then she fed Gypsy a bit of roast beef. "All right," she said. "Moment of truth." She picked up her sandwich and dunked it in the au jus, really soaking up the sauce with the bread.

Ty couldn't look away from her. She made him feel so alive that he hadn't even realized how sluggish and dull his life had become. But she possessed an energy he didn't have all the time, and he wanted it.

She grinned as juices dripped down and she bent toward her sandwich as she lifted it up. She sank her teeth into it, really committing to a full mouthful of bread and meat. Ty couldn't remember the last thing he'd eaten with that much gusto, that much anticipation.

Sage's eyes drifted closed as she straightened and moaned. "Oh, yeah," she said around the mouthful of food. "That's good."

He laughed at the garbled quality of the words, though he still got the gist of them. He picked up his enormous sandwich piled with turkey, stuffing, mashed potatoes, gravy, with a cranberry relish instead of mayo or mustard and took an equally big bite.

He groaned too, because he hadn't had this sandwich in a long time, and it was just as meaty, tangy, and salty as he remembered.

"Can I try it?" Sage asked, revealing herself as a food-sharer.

Ty didn't normally like to share his food, but for her, he

would. He pushed his plate toward her, and she nudged hers closer to him. For her, he thought he might do anything, and he told himself to *slow down.*

She'd said twenty minutes ago that they weren't dating. He hoped he could change her mind at some point in the near future, and he'd share whatever he had to in order to stay in her good graces.

"The fairy tale romance sounds nice," he said as she took a bite of his sandwich. "I've never had that either."

Sage's eyes widened, whether from what he'd just admitted or from the phenomenal Thanksgiving-dinner-in-a-sandwich, Ty didn't know. She set down his sandwich as she chewed, nodding along with each movement.

"That's fantastic," she said, and again, she could've been talking about the sandwich or his comment. She wiped her lips and added, "What are you doing tomorrow?"

His mind flipped for a moment. "Uh, Saturday? I don't know. You seem like you have a glint in your eye, so I think I'm free all day long."

"No open houses? House showings?"

"Nope," he said, though he hadn't checked his calendar. He'd started putting everything in a calendar about a decade ago, when he'd first noticed that he couldn't keep every little detail in his head anymore.

"Do you want to go to that new shipwreck movie with me?"

"Mm, I don't know," Ty said, really making his voice sound dubious. "That sounds like something two people would do if they were dating, so…"

"Yeah," she said as she picked up her French dip sandwich again. "It does."

Ty grinned at her, but she took another bite of her sandwich. Her eyes, though... Those dazzling, almost amber-colored eyes said almost as much as her mouth ever could.

"Is that a yes to the movie?" she asked.

"Yes," he said. "It's a yes to the movie—but I can ask you out sometimes, you know."

"Oh? Is that something you want to do?"

"Yes," he growled at her. "And it's what the fairy tales are made of, so if you want that, maybe just...give me a second to breathe." He wasn't sure how she'd react, and Sage sat there, holding her sandwich and gazing at him.

Then she said, "You're right. The princess doesn't ask out the prince. Forget about the movie." She took another bite of her sandwich and put it down.

He laughed, because she didn't seem upset by his mild chastisement. As he quieted, he reached across the table and took her hand in both of his. "So, Sage. Do you want to go to that new shipwreck movie with me tomorrow?"

For a moment, he thought she'd say no. Then she squeezed his hand and said, "I've been wanting to see that."

Chapter Eight

S age unclipped Gypsy's leash, and he bounded away like
he might actually go play with another dog. After five
or six leaps, he turned back to her, his shaggy face so cute
when he smiled.

He trotted back to her, ignoring all the other dogs in the
fenced-off part of the park. "No," she said. "You go on. I'm
right here. I won't lose you."

One, there weren't a ton of black dogs here. Sure, Ty had
one, but most people had tan, beige, brown, or red designer
dogs now—doodles. Sage suspected Gypsy was a doodle too,
but she'd never bothered to figure out his breed.

Two, he was enormous. As a teeny-tiny dog sniffed his
ankle, Sage appreciated how big Gypsy actually was. He
stood to her waist, and she kept his fur long and bushy. He
hadn't seemed to mind the summers too much, but she had
been considering shaving it shorter this year.

"He's not having it," Ty said, and she sighed as she

watched his golden and his black lab frolic with several other dogs their own size.

"No, he doesn't seem to be."

Ty held his dogs' leashes in one hand, and Sage rolled up Gypsy's too. "Maybe if we walk a little, he'll just come along." He took the first step, and she fell in beside him. On the second step, he caught her hand in his.

Sage smiled to the evening sky, the beachy breeze, and the beautiful day that nearly sat behind her. She didn't dare look over to Ty, and he said nothing. His skin against hers felt warm and smooth, that of someone who worked in an office and not on a construction site.

He did make her feel something, and Sage decided she couldn't dismiss that just because they didn't have everything in common. "Tell me what you do in your spare time," she said. "Besides running and eating at every hotspot on the island." She did toss him a flirty glance then, and she found him smiling to himself too.

"Well, let's see." He sighed, and it sounded like he needed more time to come up with an answer.

When he didn't speak right away, Sage asked, "You don't have hobbies?"

"I mean, I'm not out in my back shed rebuilding furniture every weekend, no. You? What do you do in your spare time?"

"Watch TV," she said without missing a beat. "I like some of the reality shows, especially the cooking ones."

He laughed for a moment. "Okay, sounds like you."

She wasn't sure what that meant. She wanted to think

she could pick something that "sounded like him," but did she know him well enough for that? "Thelma likes to go thrifting, so I'll go to garage sales and estate sales with her."

"Thrifting," he mused. "That's a new buzzword for sure. We say it in real estate like, 'Oh, you could dress up this room with a thrifted lamp for really cheap.'"

Sage grinned, her feet feeling lighter than they had all week. And for someone who spent all day on her feet, and as it was Friday, that was saying something. "There you go," she said. Gypsy wandered ahead of them, following a white doodle from the grass to the sand. Sage loved the beach in the evening, the way the water glinted with the light still trying to reach it from the Western horizon.

"I like listening to the ocean," Ty said, his voice almost getting swallowed up in the sound of the waves. "I go out on my balcony at night—that's about the only downtime I have —and I just...listen."

"What do they say to you?" Sage asked.

"I'm still trying to learn their language." He gave her a smile that seemed absolutely authentic. No masks. No mirrors. No trying to be anything or anyone but who he was.

Sage adored that, and she squeezed his hand. "Sounds lovely. I do like the beach."

"So you want a beachfront property?"

She laughed, the sound simply flying from her throat. "I do," she said. "Who doesn't? But I don't think I can afford that."

A round of barking filled the air, and Sage instantly

looked around for Ty's dogs. It wasn't them causing a ruckus, though he'd gone on high alert too. "Brother." He whistled, and the golden came toward him. Sherman followed, and Ty added, "You guys stay closer to me."

They did, even without their leashes, and Gypsy had decided he could roam ahead about fifteen or twenty feet, and then he'd come back. Sage smiled at him, trailed her fingers along the top tuft of fur along his head, and around her he went again.

"I'm looking for somewhere that I can...cultivate," she said. "I want a yard where Gypsy can run, where I can plant flowers and maybe even a vegetable garden. I want chickens. I want a little shed out back."

"For that furniture rebuilding," he teased.

She smiled, but no. "For my gardening tools. For the chicken feed." She bumped him with her hip. "I'm from Texas, you know."

"Oh, I haven't forgotten."

"I like being outside. I wouldn't be opposed to a little river running through the property. I don't have small kids or anything."

"A river, huh?" He probably had the listings on the island memorized; Sage wouldn't put that past him. Ty was a smart man, athletic, handsome...

She cleared her throat and focused. "I want two bedrooms, minimum. Two bathrooms. I don't want to share with my friends when they come over for Supper Club. And of course, I need a decently-sized dining room and kitchen."

"For the Supper Club."

"For the Supper Club," she confirmed. "My kids probably won't come too often." A sense of missing moved through her, because she did love her children. "I have three. Have I told you that?"

"Once," he said. "A boy and two girls?"

"Two boys—neither is married—and a girl. Kayla is married. She and her husband have a little boy, and they live in Santa Fe."

"Yes, that's right."

"My boys are still in Sweet Water Falls," she said. "They're cowboys. Work a farm there."

"So the outdoors runs in your blood." He wore a smile in his voice, and Sage liked that.

"That it does." She turned her face into the breeze, relieved when it cooled her face and pushed her hair back. "I love reading beside the pool." She opened her eyes and looked at him. "Just one thing you love."

He gave her a dubious look that melted away after a moment. "I love watching the sunset."

"I love reading romance novels."

He chuckled and steered her around a couple of dogs in a sniffing chain. Gypsy walked on by, his nose oblivious to other canines. For the first time, Sage thought he might be anosmic—unable to smell.

"I like to watch documentaries," he said. "Sometimes, if I'm early to something, or I just want to be alone, I'll get lunch and eat it in my car while something plays on my phone."

"You're early to things?" she teased. "You told me you

ran late a lot."

"It's an occupational hazard," he said.

They fell into silence then, and Sage didn't mind at all. Ty led her over to the corner of the enclosure, and they faced the water. He slipped his arm around her waist, and she leaned into his chest, feeling like she really belonged there.

He got to listen to the waves as the sun went down, and Sage found two more things they had in common, for she enjoyed watching the last rays of light bleed from the sky and trying to figure out what the ocean was saying to her.

"Should we go?" he finally whispered, and Sage nodded. He whistled for his dogs again, and Sage didn't have to look far for Gypsy. Despite his name, he sure didn't wander. At the gate, she clipped on his leash, and she let Ty drive her back to the apartment with only the radio on low and the panting of dogs as background noise.

"So I'll start looking for something," he said as he walked her around the corner of her building. "But you and Thelma should come in and we'll fill out the Perfect Property Survey."

"Okay," she said. Her feet ate up the distance to her door quickly, and she turned to face him. "Thank you, Ty. This was...really great. I had a fun time."

"So did I." He gazed down at her. "So the movie tomorrow. Do you have brunch plans on Sunday?"

She wanted to stop the smile that curved her lips, but she wasn't fast enough or strong enough to do so. "No," she said. "Who has brunch plans on Sunday?"

He laughed, his head tilting back a little as he did. "Well, we can, if you'd like to go. If you want a day off from me, that's okay too."

"I think I could stand to see you for brunch," she said. "But let me talk to Thelma, okay?"

"Of course." He leaned toward her, and Sage's heartbeat banged like a big steel drum. Was he going to kiss her? Would she let him?

His lips brushed her cheek, moving from near her nose out to her ear. "I sure do like you, Sage," he whispered, his lips practically catching against her earlobe. "You...rev me up and then calm me down in a very good way."

Excitement pranced through her, because she wanted to be good for someone. She wanted to make a man's blood flow hotter. She wanted to have every good thing a passionate, loving relationship had to offer.

"Good night," she whispered, and then she slipped away from him by opening the door and letting Gypsy trot in first. She stepped into the apartment too, and then turned back to him, offering him one more smile she hoped told him that she'd let him kiss her next time.

Then the door closed, and Sage twisted the lock and leaned her back against it. She felt nineteen again, with her first hot and handsome college boyfriend, instead of forty-nine-about-to-turn-fifty trying for a second chance at happiness.

"How did it go?" Thelma asked as she came down the hall. "Oh, you're leaning against the door." She stopped and folded her arms, her silky pajama pants still fluttering after she'd paused. "Look at you."

"What do I look like?"

"Like someone is falling hard, even though you told me you weren't dating him."

"Things change," Sage said as she pushed away from the door. "And I'm not falling hard. He's doing everything right." She grinned as she approached her sister. "I'm not moving too fast, am I?"

"Who cares if you are?" Thelma asked. "Sometimes, you just know. Sometimes, it just feels right."

Sage nodded, because that was something she'd told Thelma once-upon-a-time. They'd said that when they'd decided to move here. Of course, Thelma had needed to get out of Texas—and truth be told, so had Sage.

She missed the farms and cattle ranches sometimes. She craved a good Texas thunderstorm. She loved being outside with the hills, the puffy white clouds, the feeling of home surrounding her. But she wanted a patch of land here in Hilton Head, not Sweet Water Falls.

Ty would find her one, and then Sage would be able to start living a new way of life. As she went down the hall to her bedroom and changed into her pajamas, she murmured, "The waterfront way."

A completely new, reimagined and reinvented version of the Sage Grady she'd been for so long. She'd be the same woman—only better.

Chapter Nine

S age grinned at Ty with all the wattage of the sun beaming from her. "I can't believe I'm doing this." She clutched the railing on the boat and tried not to picture herself falling overboard. "I'm a little scared of boats."

"You're a little scared of boats?" he repeated. "And we're going whale watching—out on a boat in the open Atlantic —for your birthday?" He looked aghast. "Why? Are you trying to prove something?"

She wasn't, and she shook her head. "I genuinely thought it sounded fun."

"And now?"

"Now, I'm a little worried it might not be so fun."

Ty took her elbow and gently coaxed her away from the edge. "Let's sit in the middle until we get further out."

"All right, folks," the tour guide said. "You can stand anywhere on the boat but the bottom and the top of the steps. There's a yellow square marked off, and we don't want anyone to stand there, ever. There are seats up front, in the back, and along the sides. Sit, stand, move around the boat. This is your tour."

Sage sat heavily on a long bench seat still near the edge of the boat, and Ty plunked down next to her.

"We have a bit of a drive out to where we've gotten some reports of a humpback out here, and that should be exciting."

"We should see a lot of dolphins too," Ty said. Sage reached for his hand, glad when it was easy to slide her fingers between his and hold on. She didn't normally get seasick, and she just needed to calm down. Take a couple of deep breaths and settle her stomach.

All that undulating water below... She shouldn't have looked over the edge, that was all.

"I heard there might be some right whales around still," she said. "Or moving back north."

"We've also seen some right whales in the past few weeks," the tour guide said as if spurred on by Sage's comment. "But nothing this week so far. Today might be our lucky day, though."

Sage really wanted today to simply be a great day. She didn't need luck; she didn't even really need to see whales; she just wanted to feel like she was turning a new page. Starting a fresh chapter, now that she'd turned fifty. Embarking on a new journey.

So of course she'd booked something she'd never done before. She'd told herself she might like boating in this new phase of her life, and as the vessel started to move, she didn't feel like throwing up. She felt like celebrating.

Ty had not kissed her after the movie and lunch on Saturday. Nor after brunch on Sunday. She hadn't seen him on Monday, Tuesday, or Wednesday, but her fingers felt a bit stiff for how much she'd texted him in the evenings.

Now, today, she wondered if her new, exciting, adventurous life started with a kiss on the first page. She'd never been one to rush into anything. She didn't mind taking her time and learning the ropes, where to put her feet, and how to do something. Ty had been playing all of his cards right this second time around, and Sage suspected that might be because of her attitude about the whole thing.

She'd come at it differently. Instead of expecting things to be a constant stream of sparks and heat, she'd wanted to relax into a warm bath. Things could heat up from there—and they certainly were. She also felt the sparks and heat between them, and she only had to lean in closer to Ty to say something to him to know he did too.

"I really like dolphins," she said, his head bent very close to hers.

"Are they your spirit animal?" he teased.

She shook her head, her hair brushing her forearms, and the wind doing so hard enough to make her shiver. "No," she said. "But I like how they look happy, like golden retreivers."

"I like them too," he said.

"And we've got a pod of Atlantic bottlenose dolphins already with us," the guide said. "On our left side, near the front, about two o'clock. Don't everyone rush over there now. They move back and forth."

All Sage had to do was gain her feet to look toward two o'clock on the boat, and she did that. Sure enough, one, then two, then three dolphins surfaced, skimming along the water as they swam with the boat. Pure joy filled her, and she leaned into Ty's arms as he encircled her.

"Mm, you're warm," she said.

"It's windy today," he practically yelled above the wind, the splashing of the water agains the hull, and the chatter of those around them. "They're amazing, aren't they?"

The dolphins—there had to be six or seven of them—darted in and out of one another, almost like they had an underwater obstacle course only they could see. One kept his fin above the water, but nothing else on him, and two of them seemed to like coming out of the water every few seconds.

Sage could watch them all day long, but eventually, the captain turned south, and the dolphins receded away from the boat.

"Coming up here," the tour guide said. "We've had reports of a humpback. We don't see them all that often off the coast of South Carolina, but we have had a few sightings in the past couple of decades. This one is on the register as Cyclops, and he's been here for about a week, feeding on the schools of Atlantic mackerel here right now. Of course, the humpback whale is one of the most diverse feeders..."

Sage tuned out the guide, though she normally liked what they had to say. She knew a little bit about humpback whales, and the thought of seeing one had her nerves in a pitter-patter. "This is so exciting," she said, still standing at the railing and watching the blue-gray water as if she alone would spot the humpback first.

"The humpback is a bulk eater," the guide said. "He dives down below and then comes up to get his fill, in what we call a lunge feed. But usually, he's just down there, swallowing up krill and plankton and as many fish as he can."

"A lunge feed," Sage said. "I feel like that's how I eat too." She laughed as she turned into Ty's chest. Her hands shook, and she wasn't expecting to be so cold on this tour. He wrapped his arms around her, infusing a bit of warmth into her. She didn't want to put on a show, so she sat back down, and Ty joined her.

"You don't lunge feed," he said.

"Maybe we should try it." She gave him a bright smile and went back to watching the water. The guide continued to talk about Hilton Head Island, South Carolina and the many species of fish, birds, and mammals the coastline supported as the boat moved through the water.

Several minutes later, the engine slowed, and that perked everyone up again. "So Cyclops has been here," he said. "Another tour radioed us right when we were leaving, and they'd just seen him."

A hush fell over the boat, and though the sky was blue, Sage once again experienced a shiver from the chill in the air. The wind in beachy places could never been underestimated, she supposed, and she should've packed a jacket.

She'd only brought sunscreen for this mid-morning

adventure, as well as a bottle of water, and she and Ty would get lunch once they returned to land.

"There he is," the guide said suddenly, and Sage twisted to see if he was pointing somewhere. "Twelve o'clock. He just went down, and these whales can hold their breath for up to an hour. However, he's feeding, which means he'll dive down for four or five minutes, and then come back up for several breaths. This is when we'll see him.

"Once he returns to the surface, you'll see his hump-back as he swims along, coming up to breathe. Usually they take six or seven breaths and dive down again. Sometimes we'll see the flukes when this happens."

The general atmosphere on the boat held electricity, and Sage looked at Ty. "I love this. Thank you for coming with me."

"Of course." He pressed his lips to her cheekbone again. "Would you have had just as much fun with Thelma?"

"Maybe," she teased. "But I wouldn't be as warm." She watched the water in front of the boat, and only a minute later, someone pointed. She looked; the humpback was there.

"Oh, my goodness," she breathed as she saw the spray from his spout at the same time the tour guide announced it. "There he is." She stood, and Ty came with her.

He stuck right at her side, saying, "Wow," in the same awed way that she felt.

Such a huge, magnificent animal. He did "hump" along for a few swimming strides, and the tour guide said, "There he goes, folks!" as the whale dove down, down, down, his back fins coming up out of the water.

People cheered and gasped, and Sage certainly joined them. She turned toward Ty, who wore a smile as big as any she'd ever seen on his face. "This is incredible. A humpback."

The boat stayed with the humpback for a while longer, and then they started back to the island. They didn't see anything else—no right whales, no sharks, and no more dolphins either. Sage didn't care at all.

She'd seen a humpback on her fiftieth birthday, and that was the perfect thing to start off her new chapter. On land, Ty took her back to his SUV, and he opened the back passenger door instead of the front one where she sat.

"I got you something," he said as he lifted out a pure white gift bag. White tissue paper had been stuffed in the top too, and it looked clean and crisp and pure.

"Ty," she said, but her heart was currently melting like a chocolate bar left out in the sun.

"You only turn fifty once." He gave her the bag, a handsome—if a little shy—smile on his face.

She took it but didn't immediately rip the paper out of the top of the bag. "What did you do for your fiftieth birthday?"

A frown crossed between his eyes. "I worked."

She tilted her head, sure there was more to the story. "Really? That's all?"

"I had a big client at the time." His voice lowered in volume with every word. "I, uh, maybe need some more excitement in my life too." He raised his eyes to hers. "I've been working so much, and it's all I've ever done. I've been thinking about how you said you want grand adventures, and I think—I need that too. I *want* that too."

"Ty." She didn't know what else to say, but going on a grand adventure with someone who willingly wanted to be there sounded amazing to her.

"So thank you for letting me come with you today," he said. "I've never seen a humpback before, and though he didn't lunge feed, it was incredible."

"Wasn't it?" She looked down at the bag. "Should I open it right here, or get in the car?"

He looked over her shoulder. "Okay, let's get in the car. It's kind of hot out here, even with the wind." He did open the right door for her then, and she slid into the passenger seat. While he went around the car, she pulled out the paper to find a regular-sized envelope in the bottom of the bag.

She glanced over to Ty as he got in the car. "What's this?" She reached inside and pulled it out. It wasn't sealed and it didn't have her name on it. She flipped up the flap and removed several sheets of paper.

Ty turned on the car, but otherwise remained silent. He didn't pull out of the parking lot at the marina either.

"This is a day pass to Hunting Island State Park," she read.

"It's good for twelve months," he said. "I figured it could be our next adventure."

She smiled at him, because she hadn't heard of it, and that was exactly the kind of thing she wanted to do. *He's been listening*, she thought, and that was a powerful gift too.

Sage shifted the papers, and she pulled in a breath. "This is a receipt for two nights in the historic South Charleston Hotel." She looked at him, eyes wide. "Ty."

"You can go with Thelma," he said. "It's a voucher. No dates on it. Doesn't expire, but they have to have a two-queen room for you to book it. It comes with—"

"Don't ruin it for me." Sage smiled at him and went back to the pages. She flipped to the next one, her heart beating faster and faster. "It's a food tour in Charleston."

"I've heard they're good."

"You haven't gone?"

He shook his head, and for someone who loved food as much as him, Sage knew—she'd be taking him on this weekend trip to Charleston. She wasn't sure when, and she wasn't sure how to ask him, but they'd be traveling there together, staying there together, and taking this food tour together.

"Thank you," she said as sincerely as she could. "This is all incredible."

"You didn't look at the last paper." He finally started to back out of the stall while Sage flipped to the last piece of paper in her gift.

"A pedicure." She spun toward him, somewhat surprised at his amazing gift-giving skills. "This is perfect. I haven't had one in so long."

"And for someone who works on their feet all day, making others feel beautiful and pampered, I figured *you* could use a little pampering."

She wanted to lean across the console and kiss him, but

he'd already started driving. So she grinned and grinned at her papers for a few extra second before she folded them up and put them back in the envelope.

"Thank you, Ty," she said.

"Happy birthday, Sage," he murmured, and she sighed as she sank back into her seat. He'd just given her the perfect gifts, and she couldn't wait to carry most of them out...with him at her side.

Chapter Ten

Beatrice Turner bustled around her house, checking on the last-minute details for one of her best friend's birthday parties. The table had been set for fifteen, and that included her, Grant, and Shelby.

Cass and Harrison would be here at any moment, and Cass had promised to bring the lilies that Sage loved so much. Bea had left a spot for them on the credenza that sat next to the front door.

"I love this house," she said to Grant when she went into the kitchen. He stood on a chair, currently hanging a big gold balloon in the shape of a zero next to the one of a five he'd already put up. "Oh, those are perfect on the pot rack." She smiled at the fifty, hoping Sage wouldn't feel overwhelmed by anything at this party.

She was one of the more low-key ladies in the Supper Club, something that Bea always appreciated. She could go to Sage with anything, and she'd always been met with a rational mind and kind questions. Then the best, most calm advice.

Bea knew that Sage and Bessie had deliberately saved their Supper Club, and a slip of guilt pulled through her. After all, she'd been the first to come here, fall in love, and make the twelve-hundred mile move away from her friends. Away from the life she'd known in Texas. Away from all the heartache and sorrow that she'd endured.

Sometimes she still yearned for the Lone Star State, but she wouldn't give up Grant and Shelby for anything. "Where's Shelby?"

"She went to get some ice," he said. "I definitely think there's something wrong with the icemaker in that fridge, but now isn't the time to be fiddling with it."

Bea nodded, her lips pursing a little. No, she didn't want to deal with a broken appliance either, especially not tonight. "Okay, well, that's fine. Cass should—" The doorbell rang, cutting her off. "That's probably her."

"Bea," a woman called, but it wasn't Cass. "I'm walking in."

"Come on back." Bea left Grant to finish hanging the decorations, and she went to greet Bessie. Turned out, she carried more bread than Bea thought any one human being could, and she rushed to relieve Bessie of some of the loaves.

"I come bearing butters and jams," Oliver said as he entered the house behind his fiancée. "And Cass is ten feet behind me. She might could use some help."

But now Bea's hands were full of bread. "Grant," she called.

"I'm fine," Cass said as she stepped into the house. "The flowers go right here." The vase landed on the credenza with a thump that unsettled Bea, and she turned back to make sure Cass hadn't fallen and broken a hip.

"It's fine," she said crossly. "My hands are just a little slippery." Harrison, her husband, had joined her, and Bea let them handle the flowers. They came from a nursery next to Harry's construction office, and Cass had become quite chummy with the owner. She'd taken up Lauren and Joy's hobby of gardening now that she lived here in South Carolina, and she'd gotten all of her bulbs, shrubs, and flowers from the nursery.

"Right here," Bea said, indicating the space she'd left for the bread bar. Sage had requested it specifically, and she'd wanted only maple-frosted doughnuts from Gourmet Goods for her "birthday cake."

"I have the doughnuts," Harry said as he entered the kitchen with an enormous pastry box. It was light blue, so clearly from Gourmet Goods, and he pushed it into some of the jars of jam Oliver had put down as he made room for it on the counter.

"What's for dinner?" Bessie asked.

"She said she didn't want a big thing," Bea said.

"Right," Bessie said slowly, brushing her newly cut bangs out of her face. "So...what's for dinner?"

"She catered," another woman said, and they all turned toward Lauren as she breezed into the kitchen with a sombrero on her head. She wore a bright smile to match the red, green, and yellow headgear, and Bea sputtered at her.

"I—it's not Mexican night."

"Did you or did you not order a taco bar?" Lauren put an oversized bag of tortilla chips on the blue box of doughnuts.

"That's her cake," Bea said, quickly swiping the chips off the box lest the weight bow in the top and ruin the frosting. "And yes, I ordered a taco bar. It's barely food."

Lauren's eyebrows went up, disappearing under her ridiculous hat. "Barely food? You should see how much stuff they have in the van outside then." She glanced around the kitchen, and while it was four times bigger than the house Grant and Bea had lived in previously, it still wasn't huge. "We better make some room. I told them to start bringing everything in."

"Let's put the cake over here," Bea said, nodding to the counter beside the sink. "Harry?"

"Yes, ma'am."

Grant put the chair he'd been using back at the table. "There's more room now that I'm out of the way."

"Breads first," Bea said. "Move it down to the end here, Oliver."

He started doing that, and Bessie weeded out more than half the loaves, opening the cold oven and tossing them inside. "Those are for you guys, and they don't need to be out," she said. "You can take them home later."

Bea grinned and turned her attention to Cass as she came in. "Everything good out there?"

"Right as rain." She took in the decorations, which consisted of the golden age balloons, as well as a brightly colored banner that read "Happy Birthday!" that Grant had hung across the sliding glass doors. The tableware matched that of a fiesta, and Cass's eyes landed on Lauren. "I didn't realize we were dressing up for this."

Lauren rolled her dark eyes and took off the hat. Her dark hair clung to it a little, some of it rising due to some static. "Happy now?"

"I just think a sombrero will be hard to cram in at the table," Bea said as she plucked it from Lauren's hands. "I'll put it in the bedroom." She ducked out of the kitchen to do that, catching sight of the Mexican restaurant workers coming down the hall. "Food's incoming!"

She hurried into the master and threw the sombrero, not caring where it landed. As she returned to the main part of the house, she found Joy and Scott had arrived in that split second she'd been gone. "Hey, you." She put her arm around Joy and squeezed. "How's school going?"

Joy grinned at her. "Good."

Scott had Ghost on a leash, and the dog stayed right at his side. "Is Sage bringing Gypsy?"

"The real questions is if Sage is bringing Ty," Joy said, her eyes wide and questioning.

"She told me to set her a plus-one," Bea said, not wanting to give away any of Sage's secrets.

"But that's for Thelma."

Bea put her nose further into the air. "Thelma RSVP'ed on her own."

"Oh, boy." Joy squealed. "That means she's bringing him."

"Are you Bea?" a man asked, and she took the invoice he extended toward her.

She barely looked at it, because she trusted they'd brought the beans, rice, and meat she'd ordered. She signed on the line and smiled at them. "Thank you so much."

They left, and the front door got closed for the first time in several minutes. The house smelled like spicy meat and cheese, with just a hint of maple underneath that. Bea just needed to give everyone a ten-second lecture before Sage arrived.

She didn't want them teasing her about Ty. She didn't want her relationship with him to be a big deal. She just wanted to enjoy her birthday with her friends—and technically, Sage had turned fifty two days ago. They were lucky they were even getting her to this party.

"All right, you guys," she started, but chatter had broken out in the kitchen and no one except Joy and Scott heard her. "You guys," she yelled louder.

"Knock, knock," Sage called, and Bea spun toward her. She'd lost her window to give the lecture, and as she went down the hall to greet Sage, she decided everyone knew how to act already. They didn't need her to tell them.

Well, maybe Lauren, if that sombrero was any hint at how tonight would go.

"Sage," she said, glancing over to the handsome blond man at her side. "Happy birthday, my friend." She grinned and hugged Sage, who gave some of the best hugs in the world.

"Thank you, Bea," she said in her soft, kind voice. She stepped back and indicated Ty. "You know Ty, of course."

"Of course I do. Hello." She hugged him too, and then she moved past them to welcome Thelma as well. She linked her arm through hers as they followed Sage and Ty down the hall to the back of the house. "So, do you have any handsome boyfriends hiding out somewhere?"

Thelma laughed and shook her head. "Nope."

Bea noticed Sage turn and look at her sister, but she didn't say anything. She entered the kitchen and choruses of "Happy birthday, Sage!" and "Sage is here!" rose into the rafters. Bea simply stood back and watched it, enjoying the love and friendship raining down on all of them there.

"I've got the ice," Shelby called. "Can I get some help?"

"I've got it," Tommy said, and Bea hadn't seen him in the house yet. Where he'd come from, she didn't know. He, Shelby, and Thelma made the extra three to the Supper Club women and their significant others, and Bea went to take one of the bags of ice from her step-daughter.

She and Grant had used one of the biggest, longest table from one of his rentals for tonight's dinner, so they could all sit together. She hated having more than one table, or one of different heights, and this way, she didn't have to.

"It smells like tacos in here," Sage said as Bea passed.

"It's dinnertime," she said in her defense. "You can have as little or as much as you want."

"It's a build-your-own-bar," Bessie said. "First up—bread." She grabbed onto both of Sage's hands and beaming, pulled her forward. "Come on, Sagey. I brought your favorite one."

"Yeah?" Sage laughed. "Is it cinnamon chip?"

"And you should see what's in the oven," Oliver said.

Sage gaped at him. "What's in the oven? Bess, did you bake here?"

"No, of course not." Bessie waved her off.

Oliver moved the two steps to the oven and opened it, revealing the dozen loaves of bread inside. "All cinnamon chip."

Sage blinked at the bread, then Bessie, and Bea stepped to Bessie's side. "Happy birthday, Sage. Should we sing, everyone? Then we can have cake or food or whatever."

"Yes, let's sing," Cass said at the same time as Lauren.

Grant got up on a chair, ever the extrovert who didn't mind the spotlight. With these people—her best friends and closest confidantes—Bea didn't either. Her eyes filled with tears as the fifteen of them started to sing *Happy Birthday* to Sage.

She knew Sage's life wasn't exactly what she wanted it to be. She'd been through some hard things; she worked a long and tiring job; she wanted more space and more freedom to be her true self.

She looked around, so much love for each of the women here filling her heart over and over. Then again for all of the men who'd chosen to join them, who loved her friends with such tenderness and care. For this family of hers that Bea had somehow lucked into belonging to.

And when Bea watched Ty's smile and the way his eyes

lit from within as he sang, his eyes never leaving Sage, she thought maybe, just maybe, Sage would be closer to her ideal soon enough.

"All right," she said with a clap as the song ended. "Let's eat."

"Hey, brother." Grant eased into Ty. "I don't know you were dating Sage. When did that all start?"

Bea dang near choked on her own breath. Her own husband. How could Grant say such a thing, and what could Bea do to mediate the situation?

She sensed some tension in the vicinity, and she glanced over to Cass, who'd also clearly heard Grant's seemingly innocent question. Then Ty chuckled and said, "It's really new, Grant. It's..." He looked thoughtful for a moment. "It's good. We're just seeing how things go day-by-day for right now."

"I love these maple bars," Sage yelled into the house, and Bea found her with frosting in the corner of her mouth and a big old bite taken out of one of the maple doughnuts. Several people laughed, and that seemed to break the tension.

"I guess she's going for dessert first," Ty said with another chuckle. "Maybe I should do that. Excuse me." He moved over to Sage, and both Bea and Cass stood side-by-side and watched as he slid his arm around her waist and leaned into her.

"Mm, yeah, I see how it's going for them," Cass murmured.

"Yeah," Bea whispered. "I see it too."

Chapter Eleven

~∽~

Ty sat back from his computer, his irritation starting to get to him. The air conditioning had been firing almost all day lately, and he still felt too hot. "I can't believe there isn't anything on the market for her."

It had been almost three weeks since Sage had told him about the type of property she wanted. Two or three bedrooms shouldn't be that hard to find. Two bathrooms. A yard big enough for a giant, shaggy dog and a handful of chickens. "And a shed," he said with plenty of disdain in his voice.

True, she wasn't going to get that in one of the newer plantation neighborhoods, but those communities were the opposite of what Sage would like. He knew her well enough to know that. She also wouldn't get beachfront property with land and animal rights either, and she'd been okay with that.

She'd even leaned into his chest and said, "I'll have to

come stand on your balcony to hear the waves talking at night."

That had caused quite the fantasies to spring into his mind.

He got up from his desk, because all Ty had at this point were fantasies. He still hadn't kissed Sage, and he honestly wasn't sure what he was waiting for. Since he'd told her at Nightingale's that he'd like to ask her out, she'd let him dictate every move of their relationship.

She wanted the fairy tale type of happily-ever-after. He wanted to give it to her, and that meant he had to figure out how to be a prince first. The more time he spent with her, the more he spoke with her, the more he wanted adventure in his life too.

The more he saw the nuanced colors of the sunset, which he'd never seen before. The more he saw how much he worked and how little he got from it. The more he saw the loneliness in his life—and how Sage erased it.

He paced over to his office window, which had water stains from the sprinkling system. He could focus past them, past the greening grass, and out past the parking lot too. He didn't entertain many people in his office. Usually only clients who came to fill out his Perfect Property Survey. After that, he met them in houses, restaurants, and at the lender's office to sign paperwork.

"What about Thelma?" he wondered. There seemed to be far more smaller houses available for sale right now, and he returned to his computer, a new goal in mind.

He just needed to find one house to show the sisters.

He'd like it to be for Sage, but if he couldn't do that, he'd have to take the win in another way. Thelma's file sat near the top of the stack of folders on his desk, and he plucked it out.

"Two bedrooms," he muttered. "Two baths." She had cats, and they didn't need a yard. Thelma was more reserved than Sage, and she'd looked to her older sister for a lot of the answers on the survey. Ty sensed something...scared in her, but he didn't know what, and he hadn't asked.

She'd like an attached garage, and sometimes that was hard to come by. Still, Ty should be able to find a dozen properties for Thelma, and his fingers flew over the keyboard as he typed in the requirements.

Sure enough, option upon option bloomed on the screen, and he started sorting through them by price and neighborhood. Ten minutes later, he had a list of eight homes that would be perfect for Thelma.

She'd put her number on the survey, and Ty tapped in the digits to call her. Perhaps they could go house hunting soon. Thelma didn't answer, and Ty honestly spent a lot of time talking to voicemail inboxes.

"Hey, Thelma," he said as cheerfully as he could. "It's Ty Parker. I've just gone over the system, and I've found quite a few options for you that I think will be perfect. When do you think you might be able to go look at them? If you let me know, I can start contacting listing agents and setting up showings."

He rattled off his number and ended the call. While still at his desk—he had to get out of here—he texted Sage. *Still nothing that I think is good for you, but I know something is going to come up that you'll love.*

Sage responded immediately, which was a little odd for her. She didn't carry her phone around with her at the salon, and she worked there every day except Sunday and Thursday.

I'm sure it will, she said. *People list their houses closer to summer. I think someone very smart told me that once.*

Ty grinned at her message, at the flirty quality of it, at the way she always made him feel so good about himself.

Dinner tonight? he asked. *I'm meeting a broker friend for lunch, and then I only have paperwork to do today.*

I've seen the mountains of paperwork on your desk, she said. *But if you can get away for dinner, then yes.*

There's a luau at The Heartwood Inn tonight, he said. *I know the owners, and I have tickets. It's a drive and a ferry ride away...*

I'm in, she said, and Ty leaned back in his chair, thrilled he'd get to see Sage in person that night. Sometimes she had something with Thelma. Sometimes she went to Supper Club or something else with her friends. Sometimes she just wanted to stay in.

Ty had started attending some of the dinners and parties with her friends, and he couldn't say he hated them. In fact, it felt good to be social with people who didn't talk about interest rates, the newest listing in Royal Farms, or how many houses they'd sold last month.

In fact, maybe Ty could put his relationship with Olympia Heartwood to even better use and invite along

Bessie and Oliver to the luau tonight. He had four tickets... why should two of them go to waste?

He'd rather call than text, and the only person he made an exception for was Sage. She liked texting more than calling, because she could fire off an answer or a question in the few seconds she had while a client was under the dryer or when they went to the bathroom.

But for Oliver, he dialed the man, hoping he hadn't put himself on the evening shift at The Mad Mango, the smoothie shop he owned.

"What's up, Ty?" he answered, and it definitely sounded like he was working the line at the shop.

"What are you and Bessie doing tonight?" he asked.

"I don't know," Oliver said grumpily. "Probably something for the wedding. Why?"

"I have two extra tickets to a luau at The Heartwood Inn. Thought maybe you guys would like to double with me and Sage."

Oliver sat there for a moment; someone yelled on his end of the line; then he said, "Let me talk to Bessie. I think she'd like that."

"You haven't taken her to a luau there, have you?" Ty asked, because he knew Oliver, and the man took dating very seriously. He planned the things he did with women down to the T, and Ty was convinced that was how he'd gotten Bessie to fall in love with him.

He grinned even as he thought it, because Oliver was a pretty great guy too. Grumpy, but great.

"No," Oliver said. "And she was semi-complaining last

week that she's ready for something beachy, so this might be perfect."

"It starts at seven-thirty," he said. "With the drive, the ferry...We should probably be leaving the island about six-thirty."

"I'll talk to her," he said. "She doesn't stay out late very often, and tomorrow is Saturday."

"Let me know," Ty said. "I'm not going to ask anyone else, so even if you show up at the luau and text me you're there, I can run out and get you in."

"Thanks, brother." Oliver said good-bye, and the call disconnected. Ty purposely kept his Fridays light, but he did have a lunch he needed to get to today.

Once he'd arrived at the agreed-upon restaurant, he straightened his tie and pulled down the cuffs of his jacket. Steve Hammel did a lot of business on the island too, and he even knew the neighborhoods and towns on the mainland and all the way down to Beaufort.

As Ty walked toward the entrance to Mead's, a popular place among the locals, he ran through his list of clients he was currently involved with. Sometimes people texted him to "watch for" a certain type of property and let them know if it came up.

Ty felt like all he did was watch for something to happen in his life. As he pulled open the door and got the first breath of blessed air conditioning, he wanted to *make* something happen for him. He wanted to *do* something.

"Hey," he said with a chuckle as Steve turned toward him. He didn't expect to find the other real estate broker dressed down for Friday, and he didn't. Steve wore black pants, a white shirt, and a purple paisley tie surely his wife had picked out for him.

"Ty." He grinned and man-clapped him on the back too. He held up two fingers to the hostess, and they got seated immediately. The lunch crowd on a Friday put out plenty of noise, but the booth where he and Steve sat still felt a little isolated to Ty.

"What's new?" Steve asked, even before anyone had brought water. Ty liked the no-nonsense part of him. He was probably six or seven years older than Ty, and once-upon-a-time, Ty had wanted to *be* Steve Hammel.

Have the huge house in the most prestigious gated community. Be the face of real estate in South Carolina. Have his name on the tip of every tongue whenever anything was brought up around town.

But now, seated across from him, Ty didn't feel any of that. "You know what I need, Steve? Maybe you've got a client who needs an extra push to sell, or maybe you know of a property that's not on the market yet."

Ty unfolded his napkin and put it on his lap. He could still charm people, and his charisma had won him more than one house in a bidding war. He grinned across the table to Steve, who wore that wolfish, competitive light in his eyes that told Ty he could get the information he wanted.

"I've got a client who wants to live on the island. Maybe just off of it, but not very far. But she wants chickens. A big yard for her dog. A little shed to keep her tools in for the yard, the chickens, all of that. There's nothing listed." He sighed in mock frustration, though he'd certainly been irritated that morning.

"How big?" he asked.

"Three bedrooms, two baths," Ty said as a waitress set down a glass of ice water. "Thanks." He waited until she left, and he noted that neither he nor Steve had looked at the menu. Here, Ty didn't even need one. He had it memorized.

"She's looking for something maybe even a little rundown. She's okay fixing it up. She says it'll renew her as she renews the property."

"Acreage?"

"Not specified. Enough for the dog to romp around. The chickens. Maybe a vegetable garden." He considered Steve. "Half-acre?"

Steve looked like a big black cat who'd just eaten a tiny yellow canary. "I might be able to show you something. It's not on the island, though."

Ty sat back in his seat as Steve leaned in. "How far off the island?"

"Right across the bridge."

"It's in the swamps."

"No," Steve said instantly. "But it does have some waterfront to it."

"Waterfront? Like it flooded?"

Steve pressed his mouth together, and Ty wondered what he'd find if he ever got the address from his broker friend.

"Why isn't it on the market?" Ty lifted his water to his

lips, though he wanted the peach sweet tea. "Is it going to be expensive?"

"The owner is…a public figure. Bought the land thinking it would be the next big thing, and well, it wasn't."

"Is there a house on it?"

"Yes," Steve said. "It's not quite a fixer-upper, but there are some improvements that could be made—especially along the waterfront."

Sage had told him she wanted to find "the waterfront way," and maybe a property like this would be exactly what she needed. Ty wasn't sure what she wanted to knock down, rearrange, or rebuild inside herself, but he hoped he could be at her side every step of the way.

"Asking price? My client has a budget."

"It's…negotiable," Steve said. "No one lives there, but they do have someone go in and keep the house clean and the yard looking good. You can go by anytime."

"Great." Ty grinned at Steve, already planning to stop there as soon as he finished this business lunch. "Text me the address?"

Steve already had his phone out, and Ty could usually imagine a home and property simply by seeing where it was located. "Done." Steve put down his phone and smiled across the table to Ty. "All right, my turn. I know you've got a client down in Astor Pines with a house they use maybe once a year."

Ty leaned forward now, because he knew exactly the house and people Steve was talking about. "Yeah?"

"I have a client who wants a place there. Willing to pay top dollar."

"Oh, boy." Ty laughed and looked up as a waitress finally arrived. And thank the heavens, she already carried a peach iced tea for him and a Diet Coke for Steven.

"Hello, boys," Jean said, though Ty was so far from being a boy. "Another business lunch commencing?"

Yes, it was, and Ty glanced at his phone while Steve laughed with Jean and put in his order. The address he'd been sent...yeah, this was going to be an interesting property. Ty couldn't wait to see it—and then hopefully show it to Sage.

Chapter Twelve

S age stepped onto the ferry, her feet wobbling beneath her and the ripple moving all the way up her legs. She grunted, trying to find her balance. Thankfully, Ty had his hand on her upper arm, and he nudged her forward.

"Keep going, sweetheart. You'll get used to it." He climbed on after her, his steps even and sure though the surface of the ferry shifted. It *moved*, and Sage did not like that.

She let him guide her to a seat, and she sat down hard in it, much the same way she had on the whale-watching boat. "I don't think I like boats."

Ty chuckled and took her hand in his. "No, I don't think you do. This one doesn't take long. Twenty minutes. It's on and off."

"It still moves strangely." She closed her eyes, but that didn't help. She opened them again and focused on the horizon. "This luau better be worth it."

"There they are," someone said, and Sage looked up at the familiar voice.

"Bessie," she said as one of her best friends sat down on the other side of Ty. "What are you doing here?"

"Ty has tickets to the luau," she said at the same time Ty said, "I invited them to the luau." Bessie and Ty looked at one another, and then they both looked at Sage. "I guess I forgot to tell you," he added. He put his arm around her and leaned closer. "Is that okay?"

"Well, I'm not belly-dancing in front of Bessie," she quipped.

"What?" Bessie's eyes rounded and held surprise. "What does that mean?"

"Have you seen your dance moves?" Sage grinned at her, hoping to get across the message that she was teasing. "She'll make me look bad."

Bessie caught on, and her expression softened. She smiled and said, "That's the most ridiculous thing I've ever heard. Did you know that Sage took a hula hooping class in Texas once? No one could beat her."

Sage laughed, because that had been a good time.

"The woman has mad hips." Bessie looked up as Oliver joined her, and he kissed her quickly on the mouth. "You made it."

"Barely," he said, throwing a dark look toward the entrance to the ferry. "Apparently, this thing is going to be full-full, and they almost didn't let me on."

"Mad hips, huh?" Ty murmured in Sage's ear, sending a shiver all the way down to her tailbone.

She snuggled into him despite the evening heat, and soon enough, as the ferry started to cut through the water from Hilton Head Island to Carter's Cove, the breeze coming off the ocean cooled her.

Once there, they queued up to get a ride on a golf cart of all things, from the ferry station to a beautiful, beachside inn that practically glowed in the sunset. "This is gorgeous," she said as she took in the magnificent building that seemed to grow right out of the sand.

The windows glinted like gold, and the palms looked like they didn't get beaten up by wind or storms. The golf cart took them through a circle drive, where two men in suits were directing people where to go.

"We're here for the luau," Ty said as he disembarked from the golf cart.

"To your left, sir," the man said, indicating with his white-gloved hand the path that had been marked by a sign and a tiki torch. "Around to the beach, then straight ahead." He smiled and moved to the next party, and Sage put her hand in Ty's as they started to walk.

Tonight, he'd dressed down, and she felt like they were a perfect pair. Her, in her flowered maxi dress and him in a pair of khaki shorts and a Hawaiian shirt. "Where'd you get that shirt?" she asked him now, as her sandaled feet moved from concrete to another semi-moving surface: sand.

He grinned at her. "Believe it or not, I own it."

"Did you thrift it?" she teased, because it did not look new.

"I bought it new," he said. "About twenty years ago,

right when I moved to Hilton Head permanently." He laughed, the sound flying up into the evening sky and making the colors in it seem deeper, more meaningful. "I suppose I thought I'd wear it on weekends."

"Did you?"

"Not even once."

"So now you pull it out for luaus," she said.

"That's right." The path widened, and Oliver and Bessie caught up to them. Oliver too wore proper beach attire with a pair of navy shorts and a short-sleeved white shirt. If he'd open another couple of buttons at his throat, he'd be the picture of sexy male walking the beach.

Bessie wore a palm-tree top and jean shorts, and Sage liked how they all somehow had interpreted the theme of tonight without having to communicate about it. Music met her ears, and Sage got transported right to the tropics with the steel drum beat, and the high-pitched ukulele, and the Hawaiian singing.

She gripped Ty's hand tighter, sure this adventure tonight would be the best one they'd shared yet.

AN HOUR LATER, SAGE TIPPED HER HEAD BACK and laughed as Ty caught her around the waist. He laughed with her and brought her closer, both of them in bare feet in the shifting sand. "You think that's what makes a movie good?" he teased. "If the hero is worth cheering for?"

"Absolutely," she said as she leveled her gaze at him. "If I don't want him to get the girl, why am I watching?"

He grinned and grinned at her, and she couldn't stop herself from doing it back. The moment sobered, and Sage fiddled with the collar on his loud-print shirt. "Thank you for this," she said. "It's been—" She glanced around at the other couples dancing by firelight.

Torches burned on the sand every several feet, and the waiters and waitresses cleared away the dinner dishes. Dessert had already started to be set, and she couldn't wait to taste it.

"Magical," she said.

Ty brought her a little closer, saying nothing, and Sage's heartbeat picked up speed.

"The pork was so good," she said, trying to fill the awkwardness blazing through her.. "I don't think I've ever had Kalua pork. And the shrimp." She moaned, and Ty chuckled in her ear. He lingered so close, so close, and she did everything in her power to stop herself from leaning into him further.

"I'm glad you liked it." His voice hummed through her soul, and Sage loved the vibration of it deep in her lungs.

"I so could be a fire-dancer," she said next.

"That was an amazing show," he said. "I think they're going to do an encore during dessert."

"One more dance," someone said over the loudspeaker. "Then we'll ask you to return to your seats for your final offering from tonight's luau."

Ty ducked his head and swayed with Sage now as the

music turned soft and slow. She hadn't anticipated there being a dance like this at a luau, but as she settled into his arms and into the rhythm of the song, she thanked all the stars in heaven for it. Standing in his arms was the best feeling in the world, and she pulled back a little to look at him.

His eyes met hers, and her first instinct was to thank him again. She realized he didn't need to hear it, so she kept her mouth closed. Instead, she reached up and trailed her fingers down the side of his face.

His eyes closed, and he dropped his chin. Sage had been kissed before, and she let the moment linger as her eyelids drooped as well. When his lips touched hers, the magic of the night imploded, filling her with warmth and passion and sparks.

Then it exploded, firing out in all directions until she was certain she and Ty lit up the entire island of Carter's Cove by themselves.

Sage had been kissed before, but never like this. Never with such a strong stroke that also spoke of tenderness, of gentleness, of love.

The song ended; the kiss ended; the magic faded.

Ty whispered, "We should go sit down, sweetheart."

"Mm." She pressed her lips together, sure she couldn't eat right now. If she did, the taste of him would be erased. She finally opened her eyes to find that the sandy dance floor had mostly been abandoned, save for a few stragglers about to step back onto the stone patio where they'd eaten dinner.

Part of her wanted to hurry after everyone else, so no one

would look at them. The other part of her gazed at Ty, a soft smile coming to her face. He looked back, and so many doors opened between them. She wanted to walk through all of them, and that surprised her a little. Enough to get her to duck her head, breaking their connection, and then take his hand as he turned to lead her back to their table.

"There you are," Bessie said as Sage retook her seat. "I couldn't see you, and I thought maybe you two had left."

"I would never leave before dessert," Sage said as she picked up a fresh napkin the color of the inside of a conch shell and spread it in her lap. She grinned at Bessie. "Too bad they didn't have a dance-off tonight."

Bessie smiled and shook her head. "Yeah? Would you have gotten up there?"

"Maybe," Sage said as she faced the stage again. The emcee for tonight raised the mic and started introducing the dessert on the table in front of them. "I've been...trying new things."

"Yeah, looked like it," Bessie said almost under her breath.

Sage pulled in a breath and turned to her friend. "What does that mean?"

Oliver leaned in closer too, and he muttered, "It means Bessie's a big, fat liar. She saw you kissing Ty out on the beach, and she'll talk to you about it later, because he's talking about a guava cheesecake and some of us want to hear this."

Then he straightened, gave Bessie a look out of the corner of his eye, and looked at the emcee again.

Sage's heartbeat flashed through her body as she looked at Bessie too. They both stared at one another with wide eyes, and then Bessie started to laugh. Silently, but her shoulders shook and shook and shook, and that struck Sage as funny too.

Maybe not the kissing-in-front-of-everyone thing, but definitely the way Oliver had just called her and Bessie out for not listening to the dessert ingredients.

When the emcee finally said, "Go ahead and try it," Sage picked up her dessert spoon to do just that. The guava was subtle, that was for sure, but the bright red raspberry sauce brought a tartness to the sweet cheesecake that made it perfectly balanced.

"This is fantastic," she said, looking over to Ty.

"I love the dark cookie crumb with it," he said, already scooping up his second bite. "Who knew they put coffee in that to make it richer?" He'd obviously listened to the emcee too, and Sage ducked her head and focused on her cheesecake lest she start giggling again.

So Bessie had seen her kissing Ty. Big deal. A former version of herself would've cared, but this new, adventurous woman she was becoming didn't mind. It was kissing, not something super scandalous, and Bessie didn't have to know it was their first kiss.

It had been the best kiss of Sage's life, and she couldn't wait to repeat it when Ty dropped her off later.

Chapter Thirteen

The following week, Sage washed her hands in Joy's kitchen sink, the water getting hotter than she liked. She reached to push the handle down to make it cooler as someone yelled from the front door.

Joy herself.

She turned just as the blonde woman entered the multi-purpose room at the back of the house. Living room, dining room, kitchen, with a half-bath off of it. The sliding glass doors led outside to a beautiful garden, which Lauren had once taken care of, and which Joy now did.

She and Scott had bought the house from Lauren, gotten married, and settled down into their happily-ever-after. Scott ran his landscaping business—which also kept this yard looking phenomenal—and Joy taught second grade at one of the local elementary schools. They'd been married for seven months, and Sage could still see and feel how much they adored one another.

"What are you doing in my house?" Joy had frozen, but as she spoke, she marched forward. Her school bag clunked down on the island, and she peered past Sage and into the sink. "Where are all my dirty dishes?"

She looked at the dishwasher, which had a bright orange indicator light on it, telling both of them what Sage already knew—it was doing its job.

"Sage."

"It's Supper Club tonight," she said. "And I picked up on all the cues in your texts. It's parent-teacher conferences next week, and you're already exhausted. I came over to help, because my last client for today canceled last-minute."

Joy slumped onto a barstool. "Thank you, Sage." She sniffled, and Sage simply turned and bent to open the oven.

"I got three lasagnas at Rudy's," she said. "One is Italian sausage. One is ground beef. One is a chicken Alfredo." She looked at each of them, and the two on the outside had started to bubble around the edges. After closing the oven door, she said, "They should be ready on time."

"Rudy's." Joy shook her head. "You're a life-saver."

"I love all their pre-made meals," Sage said. "Thelma and I eat them all the time."

"Scott likes their chicken cordon bleu." Joy scraped her hand through her hair, disheveling it a little bit. Otherwise, every piece of her sat in place, from her makeup to the collar on her blouse. "It'll do, right?"

"It's going to be amazing," Sage said. "Eating from Rudy's is like making it yourself without having to make it yourself."

"Cass caters," Joy said faintly.

"Which would be boring month after month," Sage fired back quickly. "We aren't all Cass, nor should we want to be." She gave Joy a very firm look and then moved over to the drawer with the utensils. "Thelma's not coming tonight, so we just need to set the table for six, and I'll save some food for Scott, and when it's almost time, I'll make up the salad."

Joy simply blinked at her with those blue eyes. "I'll switch you. When are you? July?"

"June," Sage said with a smile. "And you're not switching with me. I'm hoping to be in a new house by then." She gave Joy another knowing look and then abandoned the idea of setting the table right now.

Supper Club didn't start for another hour, at which time, the lasagnas would be melty and browned, Joy would be changed and rested, and Sage would be setting the last plate down as the first of their friends arrived.

Instead, she moved around the island to Joy and said, "Now, I know Scott won't be home for a couple of hours, and that you're tired. Go lie down for thirty minutes, then change your clothes, and come help me finish getting ready."

"Sage," she protested, but while she and Joy were only a couple of years apart in age, Sage could see her with a mother's eyes. She loved her like a best friend and a daughter, like someone she wanted to protect.

"Go on," she said. "What are you going to do out here?" She picked up Joy's bag and started across the room to the hallway. "I'll put this in your office."

This house wasn't big, but it fit Joy and Scott

perfectly. Sage deposited Joy's work bag on the desk, glanced at her friend's sewing machine, and left the small office. They had another bedroom and master bath down the hall, and they didn't need much more. They wouldn't have children together, and Joy's two boys still lived in Texas.

As Joy hugged her and then departed down the hall, Sage thought about Ty. Assuming they ended up together, married like Joy and Scott, where would they live? He had a nice house in a neighborhood that had beachfront access.

She'd never been to his house, but she knew it was close to the apartment where she and Thelma lived. He could stand on his balcony and hear the waves. Perhaps even see them. She had no idea if he had a one-bedroom bungalow or an expansive beach house.

Maybe you should ask him, she thought. He'd called earlier that day about some good news on a property he wanted to show her, but Sage had been saving it for the shares tonight. Everyone wanted to know what was happening with her and Ty, but she hoped to show them a house listing too.

Indecision raged inside her, and she quickly tapped to call Ty. His line only rang once before he said, "Hey, sweetheart."

Sage smiled at the endearment. "Hey, so, I've been thinking."

"I love it when you start sentences that way." He chuckled, and Sage turned toward the doors that would lead her into the backyard. A patio set waited outside, and she left the door cracked an inch so she could hear the timer should it go off.

"Not only that, but you're calling," he said. "Feels significant."

"I was just thinking—I haven't been to your place. Is it big? Small?" Her unspoken question hung in the air around her. *Do I even need a house? Maybe I'll just move in with you.*

Not right now, Sage told herself. Of course not. She wouldn't move in with Ty at this moment. Their relationship had been progressing, if slowly, but she wasn't to the point of accepting a house key from him.

"You want to come to my place?" he asked.

"I'd like to see the castle, yes," she teased. The breeze whispered gently in the backyard, and Sage sighed into it. "I do love Joy's place. It feels so peaceful."

"We're still going to look at the place I found, right?" he asked, some measure of alarm in his tone. "You said you could go this weekend."

"Sunday," she confirmed.

"Do you want to have lunch at my place after?" he asked. "I'll cook for you."

She laughed, the sound bordering on a giggle. She pulled it back, because she didn't want to come across as a giggly fifty-year-old. "You can cook?"

"Believe it or not, I can. I was voted best cook in my apartment in college."

"Oh, wow," she said between laughter. He chuckled with her, and Sage liked these easy conversations with him.

"So I'll grab some fresh fish in the morning, and we'll go

see the place, and then come back to my house, and I'll cook for you."

"Sounds amazing." Sage sighed as she heard the sliding glass door open. She twisted to see Lauren coming outside, and she said, "I have to go, sweetheart."

"Have fun at Supper Club."

"Sweetheart?" Lauren's eyebrows didn't rise quite as high as Sage had seen them before. She pulled out the chair next to Sage's and sat. "I'm exhausted."

"Yeah?" Sage reached over and covered Lauren's hand with hers. "Why? Is your new client keeping you up at night?"

"Tommy's new dog is keeping me up at night." She threw Sage a dry look, but a moment later, a smile accompanied it. "He loves him though, and Chloe and Oscar will come around...eventually."

Sage grinned at the mention of her two cats. "Thelma's cats love Gypsy."

"Well, Gypsy isn't a puppy constantly trying to get them out from under the bed." Lauren yawned, covering her mouth as she did. "I do love this house."

"It was a keeper," she said.

"Is the party out here?" Cass asked as she stepped outside too, and Sage turned to greet her too.

"No, we're eating inside. I told Joy I'd set the table. She looked bushed too." She retreated from the patio, afraid she might blurt out her news if she stayed. Inside, she made up the salad and pulled plates from the cupboard. She only had glasses and napkins to finish up with when the timer went off, and Sage left them for a moment to go check the food.

Everything looked browned and bubbly, and she smiled at the ooey gooey cheese on top of the lasagnas. She pushed a button to turn off the oven, and she lifted the tray out and slid it on the stovetop.

"Mm, smells good in here, Joy," Bea called, and Sage quickly removed the oven mitts from her hands. She'd taken a few steps away from the food when Bea and Bessie came around the corner from the front door, and her heart brightened with their addition.

Sage loved her friends, and she once again felt like she'd made the right move by leaving Texas behind and becoming a resident of South Carolina.

"All right," Joy said as she came down the hall leading to the bedrooms. "Who's ready for some lasagna?"

"Oh, did you get these at Rudy's?" Bea asked, stepping over to the steaming food.

Joy met Sage's eyes, hers blank. Then she blinked and said, "Yep. Yes, I sure did."

Sage didn't care if Joy took credit for tonight's dinner. She'd literally driven by a gourmet grocer and picked them out, then heated them in the oven. It wasn't rocket science.

"Did you work today?" Bessie asked as she joined them. "I thought these took a long time to bake."

Cass and Lauren came back into the house, and Cass said, "I brought wine, so I hope everyone is ready to talk." She sing-songed the last word and nudged Sage, her smile huge.

"I'm already prepared for this entire night to be about me," Sage deadpanned. A couple of the women laughed, and even Sage could admit she was ready to talk about Ty.

"In fact," Joy said, and Sage's eyes flew to hers. She shook her head, but Joy had already started to speak again. "Sage brought the food and baked it for me." Tears filled her eyes, and Sage hadn't been expecting that.

Silence poured into the room, and then Bea said, "That's so quintessentially Sage."

Her eyes volleyed over to the other blonde woman now. "What do you mean by that?"

"I mean, Sage." Bea wore the warmest, brightest smile as she moved over to Sage and linked her arm into hers. "That you always know exactly how to take care of all of us."

"I'm not that much older than any of you," she said crossly.

"No," Bea said. "But you do take really good care of us." She looked around at the others. "Doesn't she, ladies?"

"Yes," Cass said softly.

"I agree," Bessie said.

"Always," Lauren said, and Sage's heart started to swell then.

Joy moved into her and hugged her, and with Bessie practically doing that on her arm, Sage felt loved and valued. With these women, she felt seen and whole and appreciated. "Thanks, guys," she said as they all piled into one big group Supper Club hug.

As they started to break up, Joy said, "She'll tell us what she bought and baked."

Sage surveyed her friends and said, "I kissed Ty a couple of weeks ago at this amazing luau. You guys, he's amazing, and while we're both going pretty slow, I feel—he makes me feel like I'm *alive* again."

She swallowed, her throat sticking together far more than she'd like. "I feel more like myself—or this new woman I'm trying to become." She nodded, really needing some of that wine about now. "Thelma and I are also going to be living apart again. She's—been through some hard things, but we're both ready. I'm going with Ty on Sunday to look at a new place for me, and she's gone to see several places already. She's—" Her throat closed, and Sage took a breath and swallowed again.

"She's found somewhere, put in an offer, and it's been accepted. She'll probably move out in five or six weeks." Sage nodded, all of her news now out. Thankfully. She felt like she'd kept it bottled up for a long time, and then someone had grabbed the bottle and started shaking it. So when uncapped, everything had just come gushing out.

"Wow," Lauren said. "I'm going to start, because everyone else is gaping still." She grinned at Sage with all the smugness of someone who'd successfully snuck a handful of cookies out of the jar. "You kissed Ty *two weeks ago*, and we're just *now* hearing about it?"

Cass turned and opened the wine, the *pop!* from the cork really echoing through the small house. Then Bea said, "Yeah, I'm going to need more details on this luau."

"I was there," Bessie said. "It's been *killing* me, keeping this to myself."

"You were there?" Joy roared, spinning toward her. "And we didn't get a text?"

Sage grinned at her friends and took the glass of wine Cass handed her. She swirled it and took a sip, sighing into the liquid as it coated her tongue and throat. "All right, all right," she said among all the bickering going on. "Can we at least get food before Lauren tells us why she's so tired?" She moved over to the food. "I got three lasagnas and a big Caesar salad. Italian sausage." She pointed to one lasagna. "Ground beef. Chicken alfredo."

Joy got out a knife to cut into them, and wine glasses went around as the talking started up again, and Sage's suspicions about Lauren only doubled when she didn't take a glass of wine.

Oh, how she loved Supper Club.

Chapter Fourteen

～～

L auren Williams glared at Sage while the others grabbed plates and forks and napkins. She liked the buffet-style of Supper Club too, though she'd done a fully served sit-down dinner once, back when they all lived in Sweet Water Falls, Texas.

Sometimes, Lauren had snatches of that life that she missed. She couldn't believe it, because she had an ex there who'd been no good for her that she'd gone back to a few times. Her job there had turned out to be one big ball of fraud. And all of her friends were now here.

But still, sometimes Lauren missed the big Texas sky, because it didn't feel the same in Hilton Head.

At the same time, she wouldn't trade the life she'd been building here with her husband, Blake, and his son, Tommy. She'd never been married before, and there had definitely been some challenges in merging her life with two others. Two males, one of whom was fifteen years old.

Not only that, but Blake's ex-wife had found herself in a terrible predicament, and she'd needed somewhere to stay in an emergency. That "somewhere" had turned out to be Lauren and Blake's house, and Jacinda had stayed with them for seventeen days before she'd been able to sort through everything and find her own place.

Ty Parker had helped with that, and that was another reason Lauren couldn't look away from Sage. She did seem different, but Lauren couldn't put her finger on why. Sometimes Sage showed up to Supper Club in wigs or with a new hairdo, because she'd had some downtime at work.

If there was one thing Lauren knew about Sage, it was that she didn't like downtime. She seemed very busy at her salon, and she walked her big dog every morning, and she always came when any of them needed anything. She'd been a steady and trusted friend for a long time now, though she was almost a decade older than Lauren.

She went through the line right behind Sage, who only half-turned her head toward her and said, "Sorry, Lauren. I can try to steer the conversation toward something else."

Lauren wanted to share her news. She looked forward to Supper Club every month, as it was something that cleansed her soul and renewed her spirit. "It's okay," she murmured. "It's time I told everyone anyway." She put a slice of the chicken Alfredo lasagna on her plate, but it didn't look appetizing at all.

She filled the rest of her plate with salad, hoping she could eat a little bit and push the rest around enough to make everyone think she'd eaten more than she had. Cass ate very little too, and Lauren wished she'd taken half a piece of lasagna.

Conversations had broken out at the table by the time Lauren took her spot between Sage and Joy, and she looked over to Joy. She'd been such an amazing friend over the years too, and Lauren had sold this house to her and Scott so they could have their own little piece of paradise on the island.

"Tell us about the wedding, Bess," Sage said to the woman on her other side. "Where are you in the planning stages? Is Oliver being his usual grumpy self?"

Bessie beamed with all the power of the sun. "We did the cake sampling a few days ago, and he was on his best behavior." She laughed lightly as she forked off a corner of her Italian sausage lasagna. "I can't believe I'm getting married again."

She paused and stared straight ahead for a moment. "Do any of you feel like that? Like...I don't know. It's this big, heavy feeling, and it just sits in my head for a while. I'm *getting married again*. It's like I'm living a completely different life than I had before."

"That's because you are," Bea said gently. She too looked around the table of women. "We all are."

"I understand this feeling," Cass said. "After West died, I'd lose hours and even days just sitting and thinking, 'My *husband died*. He *died*.' It was like my mind didn't understand the concept."

"Yes," Bessie said. "That's how I'm feeling."

No one said anything for a beat, and Lauren took a breath. "I feel like that," she said. "For a while there, I'd given up on the idea of being a wife. Of ever getting married and having a family."

Family. She was still learning the meaning of that word, and motherhood? Lauren had no idea how to even start conceptualizing that.

"You guys." She cleared her throat. "I'm going to have a baby."

That brought the conversation and the consumption of food to a complete halt. Lauren's eyes filled and overfilled with tears, and she let them slip down her face. "I'm so scared. I have no idea what to do. Like, I never thought this could be my life. I'm *going to have a baby*."

"Lauren," Cass said with plenty of shock in her voice. Thankfully, a healthy dose of celebration mingled with it. "This is the best news ever!" She got up and came around the table to hug Lauren.

"Yes," Joy said quickly. "Lauren, you're going to be the best mom in the world." Her eyes shone with tears too. "When are you due?"

"September," Lauren whispered. "September tenth."

"I'm so happy for you," Bea said, her voice choked. "Being a mom is the best thing in the world. It's everything I've always loved, and you'll love it too."

Lauren nodded at her. "Thanks, Bea."

Sage simply covered Lauren's hand with hers, and Bessie wept too. "Lauren," she said. "How exciting! Are Tommy and Blake excited too?"

That was the understatement of the century. She gave a half-laugh and a half-sob. "You should see Blake. We went to the HomeBox the other day, and he has the crib, changing table, and rocking chair picked out for the nursery."

"I get to be the honorary aunt," Cass said.

"That's not fair," Bessie argued. "You live the furthest from Lauren. I should get to be the honorary aunt."

"It's not about how close you live to someone," Cass said with a hint of disdain in her voice. "Can I please decorate the nursery, Lauren? I've been wanting to do a baby's room. All the Country Club rooms are so...stuffy."

"Sure," Lauren said, lifting her napkin to wipe her runny nose. She looked around at everyone. "You're all my very best friends in the whole world." She joined her hand with Sage's on her left and Joy's on her right. Automatically, they all joined hands, until they were united as one. Six women. Best friends.

"I don't have much family," she said, her voice turning tinny and high-pitched. "You're all I have. And Blake and Tommy, of course. You'll all be her honorary aunts, okay?"

"Absolutely," Bea said.

"Yeah," Joy said.

"I'd love that," Bessie said.

"Of course," Sage said.

"I guess I can share," Cass agreed. "Do you know it's a girl this early?"

"No." Lauren didn't want to let go of this moment, so she stayed there, present, holding hands. "I just call her a her." A soft smile came to her face. "I'd like a little girl, I think."

All of her friends smiled that same wistful, joyful smile

back at her, and Lauren wished there was a way to press pause on life and see the situation from above. She'd do that right now, and she'd be able to see herself and her friends at this happy moment in time for all eternity.

She took a breath and the moment broke. "All right," she said. "Who else has something? Bessie, what else with the wedding?"

"Mm, nope," Bessie said as she finished her bite of salad. "It's coming along. Nothing to share." She looked at Sage meaningfully. "We need to hear all about the luau and one Tyler Parker."

Sage grinned even as she shook her head. "You were there."

"No one else was," Bessie said as she glanced around. "And it was pretty amazing, guys. If they do another luau at The Heartwood Inn, I highly recommend us all going."

"What was good about it?" Cass asked.

"They had delicious food, for one," Sage said. "One of the sisters is a master chef, as is her husband. They cook for the whole inn, and I'm still dreaming of that Kalua pork." She looked over to Bessie, who grinned and grinned. "And that cheesecake."

"They made Hawaiian rolls from scratch," Bessie said. "And those are hard to make. It's hard to get the exact right sweetness. I dream of those." She laughed, and a few others giggled with her.

"They had a program," Sage said. "With fire dancers. Hula, all this just—perfectly relaxing island music. I really felt like I'd been transported from one beach to another. It was just...magical."

"And you kissed Ty out in the open during this magical program?" Cass asked. "That doesn't really sound like you, Sage."

It sure didn't, but Lauren took a bite of a crouton and stayed silent. Sage sure had come alive, and she could see what she meant about Ty making her feel like living again. Blake had done that for Lauren too.

"While they cleared dinner and set dessert," Sage said. "They held a dance out on the sand. With flickering fire tiki torches, and the most romantic music...I kissed him out on the dance floor, in my bare feet." She laughed like she'd just had the greatest adventure of her life.

Lauren wasn't the only one semi-gaping at her. She brushed her hair out of her face, which had started to turn a shade of deep red. "All right." She cleared her throat. "Enough about me."

"Sage," Bea said. "You're being...responsible with him, aren't you?"

Lauren pulled in a breath, and her eyes flew to Sage's. Some of her light had dimmed, but she waved away Bea's question. "I'm fifty years old, Bea. I'm not going to get pregnant."

Cass exchanged a look with Bea, and it annoyed Lauren. It obviously did Sage too, because she added, "I'm fifty years old, you two. I don't need you mothering me to death. Besides, I said we were both taking it slow. So calm down."

She gave them both a pointed look and then switched her gaze to Joy and then Bessie.

"Someone else say something."

"I'm just glad to still be in business," Bessie said. "And in case the mother hens want to know, Ollie and I are being responsible."

Lauren snorted and reached for her water glass, and the six of them looked around the table at one another.

"I just—" Bea started, but she quickly got drowned out by the loud laughter that spilled from every mouth except hers.

As they quieted, Lauren tugged her phone out of her pocket and, under the table, sent a quick text to Blake. *I told them. They're all thrilled for us. I love you.*

And she got the best text back, only a moment after hers had gone through.

I love you too.

Chapter Fifteen

Ty worried the steering wheel by gripping it to the beat, releasing his fingers in between. Sage rode in the passenger seat, and he had no idea how she'd respond to seeing the property in person. He'd been here—twice now—to go over things with the listing agent, and he'd taken a few pictures for her.

But contrary to what people thought, a picture was not worth a thousand words. Sometimes seeing something in person needed to happen. Ty had sold plenty of properties via video, but he firmly believed a client should be able to see the house and land they might potentially be investing hundreds of thousands of dollars into as many times as they wanted to.

Sage had been very busy at work in the past couple of weeks, and it had taken Ty some time to get this showing to come together. Now that he had, he could probably bring

Sage back as many times as needed for her to know if she wanted this waterfront piece of property or not.

"All right," he said as he eased up on the accelerator. "We're going to be making a turn up here, and the road slopes down to a really pretty lane. Your house is just off of that. Don't let the greenery overcome you. It's springtime, and we've had a lot of moisture and then sunshine this year. Everyone's yards are overgrown."

"Just ask Scott," Sage said with a smile. "I know, Ty." She looked at him, and he couldn't conceal his nerves fast enough. "Why are you so worried?"

"There's literally nothing on the island like what you want," he said.

"This technically isn't on the island either."

"It's still in the zip code," he said. But yes, they'd crossed the bridge from Hilton Head and back to the mainland. He'd driven another quarter of a mile, and now he made the right turn and started down the gently sloping road.

Sage looked out the windshield instead of her window, and Ty told himself to just drive them there. Look ahead and worry about her reaction later.

"If it's not for me, we'll keep looking," she finally said. "I didn't expect you to find me the perfect place in a single day, Ty."

"Well, I wanted to," he grumbled.

She reached over and took his hand. "I know you did, sweetheart. That's what makes you so wonderful."

He looked at her then, finding that sexy smile on her mouth. He'd kissed her for the first time a couple of weeks ago—and every chance he got since then. He pulled his hand back to make the right turn onto the property, and he coached himself to be a real estate agent for the next hour.

He could be her boyfriend after that.

Maybe just be both, he told himself. He'd never dated a client before, and he wasn't sure how to be both. He barely knew how to be a boyfriend, and he felt like he was learning something new every single time he went out with Sage.

She had high expectations, and Ty had always strived to aim high. He liked being with her, as their conversations were so lively and easy. She always had a smile for him, even after a long day of cutting hair, and he couldn't wait to take her back to his place after this and cook for her.

The house came into view, and it wasn't much to look at from this side. He could admit that. It wasn't built to be utilized from this side, other than to park and get into the main meat of what made it so great. The two-story walls of windows that faced the ocean. That was where the real beauty of this place sat.

It showed the waterfront way between the mainland and Hilton Head, which also had some pretty big mansions along all the waterfront property out there. Perhaps this would be the perfect place for Sage. Away from the busyness of the island, of her job, of all the tourists. More land for her and Gypsy and her freedom and friends.

"It's three bedrooms," he said. "Three baths. Two levels, but there's only one bed and one bath upstairs. It would be perfect if one of your kids came to stay, or you needed to banish Gypsy to his own room when you have Supper

Club." He smiled at her. "Of course, he'll have the yard for that. It's six-tenths of an acre, so it's not huge, but with the house right in the middle of it, there's not a giant patch of grass."

"Looks like there's plenty right in front of me," she said. She'd made no move to get out of his SUV either.

"It's fenced along the north side there," Ty said, nodding. He'd slipped into his agent-voice, and he didn't try to come out of it. "The waterfront is open, so I'm not sure how your dog does with swimming and whatnot. The sun will come up in the morning and flood your house with light, and then in the evening, all those trees actually keep the whole property shaded."

"So no full-sun foliage," Sage said.

"You could try," he said. They turned toward one another, and like kismet, he leaned toward her at the same time she moved in his direction. He cupped his hand around the back of her neck, really burying his fingers in her hair, and kissed her.

Kissing her was an earth-spinning experience, and she seemed to have some nerves or pent-up energy she needed to release, because she was the one who accelerated and deepened the kiss. Ty didn't mind one bit, and in fact, he growled as he matched her movement.

She broke away several moments later, and Ty pulled at the air desperately. "You okay?" he asked, the words almost coming out as air.

"Yeah," she said. "I just...really appreciate you doing this. This property isn't even listed."

"I know a lot of agents on the island," he said. "This house belongs to a South Carolina Supreme Court judge. They don't live here, but up in Columbia, and well, my friend said they might be willing to sell."

"Might be?" Sage turned toward him, alarmed now. "I didn't realize this might not even be for sale." She unbuckled then and got out, Ty tumbling after her.

"We just have to convince them," he said across the hood of the SUV.

"Convincing them takes money." She threw him a pointed look that spoke of her displeasure, and it stabbed right into the fleshy part of Ty's heart. "Let's just look at it."

He led her down the front sidewalk, that yes, had grass growing on both sides. "See the fence?" He pointed to his left. "It goes from the corner down to the water. You could put your chickens and vegetable garden on this other side."

Sage looked right and left, taking it all in. He wondered what she saw. He saw a piece of property that had been taken care of decently well. The judge sent in someone to mow the grass and keep things from getting overgrown by vines. But the driveway needed some weeding and re-graveling, and Ty would add more flowers and shrubs along the front of the house to increase curb appeal.

"I've not actually been inside," he said. "I was told they turned on the AC this morning for us, so we won't bake." He grinned at her and tapped in the code for the lockbox. The secret compartment opened, and he removed the brass key. That got fitted in the doorknob, and he looked at Sage.

"They might be looking to sell no matter what the offer

is," Ty said. "We real estate agents have this game we play, you know? We're always trying to make it sound like it'll take top dollar to move a property. It doesn't, probably ninety percent of the time."

Her lips tightened as she pressed them together, and then she nodded.

"I can't handle you being upset with me," he murmured.

"I'm not upset with you." She sighed.

"So it's the situation," he said. "I knew you wanted a place, Sage. You act like there's no rush, but there is. That's not fair to me either."

Her eyebrows went up. "I—there's no rush."

"But there is," he said, the key still sitting there in the unlocked knob. He gestured back to the car. "You kiss me like that? You're nervous, and you want this place to be perfect, and you're upset that if it is perfect, you might not be able to get it."

He couldn't believe all the words pouring from him, but he'd said them all. Couldn't take them back. "So there's a rush."

"There's this one property," Sage said.

"But if there's no rush, sweetheart, then why does it matter if this one doesn't work out? We'll just wait until another comes along. And then another."

She folded her arms and settled her weight on one hip. "I don't like the apartment."

"Just admit there's a rush." He started to smile at her. "I actually wish you would, because then the tension I feel about not being able to find you the castle of your dreams would make sense to me. As it is, I'm stressed all the time and checking the listings, and I don't even know why."

He definitely knew why. It was so Sage would kiss him with as much passion and enthusiasm as she just had. That was why.

"Fine, I would like to find somewhere," she said, her defenses falling fast. "Especially now that Thelma has a place and will be moving out."

"The apartment might feel bigger," he said.

"There's nowhere for Gypsy," she said. "There's nowhere for *me* to grow there."

He studied her, really trying to hear what she meant behind the words. "All right," he said. "I'm looking, Sage. I really am. No, this property isn't on the market, but my friend made it sound like we could probably get it. I don't know what it will take, but that's just part of the negotiation process."

She said nothing, and Ty reached for her again. "Okay?" he murmured as she let him pull her closer.

"Okay," she whispered back, practically in his mouth right before he kissed her again. This time, it was slow and meaningful and tender, and he enjoyed this union just as much as the more frantic, passionate one.

He took a breath and stepped back. "Okay." The door-knob twisted easily, and the front door opened into a lobby of sorts. "I did get to see the floorplan," he said. "And it's basically a long rectangle, split into fourths." He was trying to take in the cool gray tile, the eggshell-colored walls, the

South Carolina art, and all the square footage at the same time as her.

"Straight ahead, you get to the back half of the house, which hosts the kitchen, living room, and an office, all of which boast those amazing views of the water." He could see it glistening from here, and he could definitely see why someone would hope this would turn into the next big real estate investment property. "It's gorgeous," he whispered.

"Look at that." Sage moved by him on her quest toward the back half of the house. He closed the door behind them and followed her. The house was furnished, and he wondered if all of that would stay or not. The kitchen sat to his left, and it had been equipped with granite and dark, smudge-proof appliances. A pot rack hung above the stovetop, which had been built into the island.

This was a far cry from a fixer upper, and Ty gritted his teeth. He wasn't sure Sage could afford something like this, and Steve had made it sound like the house wasn't that great. From what Ty could see, it was pristine.

No carpet; only a rug in the living area, which held a sectional that faced the water view. A doorway stood in the wall to his right, which held a fireplace, and he went and peered into the office while Sage still stood at the back sliding doors, looking out.

"Nice space," he said as he returned to her. "The master suite is behind the office and living area here. Private bath, big bedroom, closet."

She finally turned, and simply by the look on her face, he knew she wanted this place. He reached for her, and she threaded her fingers through his. "Come look at the actual house, sweetheart. You can't live standing at the windows, dreaming." He grinned at her, and she ducked her head and smiled shyly back.

"I like dreaming," she said.

"I love that you like dreaming," he said as he opened the door that led into the master suite. "Oh, look at this. It's got a sitting area out front. That's a nice touch." It also separated the bedroom further from the living room, so she could get some privacy when she had guests.

The guest bathroom and bedroom on this level bore the same blonde-gray wood floor, the same color of walls, and linens in cool, crisp blue, white, green, and gray. Upstairs, the guest suite did the same job.

The whole house had been built to look east, out into the strait of ocean between the mainland and the island of Hilton Head. Just coming down the stairs could be treacherous, because Ty forgot to watch his footing as he stared out at the glorious water.

He took her outside, and the fenced area was bigger than he thought. "You could put a shed on this side," he said. "Or here in the back, or on the south side."

"Not the back, baby," she said as she stepped into his embrace. "It would block the view."

He held her in his arms, perfectly content for those few seconds. Then he said, "You're right. Not the back."

She pulled away slightly and looked at him. "I like this place, Ty."

"It's flooded before," he said. "Last time, about four years ago when Hurricane Fiona tore through here."

"Well, I'm not new to hurricanes," she said. "We had them in Texas too. That's why you don't put carpet down." She started walking toward the water.

"It used to be a bit swampy," he called after her. "Sage, be careful."

She raised her hand to indicate she'd heard him, but she kept walking. Ty wasn't sure what to do. There wasn't a dock here. Nowhere to put a yacht or even a fishing boat. None of the four houses on this lane had that luxury, because this hadn't turned into one of those gated communities with private yacht facilities.

He also needed to figure out how much this house was worth, so he could give Sage a fair, market-appropriate number. "Please let her be able to afford it," he whispered as she bent down and touched the water.

She lingered there, probably fifty yards from the house, for a few minutes, and Ty gave her all the time she wanted. When she returned to him, she said, "There's a little bit of beach. Rocky, but not terribly uneven. I could sit there and read while Gypsy swims." She smiled like she'd wile away her days doing just that when he knew she'd go stir-crazy within the first hour.

"Let me do some market research," he said. "We'll come up with a number, and I'll take it to my friend." He put his arm around her. "But first, I believe I'm about to impress you with my lunch-making skills."

"Oh-ho," she chortled. "This I'd like to see."

Chapter Sixteen

Sage closed her eyes and let the sunshine flow over her as Ty drove them back to his house. As the car slowed, she opened her eyes so she could see where he lived. He turned into a nice neighborhood, the kind where every father probably had synchronized his watch with his neighbors so they could have lawn-mowing parties at eight a.m. on Saturday mornings.

She wondered when Ty mowed his lawn, and then she dismissed that thought. Of course the man didn't clip his own grass. He was friends with Scott Anderson, and that man owned a landscaping company that couldn't keep up in the spring, summer, and fall months. Surely Ty hired Scott to get his lawn care needs met.

"Here it is," he said as he pulled into the two-car driveway of a light...pink house. There was a swooping, circular driveway, and tall white pillars that held up the roof to the second story. Perfectly sculpted shrubs had been trimmed into neat little boxes on trunks, and he had rocks in the front flower bed that probably got power-washed every day.

Not fair, Sage told herself. Of course the top real estate agent on the island would have a nice house. Ty was a neat person too, and he never had a stitch of anything out of place. Sage wanted to see if the man ever dirtied dishes, or if they simply cleaned themselves when he looked at them.

She smiled over to him. "The garage door is brown."

"The house is pink," he said. "They sort of go together. You know, the wood on the steps, and—"

"I think it's amazing," she interrupted. "It matches the shutters too." A wide set of steps led up to a concrete porch, where Ty had a potted plant trying to reach the heavens. A ferny-looking thing sat off to the right, where the grass started and went along the side of the house. Trees grew up all around the sides of the house, and she wondered what the view off the back balcony would yield.

He wasn't beachside, but close enough, and Sage grinned at him as she unbuckled and got out of the car. He came after her, and then led her into the house through the front door. She expected cool colors and crisp lines inside, and she wasn't disappointed.

Ty seemed like the type of guy to like khaki and gray and soft hues of white. Maybe some seaglass colors like blue and green and maybe even more of that pink that sang from the exterior paint.

She found it all, and more. A deeper blue on a feature wall in his office. Brightly colored nautical art adorned that wall, and when he finally took her hand and led her into the kitchen, Sage realized how very amazing Ty was.

"I got grouper for today," he said as he released her hand and moved over to the fridge. Everything he did spoke of grace and fluidity, and Sage had only seen him nervous or off his game a couple of times.

Their first date, which she now knew was an outlier in his behavior. Today at the house, where he'd been so stinking nervous. At the luau, where it had taken him seemingly a long time to kiss her out there on the sand. All other times, he was the picture of sophistication and class.

Even now, he wore a pair of light brown khakis and a pale blue polo. It actually matched the sheers he had hanging over the doors that must lead out to that balcony he'd told her about.

"If you want to look around the house, go ahead." He flashed her a smile. "I can see you chomping at the bit."

Sage smiled back at him. "I just want to hear those waves." She slid open the door and ducked through the sheers. The balcony there was made with the same dark wood as out front, and it spanned the entire back of the house. She could go right or left, and to the left was a small table-for-two. She wondered if he ate breakfast there alone before she turned the other way.

The barking of dogs met her ears, and Sage smiled as she walked along the balcony to another set of sliding doors. Ty's golden retriever and his black lab had their noses to the door there, both of them barking at her.

As she watched, they turned, which signaled Ty's arrival

in his bedroom. The dogs ran toward him, only Sherman barking still. Then the sliding door opened, and both dogs barreled outside. Sage narrowly stepped out of the way, a laugh starting down in her stomach.

Today had been amazing. She could just see herself living in that house on the water, and she could see Gypsy romping through the grass there, then jumping into the water. And there, she'd have plenty of space for him to shake himself off.

"Okay, okay," Ty said, laughing at the exuberance of his dogs. "Let me get the gate for you." He stepped past Sage by trailing his hand along the waistband of her shorts and unlatched the gate for his hounds.

They trotted down the steps to the backyard, which was fully fenced and boasted more trees, tons of shade, and not much grass. It grew in patches at best, and Sage had seen plenty of yards like this on the island. Not enough sun, too much salt, and the dogs didn't really help either.

They ran around, sniffing, and Sage leaned against the railing and watched them. She didn't realize that Ty had gone back inside until she smelled the scent of warm butter and something frying in it.

She called, "Come on, Brother," and that got both dogs to come back to the steps. Sherman bolted up them like a bullet, but Brother took them more cautiously. They were good dogs, and Sage gave them each a pat before she opened the door to the kitchen. Ty had left it open a crack, but not big enough for a dog or a person to get through, and Sage paused on the threshold of the house to watch him before she entered fully.

He stood at the stove, wielding a spatula, and looking incredibly sexy doing it. He glanced at the dogs as they approached him, gave them a smile, and then checked for her. She got moving, because she didn't want to be hovering on the edge of his house.

"Smells good in here," she said, joining him in the kitchen. She leaned into him and saw he was crisping up potatoes in the pan. "Mm, a man after my heart."

"With potatoes?" He chuckled as he flipped over one of the golden fingerlings.

"Definitely," she said. "One of my favorite foods."

"Good to know," he said. "Any other favorites I need to know about?"

"Peaches and cream?" she suggested. "What about you? Favorites?"

"Uh, well…"

Sage's interest piqued, because this wasn't a hard question. "You don't know your favorite food? You've eaten all over this island."

"I'm trying to decide if I tell you my real faves, or if you want the ones I tell all my friends."

Sage blinked at him. "Uh, the real ones, I think." She inched a little closer to him. "Are you not being real with me?"

"I am," he said, but his voice pitched up. He switched off the gas and moved the pan back. His shoulders boxed up and then dropped. "Okay, look." He turned toward her and put his hands on her waist.

They didn't start swaying, but there was something

going on with Ty. "I feel like I have to be perfect all the time," he said. "Every time I leave the house, every single thing has to be exactly right, from my socks to my tie to my teeth."

Sage smiled at him. "Your teeth?"

"I whiten once a week," he said, dropping his hands and moving away from her. "And I know you don't care—at least I don't think you do—but I'm tired of being perfect."

Sage sobered and realized Ty was being real with her. "I'm sorry if I gave off the impression that I expected you to be perfect. I don't."

"I just want to be. For you." He paced away from her and ran his hands down his face. "I want to give you the world. All the adventure in it. I want you to have your waterfront way, and I want to be right there with you when you do."

"Ty, you are." Sage took a step toward him, not sure what had set him off. "I had a great morning at the house. With you. And this lunch is going to be amazing, I just know it."

"I baked the potatoes last night. I was up cleaning until almost midnight. I—"

Sage found his frustration adorable. He was so handsome, and so good, and so...perfectly imperfect that she started to laugh. She stepped over to him and smoothed down a lock of his hair that had stuck up when he'd run his hand through it.

"You're wonderful," she whispered as she leaned in to kiss him. "I'm falling for you, whether I get that house or not. Whether we just have a quiet evening at home—in *your* home—that's full of dirty dishes and smelly dogs and…us. That's the adventure, Ty."

"Really?" His insecurity endeared him to her and she touched her lips to his lightly.

"Really."

"I want to give you the world," he whispered against her lips before moving his mouth along her ear.

"Every day should be the adventure," she said. "Just seeing you makes me smile, and I want to spend more time with you. I want to know your real favorites, not the perfect ones you tell other people."

"I'm like a ten-year-old boy," he said. "I love peanut butter and jelly sandwiches and pepperoni pizza with extra cheese."

Sage tipped her head back and laughed. "Why haven't we ever gone to get pepperoni pizza? Why are you making this fancy grouper and fried potatoes? Let's get pepperoni pizza and eat it on the front porch of your pink house."

He laughed too, and that broke the tension inside him. "I just want to do—and be—the man you deserve."

She took his face in her hands and said, "Ty, you're trying too hard. We're getting to know each other. I'm not going anywhere if you have some shoes sitting by the front door."

He scoffed, his light eyes sparkling with teasing. "Who leaves their shoes by the front door?" They laughed together, and Ty took her into his arms and kissed her sloppily.

And that only added to the adventure that today had become.

SAGE LAUGHED WITH ONE CLIENT, THEN MOVED TO the next and asked her about her grandmother. They came in, got their hair done, and left. Day after day.

Ty had put together a market analysis for the waterfront property, and because she wasn't his only client, a week had gone by. She told herself it didn't matter, because the house wasn't on the market. It wasn't like someone else was going to come in and swoop it out from underneath her.

Thelma had started bringing home boxes and packing up her things, and that only reminded Sage that she'd still be in the apartment. Alone. She didn't mind being alone, but she wanted a bigger space to expand her wings and fly.

She was halfway through applying the bleach for one of her clients when her manager said, "Sage, there's someone here for you."

She twisted to look over her shoulder, and she found Ty standing there. He grinned from ear-to-ear, and that sent Sage's pulse into a frenzy. Normally, she wouldn't just walk away from a client in this state, but something told her to get over there and talk to him.

"Could you—?" She handed Barb the brush and left her station. She semi-heard her boss's protests, but the light shining out of Ty's face blurred the words.

"What's going on?" she asked as she approached him.

He grabbed her hand and towed her right out of The Salon Mionic. "What's happening?" She laughed, but her heart pounded at the same time. "Did you sell the Keller house?"

He'd told her about this mega-expensive property that had been on the market for ten months, and he said maybe one day, he could take her for a showing of it—if she promised not to get lost.

Get lost. In a house here on the island.

"No," he said almost breathlessly. "I am closing a deal today, but it's not that one." He turned back to her. "It's yours, Sage. Judge Caldwell accepted your offer. The house is yours!"

Sage's heartbeat stopped, then accelerated quickly. "What? He accepted it?"

"You got the house!" He grabbed onto her and hugged her, and Sage started bouncing on the tips of her toes.

"I can't believe it." She laughed too, so much giddiness galloping through her. "Thank you, Ty. Thank you." She tried to kiss him, but there was too much joy between them. As quickly as their euphoria had begun, it started to subside. "Let's celebrate tonight. Just me and you. Pepperoni pizza on the back deck of the house I just bought."

She searched his face. "Do you think we could do that? I mean, no one lives there, right?"

He laughed again. "I'll make a couple of calls and let you know, okay? I have a meeting this afternoon, and I pulled you from a client." He kissed her quickly. "But I had to tell you, and I was five minutes from the salon when the text came in."

"Thank you, Ty." Sage felt like she'd had her blood replaced with coffee. Her nerves and adrenaline hummed together, and she said, "Thank you," again as he started for the parking lot.

"I'll call you later," he called over his shoulder, leaving her to turn back to the salon. She'd left her phone inside, but this news had to come out now. So she burst through the doors and lifted both hands above her head.

"I got the house!"

The salon was busy, but everyone had heard her, and cheering started. She grinned as she practically bounced back to her station, where Barb had nearly finished with the bleach. She exhaled heavily, like she'd just run a marathon while eating cotton candy and throwing back little bottles of energy drinks.

"I got the house," she said to her client, and thankfully, now Teresa smiled at her. She couldn't wait to get her under the dryer, so she could text her Supper Club.

Chapter Seventeen

"Oh, there he is," Harrison yelled as Ty entered the house behind Sage. "The man of the hour!" The crowd who'd gathered in Harrison's beachfront house cheered, lifting their drinks into the air from the kitchen.

Ty grinned and laughed as everyone who'd gathered surged forward. Sherman barked and barked, joining the fray in the large area that suddenly felt too small. Sage danced ahead of him, her dark eyes glinting with so much happiness.

She hugged her friend Bessie, then moved over to Bea while Ty shook hands with Harrison and then accepted the bottle of beer from him. "I don't know how you do it," Harry said with a chuckle. "It's like you have secret connections everywhere."

"I wish," Ty said with a laugh. He grabbed onto Grant and hugged him, because Grant was a hugger.

"Good job, buddy. Bea says she's the happiest she's ever seen her, even before, when they all lived in Texas." They grinned at each other, and Ty stepped to the next person. He felt like he'd done something great, not just his job, and this whole party seemed a bit ridiculous.

But it was what Sage wanted, and when she wanted to celebrate, Ty wouldn't say no.

"Pizza's outside," Blake said, and Ty clapped hands with him too.

"I heard you have something to celebrate too," he said, glancing around to find Lauren and failing. How he hadn't realized that all of his closest friends had found their happily-ever-after while he'd been brokering real estate deals, Ty didn't know. But looking around this house, this party, he saw it.

Blake and Lauren had gotten married last year, and they were going to have a baby this fall. Bea and Grant had just bought and moved into a bigger house—and yes, Ty had helped them. His daughter had come to live with them for her senior year, which was almost done, and Bea had three grown children with expanding families who came to visit.

"Yeah," Blake said, ducking his head like he was embarrassed about having a baby with his wife. "Kind of surprising, but we're both really excited."

"Do you want a boy or a girl?" Ty asked.

"I'd take anyone who doesn't trip over his own feet every third step." Blake laughed, and Ty joined him. Tommy was a little accident-prone, and he once again looked around, searching for the teen.

He didn't see him either, but the house was big and the crowd thick. There could be more people outside too. He appreciated the fact that the men had separated from their women, but as Ty spoke to each of them, they seemed to migrate back toward one another.

Scott and Joy were the newest married couple, and she'd just started teaching this fall while Scott continued to run his landscaping business with his brother. Another dog barked, and Ty didn't recognize it as one that belonged to him.

Blake moved to let Scott into the circle, and he bent to get his dog's leash first. "You brought Ghost." Ty bent down to pat the almost all-white dog, and his dogs rushed him like he'd betrayed them mightily by even looking at another dog.

Another golden joined them, and Ty crouched down now, suddenly feeling peopled out. But dogs? He always had time to chat with them. "And what's your name?"

"That's Cass's dog," Oliver said. "Beryl."

"Ah, he's handsome. Yes, he is." He chuckled as Brother muscled his way under Ty's arm. "You're handsome too, bud." And if he didn't praise Sherman times two, he'd get licked and barked at.

So he used both hands to scrub down Sherman's jowls as he told him what an amazing black lab he was. Then, when he couldn't avoid the humans any longer, he straightened and looked at Oliver.

"Good to see you, man." Oliver gave him a light hug too and stepped back. "We really do have pizza on the back patio. Come eat." He nodded that way, and then turned to go outside.

It took Ty another ten minutes to get outside to the patio, as he had to go through all of Sage's Supper Club friends to get there. They were incredibly nice women, and they loved Sage completely.

As he saw the four boxes of pepperoni pizza spread across the big back table, he started to laugh.

"I didn't know which place you liked best," Sage said, finally returning to his side. She wrapped her arms around his waist and leaned into him. "So I got one from four of the top-rated places here on Hilton Head."

She beamed up at him, and though all of their friends watched them, as well as Shelby and Tommy, Ty leaned down and kissed her. Everything in his life had started to align, and while he'd celebrated big sales before, there had never been a party this amazing and fun.

Because he'd never had Sage at his side before.

———

TY RAN DOWN THE BEACH, COMING UP ON THE lifeguard station where he turned around and headed back to his house. He toyed with the idea of running up the beach to Sage's apartment just to say hello before either of them started the day. When he realized it was Thursday, and Sage wouldn't be working today, he decided to definitely go stop in.

Maybe he could sit down to breakfast with her and the dogs for a couple of minutes. His fantasies ran as fast as his feet, and before Ty knew it, he raised his fist and knocked on the door. It came off like a pound, because his adrenaline hovered near the top of his head. It always did after a run, and his chest heaved, his calves cramped, and Ty couldn't stop smiling about any of it.

Sage opened the door wearing her walking clothes and holding Gypsy's collar. "Well, hello there," she said with some level of surprise in her voice. "You're not wearing a shirt."

"I never do when I run," he said good-naturedly. "I thought—well, it's Thursday, and I know you're not working today. I just wanted to see you."

"Sage, who is—?" Thelma cut off when she saw Ty standing in the doorway. A smile spread her lips and she said, "Oh, your—hello, Ty."

"Thelma," he said.

"We're packing today," Sage said, her smile stuck to her face. "Thelma is moving out on Saturday."

"Oh, that's right," Ty said.

"We could use your muscles," Sage teased. "Right, Thelma?"

"I don't know anything about his muscles," her sister grumbled as she moved into the kitchen, her head down and somewhat of a flush creeping into her face.

Sage laughed lightly and faced Ty again. "Don't mind her. She's—" Her laughter died away a little. "She'd be very grateful for your help this weekend. Grant and Harry are coming. Oh, and Blake." Sage reached up and ran her hands through her hair, which looked a little lighter this morning.

"Scott and Oliver are still trying to work out their job schedule, but Thelma doesn't have much."

"Let me check my schedule too," he said. He didn't have

to say that Saturdays could be busy for him; Sage knew that. All at once, he wondered if she really got his workload.

"You know I work a lot, right, Sage?"

"Yes," she said simply.

"It's not even summer yet," he said. "Sometimes I work all day at home and then do paperwork, more texting, put up listings, at night. It's—a lot. I know I work a lot. I'm trying to scale back."

"Are you?"

"Yes."

"Why?"

Wasn't the answer obvious? "So I have time to spend with you." He leaned one hip into the doorway and smiled at her.

She smiled right on back. "You're not wearing a shirt," she said again.

Ty laughed, his head tipping back. "All right, my thoughts of having a romantic breakfast on your day off isn't going to happen, I can see that."

"Sweetheart." She cradled his face in one hand, and Ty loved that. It felt like Sage claiming him, wanting to draw him closer to her. "Not today, but I really like this idea. And next week, I'll be home alone when you stop by." She raised her eyebrows, and they had an entire conversation without saying a word.

So he'd stop by next week—and he'd make sure he brought an extra shirt with him, though part of him wanted to know what would happen if she said, "You're not wearing a shirt," for the third time.

Chapter Eighteen

Sage had decided not to lift a single thing for her sister's move. Number one, she didn't have to. She had four strong men coming in, and Thelma had a queen-sized bed, a nightstand, and a dresser as major furniture.

Since they'd been moving in together when they'd both left Texas and come to Hilton Head, they hadn't brought everything they both owned. Sage had sold a lot of her excess belongings, as had Thelma.

Sage had owned better furniture, so the couch and love seat were both hers. She'd offered the smaller couch to Thelma, but her sister said she wanted to buy her own furniture for her new place.

Ty had found her a perfectly adorable two-bedroom house with pretty trees out front and down the side, a flowering bush with pink flowers, and a white front door and shutters. Sage had gone with her sister to see the house, and she'd known the moment they'd pulled up to the house that Thelma would love it.

The neighborhood didn't have much crime, and Ty had said the demographics were older married couples—empty nesters. Thelma had never married, but she'd always gotten along really well with those older than her.

She'd meet new people—good people—who could provide support and comfort. She might even be able to find someone who'd been through what she had. Sage had done her best, but she knew her situation with Jerry wasn't the same as Thelma's abusive relationship.

Her phone rang only moments before she expected the doorbell to ring, announcing the arrival of her moving crew. Kayla's name sat there, and Sage lit up. "Hey, baby," she drawled, reverting right back to her Texas roots.

"Momma," her daughter drawled on back. "How's the movin' goin'?"

"We haven't started yet," she said, "You must be up early."

"Oh, Daphne's had a cold for the past couple of days. She can't breathe unless I'm holding her at exactly the right angle." She sighed, and Sage had endured many of those nights herself. She'd never given much thought to how she'd always been the one to get up with the children—until she'd finally gotten the nerve to file for divorce.

It was all the little things over the many years they'd been married that had piled up, each of them—like Sage being the only one to ever do anything with the children, be that diapering them, teaching them to do chores, or helping them with their homework, class registrations, anything and everything—carrying a little bit of weight until it had all been too heavy for her to carry any longer.

"How's Bruce?" Sage asked, hating how her voice pitched up slightly. She liked her son-in-law a lot, but Sage honestly didn't know him well enough to make much more of a judgment than that. He and Kayla had only stayed in Texas for six months after their wedding, before his job had taken him to another state.

Sage had missed her daughter terribly in the beginning, but that had dulled over time.

"He's great," Kayla said. "He's home today, so he'll take Daphne, and I'll be able to go back to bed."

"That's great, baby." Sage smiled as her front door opened. Ty entered first, but Grant, Harry, and Blake—and his son, Tommy—came right behind him. "Oh, my moving crew is here." She spotted the light blue box in Harry's hand, her smile only getting brighter. "And they brought breakfast."

"Tell Aunt Thelma I'll call her later," Kayla said.

"I will, baby. Love you." She ended the call at the same time her handsome, blond boyfriend reached her. "My daughter."

"Oh, fun," Ty said before sweeping a kiss across her cheek. "You better put us to work, sweetheart. Blake was saying something about how he's not sure he can lift anything, because his son's dog was crying all night."

Sage looked over to Blake, who had already collapsed on the couch, his legs sprawled in front of him. Tommy loitered with Harry at the counter, where the doughnuts had been placed.

"Thelma," she called, because while she'd seen her sister this fine Saturday morning, she'd been running around doing last-minute things for a while now.

"I'm ready," she called from down the hall.

"She's got furniture in the bedroom, boys," Sage said, indicating the hallway like she was a game show host and there might be a brand new car behind door number one. "And all these boxes out here."

"We need to start with the big things," Harry said, leading the charge down the hallway.

Sage stayed out of the way, smiling politely at Blake as he sighed and yawned as he got off the couch and growled, "Come on, son. We're here to work, not eat."

She'd corralled Gypsy in her bedroom so he wouldn't be in the way of this move, and she helped Thelma with the smaller things—a lamp she didn't want to get broken, her cats in their carriers, and an open box of last-minute items she'd used that morning to get ready for this move.

As predicted, the men had everything out of the apartment and in the moving truck in twenty minutes, and that included all the walking around the building. Then, Sage followed Thelma out of the parking lot, and Ty, who'd picked up the moving truck, followed her. Harry had driven his truck too, and Blake had his SUV. They all caravanned to Thelma's new house, which sat about in the middle of the island.

Sage hadn't been here since they'd originally looked at it,

and that had been over a month ago. "It's nice," she said to herself this time as she pulled up to the house. It sat back off the road and had a nice, long driveway, which Thelma pulled into first.

The unloading started, and Sage texted her Supper Club to let them know things were humming along nicely. None of them had to work on Saturdays—and Sage had taken today off—and they'd all agreed to converge on Thelma's new place and help her unpack. Help her get groceries. Anything they could so she'd be set up by nightfall, ready to live on her own, no rummaging through boxes and calling for takeout.

Sage stood at the front door, directing traffic with every item that came into the house. It couldn't be bigger than the apartment, but it felt like it had astronomically more air to breathe. More room to just be and live. Better energy.

Bea and Cass arrived together, and Cass said, "We'll get the bed made up," as she and Bea headed that way. Joy and Lauren worked in the kitchen, putting away Thelma's pots and pans, her utensils, and her dishes.

Sage sliced through the plastic wrapped around a new rug Thelma had bought, and she and Ty worked together to put down a piece of sticky under-the-rug matting to keep it from slipping. Then, they laid the rug over it and anchored it with the feet on the sectional Thelma had bought and had delivered yesterday.

"It's nice," she said to no one in particular. Thelma liked far brighter colors than Sage, so she didn't comment on the pink, purple, and red flowered flooring. It wasn't what she'd pick, but she only had to visit here from time to time.

"What's this?" Harry asked as he brought in a box that looked like it had come from a home goods store.

"That's her fireplace," Sage said. "That needs to be assembled. Could you guys tackle that?" She could see a hairstyle and know where to trim and what to keep, but lining up screw B onto piece 2? Sage couldn't see it.

"We've got it," Harry said as he and Oliver started to open the box.

Bessie showed up about an hour after unpacking had commenced, and she had fresh bread, butter, and jam to go with the doughnuts Harry had brought from the apartment. Everyone paused to come have a bite to eat, and Sage's gratitude swung violently upward. "Thanks for coming, everyone," she said.

"Yes," Thelma added quickly. "Thank you so much." She caught Sage's eye, a smile flirting with her expression.

"Are you excited to be here alone?" she asked as she smeared raspberry jam on the honey whole wheat bread. That combination made Sage's taste buds rejoice, and she took a big bite as she looked at her sister.

"Yeah," Thelma said. "I think it's going to be great." The doorbell rang, and several of them turned in that direction. The house had been divided in half, with the front door opening on the edge of the living room. It expanded back and to the right, with the kitchen-dining-room-combo in the back corner.

"Who could that be?" Thelma wondered, and Sage kept

an eye on her as she navigated past her couch to get the door. A short, older woman stood there, her blonde pixie cut reminding Sage of Bea's new hairdo from when her divorce had been finalized. She'd grown it out in the past year or so, but Sage loved the pixie on her.

Thelma spoke with the woman for a few minutes, and then she turned back to the house with a literal stockpot in her hands. She even now carried it with oven mitts, and she looked like she'd been hit with a two-by-four.

"What in the world?" Cass asked as she bustled forward to help.

"My neighbor on that side." Thelma nodded to her left. "She brought me some soup." She set it on the counter where they were all feasting on bread and butter, and everyone looked at it like it might contain a trio of cobras.

"Soup?" Grant finally asked. "She knows it's already eighty degrees outside, and we haven't even hit May yet, right?"

Sage continued to blink, because those were her thoughts too. Soup? Who made soup in the summertime?

"She was very nice," Thelma said feebly. "Said she's been divorced for six years, and she's finally figured out how to be happy."

Sage snapped back to attention, her gaze lasering in on Thelma's. "You don't have to *figure out* how to be happy, Thelma," she said. "You're doing great, and you can *choose* to be happy."

Her sister nodded, and Sage suddenly wanted everyone to leave so she could be there with Thelma alone. She could make sure the coffee cups got put in the right cupboard, and she would allow Thelma to be nervous and weepy about living here by herself.

Or maybe she'd do some of the weeping. She wasn't looking forward to living by herself all that much, but she reminded herself that she had Gypsy.

And what about Ty?

The question simply entered her mind, unbidden but oh-so-loud. She didn't know how to answer it, because she'd only been dating Ty for a couple of months. She wasn't Bea, and she didn't fall in love in only a few days.

She had time, and she caught Ty's eye from across the dining room table. His eyebrows went up, but she shook her head. No, she wasn't going to tell him she was thinking about where they might live if they got married. His house was great, and big enough.

The one she'd just put an offer on was too. Would he move there with her? Why was she even buying a house right now if she thought she might vacate it in the next year?

Whoa, a year? She shook her head at herself now. Surely she and Ty wouldn't fall in love and get married so fast. Or would they?

Could be less than a year, she thought, and she lifted her gaze to Ty's again. He grinned at Oliver and said something, but neither of them laughed. She'd wanted a friend, and he'd become one quickly. She'd wanted someone to treat her right, and it seemed all Ty thought of was her needs, her wishes, her wants and desires.

Sage had always been exceptionally good at crossing

bridges only when necessary and only when she came to them. So she shelved her thoughts for now. She needed somewhere to live that wasn't the stifling apartment. She *needed* the waterfront way, and it didn't matter how long she lived in the house on the coast.

She couldn't wait to get there, and as for her and Ty... well, she'd cross that bridge when she had to.

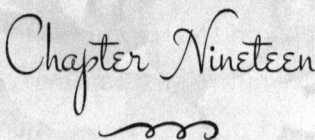

Chapter Nineteen

Ty pounded his feet against the sand, so much turmoil brewing inside him. It felt like a hurricane forming over warm ocean, the streams twirling and swirling and accelerating intensely. All he could think about was him and Sage. Sage and him.

They'd been dating for almost three months now. He'd found her sister a house, and Thelma had moved out. Sage's financing and closing had taken a little longer, but she should be able to move into her new, waterfront home the first week of May.

She'd wanted to then throw Bessie a bridal shower in her new place, and he knew she'd been planning that.

What he didn't know was why she needed him. She had plenty of friends here on the island, and while she'd told him she wanted to start their relationship that way, Ty knew she wanted more.

She wanted the world—and he'd realized he did too.

Talk to her, he told himself. His pulse started to yell the same message. *Talk to her, talk to her, talk-talk to her-her.*

He reached the lifeguard station and turned his canines around. Several minutes later, they'd gone up the beach, and Ty had walked back and forth a couple of times on the very solid concrete to give himself a minute to cool down.

Then he knocked on Sage's apartment door, expecting her to have it open for him. After all, it was Thursday morning, and he'd been stopping by for the past couple of weeks to catch a quick breakfast with her. Scheduled. Routine.

He tried the knob, and sure enough, it turned easily. He called, "It's just me," but she didn't respond. Gypsy barked and leapt off the couch like he was an antelope and not an eighty-pound shaggy dog.

Ty chuckled and bent down to say hello to the other black dog in his life. Sherman and Brother greeted Gypsy too, and with three big dogs in the small apartment living room really filled the place up. He glanced down the hallway, still didn't see Sage, and weighed his options.

He unclipped the dogs from his belt, stepped into the kitchen, and opened the cupboard above the microwave. He'd brought over a couple of T-shirts last week, and he pulled out a fresh one and tugged it over his head.

The weather kept getting warmer and warmer, but Ty hadn't adjusted his running time. He liked his routines, and as he leaned against the peninsula in Sage's kitchen and eyed the hallway, he wondered if his relationship with Sage was still as exciting as she wanted it to be. The truth was, his life was very boring. He knew terms no one else did, and he could really only have a meaningful conversation with other real estate agents.

Doubt assaulted him, and he crossed the living room to the mouth of the hallway. "Sage?"

She didn't answer, and he took a few tentative steps down the hall. Her bedroom sat in the far corner, and when he reached the bathroom door, he realized it was closed and the shower was running.

He backtracked to the kitchen and started making coffee, his heartbeat pounding at him for some reason. About the time he had a cup of coffee with sugar in it, Sage said, "Oh, Brother. Hey, boy." She appeared at the end of the hallway, wearing a sundress and her hair flowing over her shoulders. It was bone dry, which meant she hadn't washed it, but Ty still found her fresh from the shower.

"Morning," he said. "We just came in."

"I see that." She smiled and came toward him. She leaned down and gave him a quick kiss when he wanted to hold on. He wasn't sure why he didn't. Maybe because he'd let Sage dictate everything about this relationship, and she seemed satisfied with a quick peck on her way to get a cup of coffee.

Talk to her.

He watched her as she got everything put together and joined him at the small table against the wall. "What?"

"Nothing."

"You're staring at me."

Ty took a sip of his coffee, but that didn't settle his stomach. "Are you—I mean, are you happy with how things are going with us?"

Her eyebrows went up. "Am I happy about how things are going with us?"

"Yeah." Ty maintained his eye contact, because he didn't want a relationship like he'd had with Gloria, and he suddenly knew that he'd somehow gotten himself into the same situation. He wouldn't break-up with Sage; she'd end things with him. He waited for her to lead out on almost everything. He *followed*.

"Because I feel like we're turning stale," he said honestly. "And I'm..." He wasn't sure how to tell her he was tired of following a woman around. "My last girlfriend, remember I told you about Gloria?"

"Yes," she said cautiously.

"She controlled everything. She wouldn't even let me break-up with her, for crying out loud."

"Okay." Sage stirred her coffee, but she hadn't taken a single sip yet.

"I guess I just feel sort of powerless in this relationship too, and I don't like it." There. He'd said something he hadn't even realized was true until it had come out of his mouth. "I want—I want to give you everything you've ever wanted. I don't know if I'm doing that or not. I don't know if you're happy or not. I don't know if my boring, day-to-day routine will be exciting enough for you long-term."

When she didn't immediately reassure him that of course he was amazing, non-boring, and she was totally happy, Ty's frustration only grew.

"I guess I want to know what you think is different between us compared to you and Jerry."

"I don't think Jerry cared if I was happy or not," Sage said. "So that's one big difference."

"But he was boring," Ty pressed. "He got up and went to work every day. He got home and kissed you about how you just kissed me, I'm imagining."

Her eyes widened, and Ty didn't like the shock pouring into them. "I—I..."

"Yeah." Ty finished his coffee in a couple of big gulps. "I have to go. I'm meeting with Katherine again this morning. Then, I have another boring call with a client, and then I need to check on some photos that should've been taken. Then, to top it all off, I have some *super exciting* paperwork to go through tonight." He got to his feet and took his coffee cup into the kitchen.

Sage quickly joined him at the sink. "Is this about us, or about you?" she asked, gently putting her hand on his arm.

"Both, I think." He looked at the wall in front of the sink, because she didn't have a window there. "I like you a lot, Sage," he said. "But you were clear from the beginning that you want something special, and well, I don't know if I measure up." He barely looked at her as he turned. "I'll call you later, okay?"

"Okay," she murmured, and Ty bent to grab his dogs' leashes before he left the apartment. "Ty."

He turned back to Sage with his hand on the doorknob. She had not said anything to assuage his need for reassurance, and he now seriously believed he was as dry toast as they come. And Sage Grady certainly didn't want dry toast.

She came toward him, and Ty dropped the leashes. He moved toward her, took her face in his hands, and *kissed* her. None of this pecking stuff. No quick kiss on the way to something else. Nothing friendly about it at all.

Heat filled him from top to bottom, and he braided his fingers through her hair and turned her until he had her pressed up against the front door. This was the kiss he wanted when he came over, and maybe he just needed to be more up-front about it.

Maybe he should've pulled her onto his lap and *kissed* her instead of letting her walk on by him. He pulled away and said, "I didn't like the kiss you gave me this morning."

"I see that now."

"I don't want boring either." His voice turned husky as it stuck in his throat. "But I know I'm boring, so I'm just going to have to take what I want when it comes to us, because even though you haven't said it, I know you're feeling the same as me."

"What's that?" She curled her fingers through the hair at the nape of his neck, which sent showers through his limps.

"That we've turned a little stale."

"Maybe a little," she said.

"You don't want that."

She shook her head. "Jerry did get up and go to work every day. He came home and kissed me like I kissed you this morning. He might ask me about the farm a little, or how the salon was. But he didn't really *care*." She looked up at him, earnestness in her eyes. "I know you care, Ty. There's a big difference."

"We still can't agree on what restaurant to go to in the evening."

"Okay."

"I sometimes feel like you only keep me around to make sure the house is going to go through."

She gasped and stepped away from him. Her hands fell back to her sides, and she blinked a couple of times. "That is not true."

He lifted his chin. "Then, what's your plan, Sage?"

"I'm sorry?"

"Why is this house so important to you? If we're together—you're not new to this. People date to get married. Unless you don't want to get married? What do—what do you want?"

Maybe she didn't even want to get married. Maybe she wanted her waterfront house, and she'd keep him around, but she didn't want him as a husband.

"I've never been married," he said. "I'm—I'd like to get married."

Her eyebrows went up again.

"Not right now," he said. "I'm not saying I want to marry you, but I date to get married. That's my end-goal. I guess I need to know what yours is."

"I didn't have a good marriage," she said.

"You've told me."

"I don't even know what that looks like."

"Then we're on the same playing field."

Sage reached up and ran her hand through her hair, the sigh that came from her mouth frustrated. "I don't know, Ty. I'm not thinking that far ahead, to be honest."

"At least it's the truth," he said.

"I like you a lot," she said. "I don't want to break up."

"I don't want that either," he said. "But I do need to know what you're feeling and thinking. I can't read your mind, and it's unfair of you to make me try."

She folded her arms. "I'm not making you try to read my mind."

"Okay," he said. "So...dinner tonight?"

"It's Supper Club tonight," she reminded him. "That's why you have T-shirts above my microwave, so we can have breakfast on Thursdays together."

A smile twitched against the corners of his mouth. "So you want me to stay."

"I don't want you to leave."

"I'll order those bacon and egg sandwiches." He took a step toward her, his skin itching to be next to hers again. "And kiss you until they get here?"

She tipped her head back and laughed, the sound filling the apartment and Ty's heart. He'd had plenty of difficult conversations with clients, colleagues, and even exes. Sage, for some reason, had been harder, probably because he wanted her to like and respect him after all the words got said.

Ty arrived in front of her, his thumbs flying over his phone. "You don't like bacon, which I so don't understand, but whatever." He smiled at her. "Different strokes for different folks. I got you the sausage one."

"With the jalapeno jelly?"

"Adding the jalapeno jelly now..." A few more taps, and done. Ty looked up. He didn't ask her if he could kiss her again. He simply leaned down and did it, taking her into his arms and somehow moving her over to the couch and shooing the dogs off of it so he could kiss his girlfriend.

Chapter Twenty

A nother Thursday went by, where Ty showed up on Sage's doorstep, ordered breakfast from somewhere, and then kissed her until it arrived. They laughed and talked, and Sage could admit he'd reintroduced some spark into their relationship. She hadn't even realized it had gone out, and every morning when she first woke, she wondered if she'd been more of a problem in her marriage with Jerry than she'd originally assumed.

Her thoughts ran in circles this Thursday morning too, a healthy dose of worry in there as well. Could she become the woman she wanted to be?

"Why does the house matter so much?" she wondered to the ceiling, to Gypsy in his dog bed in the corner, to the barely-there dawn light, to herself.

She wasn't sure, but she felt like she'd been in a holding pattern, that she was being held back by a thick layer of plastic wrap, and she wouldn't be able to move forward until she left this apartment behind.

She needed to leave this stage of her life and step into a new one. She'd seen Bea do it after her divorce by cutting her hair and taking a vacation by herself.

Maybe Sage needed to do that.

She'd seen Cass heal and move forward after her husband's death by finally taking the vacation she'd been planning for the two of them once they became empty-nesters.

Maybe Sage needed to go back to something she'd planned to do with Jerry that hadn't been realized.

She'd seen Lauren reinvent herself after almost being indicted by the FBI, losing her job, and moving twelve hundred miles without a plan at all. She'd *made* a plan for herself, and while Sage had never really needed one of those, right now she did.

She'd watched Joy wrestle within herself about where to live, and why, and who to be with. She'd taken bold steps—in the middle of the school year—so she could find her own brand of happiness.

She and Bessie had watched them all, and they'd taken the big step of moving to Hilton Head too. Then, Bessie had confronted all her fears, opened a bread bakery, and started dating again. In only three more weeks, she'd marry Oliver, and their next chapter would start.

Maybe Sage needed to start outlining the next chapter, at least.

Her phone buzzed, and she reached for it to silence the

alarm. The clock read seven-thirty, and that sent alarm through her until she remembered she'd canceled her morning walk with Ed and the dogs today, because—

She sat straight up. "Today is the day."

She was moving today.

The next chapter started *today*, and Sage still had no idea what should be in it. What she wanted to write in it. What the plan was.

She rolled out of bed and got dressed. She started packing up the things she'd been using to live since she'd packed the last box last night—toothbrush, toothpaste, hairbrush, her pajamas, her bedding.

She took that out to her car, along with Gypsy's box of essentials that she used every single day. Then she wouldn't have to dig through her belongings to find what she needed to have somewhere to sleep and to feed her dog.

"Come on, buddy," she said to Gypsy as she re-entered the apartment. "Let's go for a quick walk, and then we have to go get the moving truck so we're ready when the boys come."

Ty and his friends were so much more than boys, and Sage thought about him every step and for every second she took Gypsy down to the water's edge and then back.

Thelma arrived just as Sage returned to the apartment, and she asked, "Ready?"

Nerves ran through Sage, and she grabbed onto her sister and pulled her against her chest.

"Oof." Thelma took a moment to return the hug. "Hey, what's wrong? I'm never the one to comfort you."

Sage had had to be the strong sister since the moment their mother had died, when she was only twenty years old. She'd never really burdened her siblings with her insecurities and problems, but her emotions swelled and overflowed. She sniffled as she said, "What if this house doesn't have all the answers?"

Thelma pulled away and searched her face. "Sage, of course the house doesn't have all the answers."

That so wasn't what she wanted to hear. Irritation fired through her, and Sage fell back a step. "I'm ready to go." She wiped her face and turned in a full circle, trying to remember where she and Thelma were going.

Moving truck. Right. Thelma was driving them there, and Sage would drive the truck back here. She didn't need keys. Just her purse.

She picked it up only to have Thelma pluck it away from her. "You've given me advice my whole life," she said. "It's time for you to take some from me." She folded Sage's purse into her arms, and Sage frowned at her.

"You've told me I can choose happiness, but you don't. You've told me that I can't hold onto the past and move into the future, but you won't let go."

"I *have* let go," Sage said. But now she wondered. She'd wanted a bigger piece of property so she could...recreate what she'd had and then been forced to abandon in Texas. The hobby farm. Her chest couldn't hold a full breath as tight as it was, and her breathing turned shallow. "I'm happy...enough."

"No, you're not," Thelma said. "You might be able to

fool your friends, and even your dog, and maybe even Ty for a while, but you don't fool me, Sage. I know what you've given up for me and Owen, and we both love you for it. But you wear everything on your face where I can see it, and you're not happy. You haven't let go."

Sage's strong façade started to crumble. "I don't know how," she admitted, her voice pinched and pitching up. "I like being outside. I like chickens, and I want to be right on the water. It...soothes me."

"Then maybe the house will help you heal," Thelma said. "I don't know, but I think it's dangerous for you to think that when you move in there, everything in your life will magically align. That's not how real life works."

Sage nodded, her walls all down now. Tears pricked her eyes. "You're right," she whispered.

Thelma gathered her into her arms this time, and Sage bowed her head and curled into her sister's shoulder. "How'd you get to be so smart?" Sage asked.

"I have a great older sister," Thelma whispered back. "Who's going to be late for her moving crew if we don't get over to the truck rental office."

Sage half-laughed and half-cried, and then she stepped back and took her purse from Thelma's outstretched hand. "Let's go."

Yes. It was moving day.

"LUNCH IS HERE," BEA CALLED AS SHE WALKED through the front door of Sage's new house. "It's so open. Look—" She sucked in a breath. "Cass. This view is better than yours."

Cass came to stand beside Bea, both of them carrying items that were too heavy to be standing around staring for very long. "Look at that," she murmured.

"You found it," Sage said as she came around the corner that obviously led into the kitchen. She wore the biggest, brightest smile Bea had ever seen on her face, and she hadn't realized how...dull Sage had been before. "Thank you for stopping to pick this up."

She arrived and took one of the heavy bags from Bea. "Come on. Come see what we've done this morning."

It looked like someone had moved into today, that was for sure, with some boxes already unpacked and broken down and some still sitting there taped closed.

"Did the furniture come with this place?" Bea asked as she trailed her hand along the back of a sectional she had never seen at Sage's apartment.

"Yes," Sage said. "Most of it, at least. The couches stayed. The dining room table. I put my two-seater one on the deck out back until I can save up for some real patio furniture."

"There's a deck out back," Bea said, exchanging a glance with Cass. They both stepped outside, and if anything, the view only got better.

"It's so gold," Cass said from Bea's side. "It doesn't look this gold from the east coast of Hilton Head."

"Maybe it's lower," Bea said. "She has way more greenery here too. Maybe that's influencing our cones and rods." No matter what, this place felt absolutely amazing and perfectly right for Sage. No wonder she'd held a massive party when her offer had been accepted and she'd officially bought this house.

"We're eating," Sage said. She ducked back inside, and Bea looked at the wooden dining room table-for-two before she returned to the kitchen too.

"Maybe we could put our money together and help her with a patio table," she murmured to Cass. "As a housewarming gift." She nodded over to Lauren, who stood in the kitchen, pulling white Chinese containers out of the bags she and Cass had brought. "We'll ask everyone in the Supper Club."

"And Ty," Cass whispered back.

"What are you two talking about?" Bessie asked with a wary look in her eye as she threw a pile of napkins onto the much bigger and much more impressive dining room table. This one sat eight without a leaf in it, and Bea could see the grandeur Supper Club would be here in this home.

"Nothing," Cass said. "We were lucky to get that sweet and sour shrimp, so whoever eats it should really love every bite."

Bessie grinned at her and stepped in to hug Cass. "Is that your way of saying 'no one touch that shrimp, because I want it all'?"

Cass laughed, said, "Maybe," and they moved over to the island too. Bea took in the fireplace and the big screen TV above it. Sage didn't watch much TV, and when she did, she claimed to like to lay in bed to do it.

"They took the rugs," Sage said. "So I'm going to go rug shopping tomorrow after work."

"Hot Friday night date," Bea said with a smile.

"You want to come?" Sage asked. "I think Ty is showing Katherine-the-Great several new houses tomorrow night, and he can't come." She spoke in a teasing yet kind tone, and Bea loved her so much.

"I'll come," Cass said. "I'm dying to pick out something besides industrial Berber carpet."

"I thought you were doing Lauren's nursery," Bea said.

"I am," Cass said. "But I need some new jobs." She sighed as if getting paid a lot of money to redesign the Country Club's conference and wedding spaces was just so taxing. Bea worked in Grant's office, answering phones and managing all the sub-contractors they needed to keep the vacation and other rental properties operating smoothly.

He updated the listings, dealt with the customers, and spent a lot of time on-site doing some of the repairs and updates himself. His management company was successful too, and they didn't hurt for money, but they didn't live in a million-dollar beach house like Cass and Harry.

"Anyone can come," Sage said. "I like the neutral color palette here, but I'm looking to add some color in some of the accessories."

"This couch is amazing," Cass said as she sank onto it. "But some colorful pillows would be amazing."

"Yes, like that." Sage turned back to the kitchen and took

a plate of beef and broccoli from Ty with a smile. Bea liked watching the two of them, as they exuded some sort of... magic that she wanted to feast on.

She wanted to introduce some of that newly-dating magic back into her relationship with Grant, and she thought about how she could do that while she got her own plate of Chinese food and joined her friends at the table.

"All right," Sage said several minutes later. "Who wants a tour?"

The only person not there was Joy, as she couldn't take a Thursday off of school in May, when all the tests were being administered. But everyone else immediately got to their feet, voices already chitting and chatting as Sage started to lead them through the house.

"What a great fresh start," Lauren said after Sage had shown them the master suite and the office. "I'm super jealous of that office."

"I'm thinking about having someone come give me a bid on adding an outside entrance into it," Sage said. "I have the driveway space for clients, and I could have my own salon, right here at home."

"That's a great idea," Bessie said. "I thought you liked Mionic."

"I do," Sage said. "Just musings." She grinned and led them upstairs. "I've already videoed my sons, and Dallen said he wants to come visit. I guess he's amassed a bunch of PTO at his farm, and I told him to come for the Fourth of July."

"That's great," Cass said. "Sariah and Robbie are coming then too."

Bea's fear-of-missing-out reared up, and she had to stuff it back down. She, Grant, and Shelby would be taking a month-long road trip with his daughter before she moved to college, and it was their goal to visit and explore at least five National Parks this summer. Grant had hired someone to take over the rentals while they were gone, and Dave would actually start coming into the office next week to get a sense of things for the next six weeks before they left.

They'd be here for the fireworks, but they were literally leaving the next day. Bea told herself not to be jealous about seeing her friends' children. She had before and would again.

"And that's it," Sage said as she led them back down the staircase that gave a spectacular view of the water beyond.

"Smart to put your couches up in the loft," Bessie said. "I would never leave that spot. It's *perfect*."

"This whole house agrees with you," Bea said as she reached the bottom step. She drew Sage into a hug. "I'm so happy for you."

"Thank you, Bea."

"I didn't mean to make you move here," she whispered, not sure where the words had come from. "I'm sorry."

Sage pulled back and studied her face, her eyes flitting back and forth between Bea's. "Don't apologize. I'm embarking on my grand adventure too—just a few years behind you." Her smile wobbled a little bit before Sage strengthened it, and Bea decided she'd said what she needed to.

No need to make Sage's moving day any harder or longer than it already would be.

"Love you, Sage," she said. "I better get back to work."

"Yeah," Lauren sighed. "Me too."

"I'll stay and help with the kitchen," Cass said, meeting Bea's eyes. "I'll call Harry to come get me later."

"All right." Bea left with Lauren, and when she arrived back at the office, she found Grant kicked back in his chair, his feet up on his desk and his phone at his ear.

"...know that, Julie."

His twin sister. Bea put her purse on her desk and moved over to Grant. His eyes met hers, and he put his feet down. "I have to go," he said. "I'll call you back." He tossed his phone onto his desk just as Bea slid onto his lap. "What's going on with you?"

"Nothing," she said, but she wrapped her arms around him and kissed him. "I just missed you," she murmured against his lips.

He matched her stroke for stroke, sending desire through Bea from head to toe. "You were gone for an hour," he whispered as he moved his mouth to her neck.

Grant didn't wear a tie to work, but Bea fiddled with the buttons on his polo as she said, "Shelby has debate practice after school."

"You want to play hooky?"

"Mm, yes, I think I do."

Grant brought his mouth back to hers for another sizzling kiss, all the answer she needed to whether or not he'd take her home and make love to her.

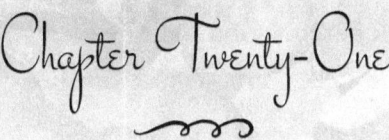

Chapter Twenty-One

Bessie Clifton wasn't sure if the bride was supposed to stop and pick up her own refreshments for her wedding, but she'd also made all the bread she and Oliver would be serving at their celebration later today too.

She also didn't care what was traditional or not. She and Oliver had planned the wedding they wanted to have, and the only person Bessie had considered more than herself was Wyn.

For her daughter was also engaged, and they'd be back for some nuptials for her and Douglas come September. She had taken longer to accept the diamond, though Bessie suspected Wyn had been in love with Douglas for about the same time Bessie had been in love with Oliver.

She'd just needed extra time to make sure things were really right, and Bessie wouldn't fault her for that. She'd been through a lot with her ex-boyfriend before they'd moved to Hilton Head, and Douglas had been the first man she'd dated since that break-up.

She hurried out of the back of the shop, pushing the cart of bread in front of her. Wyn herself got out of the car and opened the back hatch. "Got it all?"

"Yes," Bessie said. "They'd just finished slicing it, so we should be good to go."

Wyn had packed the butters and jams last night, and they waited in three coolers they'd already loaded into the SUV. Wyn helped load the three dozen loaves of bread into the back of the cart, and Bessie pushed the cart back inside. "Bye, Hillie!" she called.

"I'll see you there," her assistant baker called, and Bessie hurried back out to the car. Wyn drove them through the streets of Hilton Head, which would be bustling with tourists in only a couple of weeks, once school got out and families started to travel for the summer.

As Wyn drove by a store that had a little bit of everything for rock bottom prices, she looked over to her daughter. "Do you think we have enough toasters?"

"Yes," her daughter said decisively. "Mom, we have thirteen toasters."

"Feels like an unlucky number," Bessie murmured. She hadn't invited very many people to the wedding. Her friends in the Supper Club. All of her employees. Wyn and Douglas. Her side of the guest list had actually been quite small, as she had two sisters who would be coming by themselves, along with her parents.

But Oliver? The man had owned a smoothie shop on the

island for thirteen years now. He seemed to know every other small business owner, every local resident, everyone. He had brothers and their families, as well as his daddy coming in from Alabama.

It was his first marriage, and while he'd told her he'd do big or small, she'd sensed he wanted a big celebration where he could invite anyone he wanted. No restrictions.

So Bessie had done a little researching, and she'd found a great wedding venue that hadn't cost her an arm and a leg the way Lauren's nuptials had. Cass had gotten married at the Country Club, but she was currently in the middle of remodeling that facility now, and it sat a bit out of Bessie's price range anyway.

She'd booked The Oaks Overlook, which boasted ten acres of emerald green grass, trees, bushes, and meticulously sculpted flowerbeds for outdoor weddings. They had an altar spot right on the edge of a low cliff, with the ocean sashaying ashore below, with spectacular views any time of day.

They had two indoor chapels, and a variety of décor options for anything indoor or outdoor. Bessie had been overwhelmed at their binder of options, but she'd sat down with Joy, who spoke a love language in binders, and they'd gone through things pretty quickly.

Joy had a way of helping Bessie eliminate the things she didn't like easily, and that had only left her a few choices.

She'd gone with an evening wedding, since neither she nor Oliver wanted to be too formal and serve dinner. In fact, her off-the-cuff idea of a toast and bread bar with smoothies was exactly what guests would get.

Oh, and the cake. She'd splurged on the cake, but she hadn't been able to stop herself. She loved sweets, and both she and Oliver had agreed on the delectable, light-as-clouds, white wedding cake with a light, vanilla frosting and an orange curd filling.

It was sweet, smooth, with a bite of tartness that had make her eyes widen and brighten upon first bite. And when she'd seen the same look on Oliver's face... She'd splurged on the cake.

"Mom, look." Wyn pointed to the left, and Bessie had to lean to look across the SUV. The sky held the puffy clouds she'd been hoping and praying for. "Clouds." Wyn smiled at her, and Bessie reached over and covered her daughter's hand.

Because she was getting married at sunset, she'd hoped for clouds to hold all the pinks, violets, tangerines, and sapphires as the day ended.

"You'll be okay next week while Oliver and I are gone?" Bessie reached up and wiped the corner of her eye, where a tiny teardrop had gathered.

"Yes," Wyn said. "We're going to pick the menu for the wedding." She glanced over to Bessie. "Thank you for increasing the budget."

"I hope you only get married once," Bessie said, smiling at her daughter. "It's not that much."

It actually was a lot, but she'd discussed it with Oliver, and for a couple thousand more, Wyn and Douglas could offer a beef dish for their guests. Wyn didn't have a lot of people on her invite-list either, but Douglas had grown up here on Hilton Head.

But their venue had cost almost nothing—Wyn wanted to be married in a church—and she and Douglas had decided to host the wedding luncheon in his parents' back-yard. They apparently lived in one of the wealthier neighbor-hoods here on the island, and they had room to host the hundred-guest limit both she and his parents had approved.

The radio warbled between them as Wyn finished the drive to the south side of the island, where the bridal room at The Oaks Overlook waited. Bessie got checked in and assigned a place to park. Two men accompanied her outside, and they started taking the coolers and trays of bread.

"It'll all be set up?" Bessie asked, her nerves worrying at her like crazy. She wanted her wedding to count too. She wanted it to be as special as Joy's, though she didn't have a custom-made dress with pastel chalk on it.

She wanted it to be as spectacular as Lauren's, though Bessie knew that was literally impossible. She wanted it to be as classy and sophisticated as Cass's, which had run without a hitch. And she wanted it to be as joyful as Bea's had been, with two families joining together to celebrate the love of their loved ones.

When the men had emptied the car, she collected her garment bag, her makeup kit, and her hat box and faced her daughter. "We're in the Magnolia Bridal Suite."

"Wow," Wyn said with a grin. "A whole suite, huh?"

Bessie smiled at her and re-entered the building. She

followed the signs to the Magnolia Bridal Suite, which sat at the very back of the building. There, she found a woman wearing a navy skirt suit and holding a clipboard waiting for her.

"You must be Bessie," she said cheerfully. She had to be close to Bessie's age, with a cute, shoulder-length haircut which curled up at the ends. She shone with sunlight as she shook Bessie's hand. "I'm Linda. This whole room is yours, including all the changing rooms over here on the right."

Linda led her around the suite, which had a minibar in the back next to the door that led outside. She pushed it open and said, "When you're ready, you can go to the staging area right there under the tent. Then you walk down the aisle."

Several people were setting up chairs for her wedding, with one tying on the yellow bows Bessie had requested, and two working on filling the altar with flowers.

Everything suddenly became real, and Bessie's breath caught in her throat. She turned back to find Wyn hanging up their bags and Linda already heading over to the far wall. She made it through the rest of the tour—a bathroom and a button Bessie could push to summon Linda back to the Magnolia Bridal Suite should she have any questions or concerns.

She smiled as Linda left, and then she stood there for a moment, basking in the feelings running through her. She smiled, her mouth barely moving upward, but the gesture filling her whole body.

"Mom," Wyn said. She arrived in front of her, concern

on her face. "Why are you just standing there? Bea's on the phone, and everyone needs to know where to go."

Bessie sucked in a breath through her nose and took her phone. "Thanks, baby." She put the device to her ear. "Hey, Bea." Her emotions vibrated through her body. "It's the Magnolia Bridal Suite."

She walked away from her daughter. "It's all the way at the back of the building, and Bea, it's just gorgeous." Her voice shook, along with her hands, and she pulled in another breath to try to steady herself.

"I can't wait to see it," Bea said. "We're on the way down the hall. Sage forgot her toasters, so she's a bit behind us, but otherwise, we're good to go."

Bessie nodded, though she was on the phone. "Thanks, Bea. See you in a minute."

Sure enough, most of her friends arrived in the Magnolia Bridal Suite only a minute later, and all the hooks got filled with garment bags containing dresses, shoes, and pantyhose.

Bessie couldn't stop the tears, and she gripped Cass tightly. "Thank you," she said through a narrow throat. These women knew her, and Bessie didn't have to explain her emotions. She simply moved over to Joy and hugged her tightly.

Lauren gripped her, and Bessie marveled at the baby bump between them. She put her hand there and smiled at Lauren. "I love this for you," she whispered.

"You're getting married today, Bessie."

She smiled at Lauren, who smiled softly back at her.

There was nothing quite like a baby to bring pure joy and softness to anyone, hardened as they may be.

Bea hugged her, and Bessie said, "Okay, I'll hug Sage when she gets here, but I better start getting ready." She found her makeup bag and went to sit at the counter that ran along the front wall, the one with lighted mirrors.

Her friends joined her, and Bessie listened to them talk and laugh as she painted on her eyeliner, eyeshadow, and lipstick. She didn't want to become a completely different person, and she didn't wear a lot of makeup to begin with.

As she sat there, Sage arrived, and she put an entire hair bag on the counter next to Bessie. "I'm so sorry I'm late."

Bessie looked up and then stood to hug her best friend. "You're not late," she said. "You're right on time." She stepped back and looked at Sage. Her hair looked a little lighter than it usually did, but she'd already twisted and pinned it up, so it was hard to tell.

"Your hair is done already."

"So let's get yours done, and then I can do my makeup." Sage gave her one of her trademark smiles, and Bessie sat back down. Sage started working her magic with hairspray and curling irons and pins, and Bessie watched as she turned into a queen.

In fact, Sage set a tiara in her hair as the last thing she did, beaming as she leaned down and pressed her cheek to Bessie's. "He is so lucky." Then she turned and went to get herself ready.

Wyn was already dressed, and she helped Bessie into her wedding dress. She stepped into a pair of heels that lifted her up a couple of inches, and she watched her friends as they got their dresses zipped up, buttoned, and pinned.

She hadn't put any restrictions on colors, because she wasn't going the traditional route. She liked yellow, because it was sunny and happy, and Oliver called her "sunshine." So she'd put those bows on the chairs. She'd requested flowers on her wedding cake and the altar, but without color restrictions.

So it was that Lauren wore a light pink dress that went well with her dark hair and deeper complexion. Joy wore blue, because she was blonde and blue-eyed, and she knew how to make herself look amazing. In fact, Bessie suspected that she'd sewn this dress too.

Cass wore silver, because everything about Cass spoke of glamour and glitz, with a level of sophistication that one couldn't learn. Bea wore a soft shade of indigo that Bessie wasn't sure she'd ever seen before. And when Sage came out of the dressing room, she wore a gold dress that made her hair look even lighter. It alone was a short dress, ending at the knees, and as she stepped into a pair of black heels, her legs took such an amazing shape.

"Wow," Bessie said as Sage cocked one hip for the group. "You look like a movie star."

Sage laughed, her head tipping back in the carefree way it always did when she let loose.

"Ty's going to have a bombshell on his arm," Cass teased, reaching to flip down one of the sequins on Sage's shoulder strap. "Are you and him talking about marriage?"

"Not really," Sage admitted. "Things are..."

"You're still seeing him, aren't you?" Bea asked.

"Yes, yes," Sage said almost impatiently. "I'm just figuring some things out, that's all." She gave them all another smile. "He's being very patient with me."

"In that dress, I bet he is," Joy said.

Lauren giggled, her hand resting protectively on her baby belly. Her dress swooped across her midsection so as to hide it, but Bessie knew it was there.

"Mom," Wyn said. She stood near the door, her dress the color of green seaglass. She looked like an angel, and Bessie went to stand at her side. "It's almost time."

She put her arm around her daughter and leaned into her. "I love you."

"I'm so glad you found him, Mom," Wyn whispered. "You deserve someone who loves you and takes care of you, and I think that's Oliver."

Bessie smiled, her emotions still teeming near the surface. "Me too, baby."

She turned back to the women in her suite and opened her arms. "Come on over here and give me a hug, and then Wyn's going to get a selfie of all of us." She gestured to Shelby, Bea's step-daughter. "You too, honey. Everyone."

They piled into her arms, hugging her and congratulating her and enveloping her in the love of pure friendship.

"All right," Bea said, ever the taskmaster. "Bess, it's time to get married."

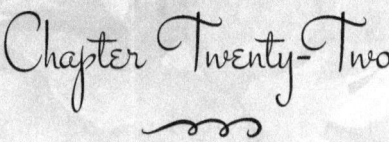

Chapter Twenty-Two

S age took the flowers an employee at The Oaks Overlook handed her, her smile stitched in place. She couldn't get it to flatten no matter what she did. This was the fifth of her friends to get married, and Sage's happiness moved through her genuinely.

She simply wasn't sure she wanted to get married again. Ty had asked her, point-blank, weeks ago, and she hadn't known how to answer him. She'd learned a lot about him that Thursday morning, mostly that he wanted to have more control in their relationship.

She hadn't even realized she'd stopped him from doing that.

Number two, he was more physical than she'd known, and she wasn't complaining about that. He liked to hold hands, wrap her up in his arms, and kiss her as often as possible. And he didn't want casual touching. Every touch was intimate and passionate and meaningful to him.

Yes, they argued about where to eat every time they went out. He teased her about her dislike of bacon, beets, mushrooms, and soft-boiled eggs. She'd taken to doing the same about things he liked that she didn't understand—namely, rare steak. Why cook it at all if he was going to eat it with so much red in it?

Thankfully, they'd managed to find things to do they both liked and could live with, and she sure did like spending time with him. Time doing things and slow, Southern time where they simply sat on her back deck and watched the water lap up on the shore.

She lay in his arms, on a loveseat her Supper Club friends had bought for her deck, and he stroked her hair. It was a beautiful life, and Sage did enjoy her time with him. Perhaps that was enough. Did they have to get married?

Bessie and Wyn went out the back door to go to the altar, but Sage went with the other women out the main door and down the hall to another exit. Ty, Grant, Blake, Harry, and Scott waited there, and Shelby tipped up onto her toes and kissed her daddy's cheek before she left first to go sit in the audience.

Sage's lungs shook as she took a breath, her eyes locked on Ty's. He was a handsome, handsome man, and she didn't want to stand in her own way. She'd heard his stories about his ex, and she didn't want to hurt him either.

"Wow," he said almost under his breath. "This is the most gorgeous dress I've ever seen." His eyes dripped down to her knees and then climbed again. "It's short."

"A little scandalous, right?" She grinned, glad Bessie

hadn't said anything about the length of the dress. She knew it wasn't exactly traditional for a wedding, but Bessie had said she wasn't trying to be conventional.

Ty took her into his arms and pressed his lips to her cheek. Even that was a passionate touch, and Sage leaned into it, silently telling him that she'd like to be alone with him to do more. Their eyes met as he pulled back, and oh, the devilish glint in those light hazel eyes...

"Ladies and gentlemen," the employee said. "We're ready for the procession. Let's go." She opened the glass door on the left, and someone else did it on the right. With them both open, they could proceed, and Cass and Harrison led them out.

Sage and Ty were last, right where Sage wanted to be. She didn't need people seeing her first, and she didn't need to make an impression. She absolutely loved Bessie, and she wanted to be there to support her. Plus, she did like getting all dressed up for an event. A glow seemed to come alive inside her when she did, and she thought she should do it more often, just to go to the grocery store or the beach. Just for fun.

Pavers led the way down the middle of the chairs that had been set up, and the sun had started to paint the sky in all the colors Mother Nature had to offer. They streaked through the deepening blue and got caught in the puffy clouds that floated through the sky. The orange could only be described as burnt, and the pink could only be called vibrant. Some violet and indigo streaked through that, with bands of light as well.

In the distance, past the altar where Oliver stood in a pristine suit of black, his dark hair slicked just-so, and his hands clasped, the world opened up.

Positively the whole world, with just sky and ocean and freedom. Sage closed her eyes and felt herself soaring through it for two steps. Then Ty's presence at her side grounded her, and she looked over to him. He wore a smile too; he wore the dark suit too; he knew a lot of people here at this wedding too.

A lump formed in Sage's throat, and she had no idea why.

When she reached the altar, she turned to the left while Ty went right, and she looked back down the aisle as Bessie and Wyn stepped to the head of it. They'd linked arms too, and they looked at one another for several long moments, each of them saying something, before they faced the crowd that had gathered and took the first step toward Oliver.

His smile grew and grew and grew with every step the women took, and when they reached him, he opened both arms and took them both into the safety of his chest. It was one of the most tender moments Sage had witnessed, only enhanced by the fact that she knew how grumpy Oliver Blackhurst could be.

For Bessie, though, he wasn't. He attended to her every need, and Sage wanted that for herself. Didn't she?

Or could she take care of herself?

In so many ways, these past years since her divorce, Sage had gotten so many things she'd wanted for so long. She didn't have to consult with anyone about what color to paint the bathroom or which rug to put in the living room.

Yes, Cass had come with her and offered her opinion, but in the end, Sage got to decide. And she liked deciding. She liked that she could eat whatever she wanted for breakfast, without any comments about how she ate too much fruit, or that she hadn't rinsed her bowl and put it in the dishwasher. Heck, if she didn't want to cook, she didn't. If she didn't want to do dishes one day—or two days, or three, or a week—she didn't.

The truth was, she'd been enjoying her independence in a way she hadn't anticipated.

You're still lonely sometimes, she thought as the ceremony started. She blinked, trying to clear her thoughts so she could be present for Bessie and Oliver.

"I always love seeing a couple at this altar," the reverend said. "Especially a pair of people who can't stop themselves from holding hands, and who aren't in their thirties anymore."

A ripple of chuckles moved through the crowd, though Sage wasn't sure what age had to do with marriage. Plenty of people got married young and had great marriages. Some people didn't, but the same could be true for people who'd gotten married later in life. Age didn't matter.

Sage felt like she should know more than she did. She was fifty years old, for crying out loud. Why was she standing at her best friend's wedding, wondering what to do with her life?

"I believe you two wrote some vows for each other," the

pastor said, and Bessie and Oliver turned toward one another.

Bessie shone like the moon, the stars, and the sun all in one, and she said, "Oliver, I know you like things to be short and sweet. You don't want to listen to a lot of words when a few will do. So I'll just say this: You came into my life right when I needed someone to challenge me, move me out of my comfort zone, and support me every step of the way. That person was you, and while sometimes I wanted to throttle you, I somehow fell in love with you instead."

She grinned at him and placed both of her hands on his chest, gripped his lapel, leaned into him. "I love the way you take care of me, and I love the way you love me." With that, she turned toward the pastor, then looked back at Oliver.

His throat worked as he swallowed, and Sage found herself tearing up too. A man who could show emotion ranked high on her chart, and she wished she still stood next to Ty, so she could cuddle into him.

She glanced at him and found him watching her too. His eyebrows went up, and she knew what he was asking. Did she want to stand at an altar like this...with him?

She gave him a smile and focused back on the couple. Oliver reached over and cradled Bessie's face. "I love you with everything I have," he said, his voice gruff and husky. "You are the ray of sunshine I've been searching for, and I can't believe you love me." His voice broke, and he shook his head, his smile there but wobbling. "I love you."

They turned back to the pastor, this time with Oliver's arm around Bessie, keeping her tucked closely against his side. The pastor pronounced them husband and wife, and Sage cheered as she tossed her flowers toward the altar.

Now, she just needed to get her head on straight, or she might lose the man who could stand at an altar like this and proclaim his love for her.

Her.

Sage wasn't even sure she knew what it felt like to be loved. Since she'd come from a marriage that had turned out to be a sham, she honestly did not know. She had not been loved, even through the dating, the wedding, bringing three children into a family.

Jerry had never loved her, and she wasn't even sure if someone *could* love her. That brought tears to her eyes, and she tried to shake them away. "Of course you can be loved," she whispered among all the celebrating. "Your friends love you."

And in that moment, Sage knew that yes, her friends loved her. But there was nothing that compared to the love of a good man, and Sage wanted it for herself. So she hurried to Ty's side and took his hand.

"Hey, beautiful," he said, and Sage simply basked in his presence. She still had some things to figure out, but Ty wasn't going anywhere right now.

***

"MONICA!" SAGE CAME AROUND THE CORNER AT the salon and broke into a little run. She grabbed onto her client from Sweet Water Falls, who'd flown here to get her hair done.

They laughed together, and Sage pulled back. "Wow, you look so...relaxed."

Monica reached up and bunched up her hair in her hands. It looked like she'd been dying it from home in the past couple of years since Sage had left Texas, but also like she'd been sleeping on the beach for a couple of days.

"How long have you been here?"

"Just came in yesterday," she said as she followed Sage to the chair. "We've had a great day on the beach, though. The kids are loving it here."

Sage pulled the drape around her friend and snapped it into place. "The beaches here are amazing," she said. "How's James handling the heat?"

Monica grinned and then rolled her eyes. "He's got a swim shirt on that goes to his chin and his wrist." She shook her head, and she did have a mane of hair. Sage had been doing Monica's hair for years, and she could hardly believe she'd flown here to get her cut and color.

"What are we doing today?" she asked, because she always asked clients what they wanted. She never knew what they'd been looking at, what changes they wanted, or if they just wanted more of what they already had.

"I want you to make it that blonde that everyone comments on," she said.

Sage knew what that was, and she grinned at her friend as she stared moving her fingers through Monica's hair.

"Take a couple of inches off. What do you think about bangs?"

"I wish they weren't so popular," Monica said, and that answered that question.

"I'll put those chunky layers in the bottom," Sage said. "Everyone at church will want to fly to Hilton Head to get their hair done." She laughed and added, "I'll go mix up."

When she got back with the lightener, Monica met her eye in the mirror. "You look really good, Sage."

"Aw, thanks." She smiled at her friend and started bleaching out her roots. She'd use the heaviest lightener there, then put on something lighter the further down she went.

"No, I mean...it's not about looking good. You seem... happier than you were in Texas." Monica wasn't grinning from ear to ear anymore, and she watched Sage in the mirror.

"Well," she said carefully, wondering what Monica saw in her. "I am happy here, but I was happy in Sweet Water Falls too."

"Okay," Monica said. "You just seem like you're thriving, that's all."

Sage flashed her a smile and kept working. The conversation moved to something else, but Sage reflected on what Monica said for the rest of the day. That night, she put together a simple dinner by opening a bagged salad and getting some precooked chicken breast out of the freezer. She opened her back door and let Gypsy out, then took her dinner onto her deck and sighed as she sat at the table.

The evening heat bore down on her, but she didn't mind

so much. The deck sat in the shade, and she got a little breeze off the water. Nothing big, like what happened on the east coast of Hilton Head. Her house was more sheltered, and she watched Gypsy sniff around the yard.

She'd eaten half her salad before she realized she'd left her phone somewhere. Sometimes, she felt chained to it, as she conducted so much business on it with the scheduling of her clients, the rescheduling, and then keeping up with her Supper Club. Today, Bea had told them all about Shelby's graduation on the video app, and that had taken her entire drive home from the salon.

So she enjoyed the slow evening of sitting on her deck, picking at her salad, and patting her dog. She thought about her sons and her daughter, a soft smile coming to her face. She smiled at Gypsy as the dog finally came and flopped on the deck next to her.

She sighed with such pure contentment, and of course, then her mind caught on how perfectly peaceful her life was in this moment. She didn't have a man at her side, but she pictured herself with Ty. They didn't have to talk constantly, and he could be here on the deck and she'd feel the same way.

Wouldn't she?

She thought she would, but she still wasn't sure she wanted to get married again, merge her life with someone else's again, and open herself up to be...unloved. Again.

Dusk fell, and Sage finally picked up her bowl and said, "Come on, Gypsy. Time to go inside."

She'd just stepped inside when the doorbell rang. Ty

called, "Sage, are you in there? It's Ty."

She hurried to put her bowl in the sink so she could go open the door, but she didn't make it that far before he called, "Sage? I'm coming in. Are you okay?"

She moved around the corner to find him striding inside, on high alert. "Hey."

He came to a complete stop. "You're okay."

"Yeah," she said slowly. "Why wouldn't I be okay?"

He frowned and continued toward her. He looked left and right, like perhaps she really wasn't okay. "I couldn't get in touch with you. None of your friends could. Thelma. No one."

"I was out on the deck."

"I called Barb, and she said you left the salon hours ago, but you didn't show up at the beach. I finally left *all of our friends* there to come do a welfare check." His eyes blazed, and not in a good way. "And you're just—out on the deck?"

Sage gaped at him. "The beach?"

"You forgot about the beach. We were meeting there tonight for Shelby's graduation party. You never showed up. Everyone is scared and worried." He shook his head and pulled out his phone. "I'll text Grant."

Sage didn't know what to say or do. "It's not like me to forget," she said, swallowing. "I even listened to Bea detail graduation on the way home." Her chest felt brittle, like her next breath would shatter it.

Ty's thumbs stopped flying as he sent his text, and he looked up at her. "I don't know how to feel right now."

Sage felt like crying, and she looked up at him, her eyes

filling with tears. They spilled over just as he swooped her into his arms and growled, "You scared me, Sage."

She held onto him, because she needed someone strong to hold her up when she felt so weak.

Chapter Twenty-Three

Ty didn't like listening to Sage cry. His chest stormed with emotions, and he kept tamping them back. His adrenaline wouldn't subside so quickly, and he wanted to lecture her for not showing up, for forgetting, for not having her phone with her.

"I'm mad at you," he said even as he held her right against his chest. "But I'm so, so glad you're okay."

She moved back a couple of inches, enough for him to gaze down at her. "What happened tonight?"

"I don't know." She shook her head, and sniffling, moved out of his arms. "I just forgot. I can't believe I forgot."

Ty looked out the windows to the deck Sage loved so much. The view. The yard for Gypsy. She hadn't gotten any chickens yet, but she'd been decorating the house to her liking. Sage had been living here for about a month now, and truth be told, Ty had seen a change in her.

She still went to work every day. She still communicated with her friends and cared about them. He'd never seen anyone sexier than Sage in that gold dress at Bessie's wedding.

But she'd changed too.

"You're different," he said as he faced the windows.

She didn't come to stand beside him, and his phone vibrated in his pocket. He pulled it out to find several texts from Harry, Grant, and Blake.

She's really there?

She's okay?

Lauren is beside herself. Can you have Sage call her?

"You need to call Lauren," he said. "She's upset."

"I don't know where my phone is right now," Sage said.

"I'll call it." Ty tapped a couple of times to do that, but Sage said, "It won't do any good. I keep it on silent at work, and I didn't turn it back on."

"That's the problem, isn't it?" He turned to face her. "I know you want room to grow. Room to be yourself, and get chickens, and eat dinner alone on the deck. But I feel like...I feel like you'd rather be alone than be with people."

Sage rifled through her purse, but she didn't find her phone. She looked up. "I like being with people too."

"On your terms," he said.

"That's usually how everyone operates." She huffed and added, "I'm going to go check my car." She left, and Gypsy came over to Ty. He stroked the dog's head absently, watching the front door.

Sage finally came back inside, wiping her nose and

saying, "Yes, Lauren, I'm fine. I swear. I just...I don't know what happened." She turned to close the door, and she kept her back to Ty. Her voice lowered, so he wasn't sure what she said to Lauren.

He had a feeling he was going to say something he'd regret later if he stayed, so he made sure he had his phone, and he approached Sage. "I'm going to go back to the beach," he said. He swept a kiss along her cheek and walked outside.

He'd made it all the way to his SUV before Sage called, "Ty, wait." She came running toward him, her purse over her shoulder. "Can I go to the beach with you?"

He hesitated, and not because he'd have to drive her all the way across the island when the evening ended. Then drive himself back home. "Do you think that's the best idea?"

"Lauren says everyone wants to see me." She hesitated near the hood of his car. "I don't mean to be distant, Ty. I don't mean to be, I swear. I..." She flapped her arms up in frustration and let them fall back to her sides.

"You do realize you've been distant since moving in here, right?"

"We still see each other a lot. You're working a lot. So am I."

"It's more than that, Sage," he said, though he couldn't articulate it any further. "I don't want to talk about it tonight. I just want to get back to the beach."

She took a couple of steps toward him. "That surprises me a little. You aren't really the beach party type."

He put his hand on her hip, unable to stop himself. "You're not the only one who can change," he said. "I'm friends with Grant, and this is his *only* daughter's *graduation* party."

She ran her hand up his chest. "Are you going to be mad at me for very long?"

"I don't know," he said, though he wasn't upset anymore. "Can we talk about it another time?"

She nodded, some measure of relief moving through her expression. "Yeah, let's get back to the party."

He said nothing about how she couldn't go back to something she'd never been at in the first place. Ty also knew that he'd lose her attention the moment they arrived on the beach, because her Supper Club friends would descend on her, and he'd be left to take a bottle of beer from Grant, sit in the sand, and stare at the firelight flickering off the waves in the distance.

Honestly, it was better than the scenarios that had been running through his head on the drive here. His muscles were still bunched and tense, and he didn't know how to get himself to calm down.

Sage is okay, he told himself. He hadn't known until now that his imagination could be so vivid. Call up such horrific things.

He got behind the wheel and waited for Sage to get in the passenger seat. Ty honestly wasn't sure how to survive this drive, but he took a deep breath and started the ignition. Thankfully, he'd been driving for a great many years, and it didn't take many brain cells.

"I thought maybe you'd been in a car accident," he said as they crossed the bridge back to the island. "Then, your car was here, and I thought *maybe she fell down the stairs. What am I going to find inside the house? Can I just go in?* It was—it was awful."

"I'm sorry," she whispered.

"I don't want your new 'waterfront way' to exclude me," he said. "I'm trying to give you the space you need, and I want you to have everything you've ever wanted. But I'm afraid that I've made it too easy for you to—to...to something."

"Fly," she said.

The perfect word for what Sage wanted. How did he catch a bird who wanted to fly away?

"You can fly," he said, shoving down the impatience and slight irritation. He wasn't sure if he was upset with himself for starting to fall for yet another woman who didn't want him, or with her for starting something with him when he didn't fit into her plans.

"I don't want to clip your wings. But I want you to come back to me, and well, it feels like you're not."

She nodded instead of disagreeing with him. "I'll do better."

"I want you to do what you want," he said. "But you just need to tell me if what you want still includes me."

"It does," she said firmly. "Absolutely, Ty, it does."

He nodded too, and he squeezed the steering wheel to try to release the last of his nerves and adrenaline. The dark beach would be welcome about now, with the dull roar of the waves to lull him back into a place where he wasn't terrified and worried all knotted into one horrible emotion.

They didn't talk the rest of the way back, and Sage held his hand from the parking lot to where Grant and Bea had set up their party. They had lanterns to light their area, and with a group as large as they were, Ty could hear them as he and Sage approached still in the shadows.

"Sage," Bea said, jumping to her feet, and that was that. All the conversations stopped, and Sage got whisked away by her friends. Ty returned to the chair he'd been sitting in before he left, and he took the bottle of beer from Harry.

"She seems okay," he commented.

"She forgot," Ty said, trying—and failing—to keep the bitterness out of his voice. "Left her phone in the car and just...ate dinner on the deck."

"Sounds like a simple mistake," Harry said.

Ty caught the surprise in his voice. "Doesn't erase the fact that she left us all high and dry."

"She left *you* high and dry," Scott said, and yeah, that was the real rub.

"I'm not...sure about us," he said, because he didn't need to get into the intricate details of his love life.

"Maybe you just need to be more patient," Blake said. "Lauren needed some time to come around."

"Cass's kids didn't like me at all," Harry said, lifting his bottle to his lips.

"Joy wouldn't even go out with me," Scott said with a chuckle. "What did Sage say when you got there?"

"She said I'm still part of her plan." Ty stared straight

ahead, because he didn't want to give away too much with his expression. He was good friends with Grant, Harry, Blake, Scott, and Oliver, but he'd always held some part of himself apart from them. That was partly because of his work schedule and partly because he didn't make friends easily.

Then, they wanted to know everything about him, and he had to tell them things about his life. Meaningful things, like how scared he'd been driving across town to Sage's house, wondering what he'd find there.

He took another long drink of his beer and then set it aside. He still had a lot of driving to do tonight, and he couldn't be irresponsible.

"I'm glad she's okay," Grant said as he returned from the group of women. He sighed as he sank to the ground.

Ty was too, and he didn't want to talk about Sage tonight. Thankfully, his friends seemed to pick up on that fact, and none of them asked him any more questions about her.

"ALL RIGHT," TY SAID AS HE BROUGHT HIS SUV TO a stop. "I think this is going to be the place, Katherine." He gave her a bright smile and got out of the car to go get her door. No, he didn't normally drive his clients to their home showings, but Katherine Tallison wasn't an ordinary client.

"I like this staircase," she said as she turned her legs to keep her knees together. She stood from the car and looked at the house, really drinking it in. It wasn't just a house, either, but a mansion.

Ty had been searching for the perfect property for her for months now, and he'd shown her several places. She'd like something different about each of them, and trying to piece together the perfect house for her was like trying to rebuild Frankenstein.

"Wait until you see the backyard," he told her. Apparently, an outdoor entertainment space was an absolute must, though Katherine hadn't put that on her Perfect Property Survey.

He kept his hand on her lower back as they walked up the sidewalk, and he pointed out the trees, bushes, and shrubs on the meticulously cared for property. The shutters matched the garage door color, and that reminded him of something Sage had said about his house.

He hadn't spoken to her since dropping her off last night, and they'd barely spoken then. He'd walked her to the door and hugged her. *Hugged* her. No kiss.

She'd been crying at the party, and he'd left her a little sniffly at her house too. She knew he had a full day of showings for Katherine, and they had no plans to get together. Of course, Ty hadn't had to make specific plans with her for several weeks now. They spoke every day, and he did end up seeing her most days, despite their busy schedules.

At least until she'd moved into her new house. He'd seen her less, but not an alarming amount. But with last night's forgetful episode, and Ty could see all the nights she'd stayed home, alone, when they could've been together.

"Big foyer," he said once he got the front door open. "Look at the height in the ceilings." Also something she'd commented on but left off her survey. "And this house has plenty of natural light…"

He walked Katherine through every room in the home, where most of the time, he let his clients look at the house without him. Then they could be honest with whoever they'd brought with them, and they found him back in the kitchen to ask any questions.

Forty-five minutes later, he led her back toward his car. Once they'd both gotten in, he said, "Well? Tell me what you're thinking." He'd really like to find something for Katherine, because she was one of his neediest clients, and he stood to make a lot of money if he could find her the right house.

She turned toward him, and her eyes shone. "I really like that house, Ty. The chandelier over the dining room table is *exquisite*."

He smiled though a certain measure of exhaustion pulled through him. A chandelier. She'd never mentioned one of those before. He made mental notes as he drove her back to her place and dropped her off.

Back in the office, he jotted down what she'd said so he didn't have to remember, and then he leaned back in his chair. A sigh bled from his mouth. He looked up to the ceiling, wondering what to do next.

A Saturday at the beginning of June usually found Ty working, and while he'd done a showing and made some notes, he didn't have to stay in his office. All the times he had in the past had been by choice.

So what did he want to do with his weekend afternoon? Sage worked Saturdays, and Ty reached up and ran his hands through his hair. He could use a trim, and he pulled out his phone and texted Sage.

As he watched the message pop up on his phone, he re-read it. Apparently, he couldn't even stay mad at her for twenty-four hours, and he wasn't sure if that made him pathetic or if he was falling in love with her.

Probably both.

Chapter Twenty-Four

Sage finished up her client and headed into the break room to get off her feet. She pulled her phone out of her pocket before she sat, because her shorts today were just a bit too tight. Probably from all of Bessie's bread she'd been eating in the past year.

She didn't care one whit about her weight, a fact only enunciated by the fact that she pulled out a bag of Doritos and was about to call it lunch. She saw her missed messages and notifications from the video app.

A sigh moved through her, because she was tired of always feeling behind. Always feeling left out. All of her friends worked too, but they seemed to be able to text at any time, day or night, and Sage simply couldn't keep up.

She found one message from Ty, and she tapped on that one first, her eyebrows going up with every word she read.

Hey, I'm wondering if I can get you to cut my hair

tonight. Just me and you. My place. I'll order in, and we'll talk.

Going to his house for dinner and to cut his hair sounded nice. Relaxing, even. If she could bring Gypsy, she wouldn't even have a curfew. She closed her eyes, thinking about sleeping in Ty's embrace. That actually sounded really nice, and she let the feelings of peace and contentment move through her.

Then the door to the break room opened, and the sound of hair dryers, women talking, and the bell on the entrance to the salon ringing shattered her safe haven.

"He wants to talk," she muttered to herself as a co-worker got out a bottle of water and left the room again. Talking could be good, but since she'd missed Shelby's graduation party, the conversations between her and Ty had been more reserved.

Stilted. Slow, if they spoke at all. She'd still seen him a few times this week, but she had to initiate everything, and she could admit she hadn't done it every day. She wanted some time to herself too, and she suspected he might break up with her if they ever truly got a chance to talk.

And he was creating that tonight.

So tell him no.

Realistically, she knew that all that would do was prolong the inevitable. No, if he was going to break up with her, she might as well let him get it over with.

To her surprise, tears pricked her eyes and her nose started to run. She couldn't lose her composure, because she still had two clients today, both with complex coloring needs, and she wouldn't be done here until at least five.

She also didn't want to lose Ty. She wasn't sure what that meant, but she had the sudden idea that she wasn't above begging. If he tried to break up with her tonight, perhaps she could beg him to just give her a little more time to figure things out.

What those "things" were, she wasn't sure, but she knew she needed more time to move into the next phase of her life. She'd just started living on her own again. She needed lots of reassurance that she could be loved, and—

Her mind stopped right there. "I need a lot of reassurance right now."

She started tapping out a message to Ty, her fingers almost flying as fast as her thoughts. *I'd love to,* she started. *I know we need to talk, and I'm going to start right now, right here. I need a lot of reassurance right now that I'm likable. Jerry didn't love me, and I lived for twenty-six years thinking he did. When I found out he didn't, it—*

She cut off again, because she didn't want to admit what had happened. Thoughts of Thelma entered her mind, and she heard what her younger sister had said.

You've told me that I can't hold onto the past and move into the future, but you won't let go.

She needed to know that she was actually loveable.

When I found out he didn't, it broke me. I haven't felt like anyone can like me or love me besides my family and my Supper Club, and I just need a lot of reassurance right now. If you're going to break up with me, well, I'd rather you just said it here, and we can skip the takeout and the talk.

Sage opened her fun-size bag of chips with shaking hands, but she wasn't going to back away from how she felt anymore. She popped a chip into her mouth and picked up her phone again.

I thought I could hide behind fun beachy things, like whale watching and luaus and walking Gypsy along the sand every morning, but I can't. I'm trying to find myself, Ty. I swear I am. I don't want to lose you, but I understand if you need me to be in a better place before you're ready to...I don't know what. I don't want to hurt you, so if you need to be done, it's okay.

It wasn't really okay, and she swallowed and stared at the words blurring on her phone. She tapped quickly to send the message, her fingers already flying again.

I mean, it's not really okay, because I like you a whole lot, and I don't want to be done. But I'll respect your decision if that's what it is.

She couldn't eat another chip, and she wiped her eyes as the door opened again and someone else entered. The notification that her alarm would go off in fifteen minutes popped up, asking her if she wanted to silence it for today. She did not, because it was her signal to get up, go to the bathroom, and clean up her station, so she could be ready for her next client.

Can you talk for a minute?

She practically dove at her phone when that simple message from Ty came in.

I have ten minutes. She got up and headed for the exit, because she didn't want to have this conversation in the salon. Her phone rang as she walked past her station, and she waited to swipe on the call until she was pushing through the glass door and into the sunshine.

"Hey," she said, that single word full of emotion.

"Sage." Ty's voice came through the line softly, meekly. "My beautiful Sage." If she hadn't just typed out everything she had, she might think he was flirting with her. "I'm not going to break up with you. I don't *want* to break up with you. I just want...I want us to be us again, and I want to hold you and tell you how likeable and loveable you are. I'll even order from Wagyu's."

The last sentence did carry a bit of teasing, but everything else had been spoken with pure truth. Sage could feel it in her gut, and she couldn't stop the small smile as it curved her lips. Her head had been bent down, and she lifted it. "Will you get the mac and cheese bites?"

"As many as you want," he whispered back.

"So I didn't break us?"

"Sage." He sighed. "I'm not working the rest of the day, and you know what? I honestly don't know what to do with myself. I'm at home, wearing gym shorts and just sort of wandering around the house. Brother and Sherman keep looking at me like I have something great planned, but I don't. It's...I have nothing planned. That's the something great."

"You've been trying to work less on the weekends," she said. "That's a good thing."

"Yeah, but not if it makes me anxious."

"Is that why you want me to come over?"

"I need a haircut," he said coolly. "And I can't say what I want to say when I'm at the salon."

"I can be there about six," she said.

"Perfect," he said. "See you then."

"Yeah, see you tonight." She lowered the phone and tilted her head back so she could fully absorb the full shine of the sun. She wanted to fly really close to it, feel the full weight of the heat of it, the gravity of it, and maybe then, she'd feel like she hadn't been ignored her whole marriage.

Why does he get to have so much power over you?

The thought filled her mind, and she wasn't sure why. Jerry had never been cruel. He hadn't cheated on her or ever really done anything mean. He simply hadn't loved her, and he'd been extremely hands-off for their whole marriage. He didn't care about what she said, thought, or did, and Sage hadn't realized it. She'd just thought he was passive, quiet, and conflict-averse.

He was all of those things, and he'd tied her to the ground for decades.

She didn't want to be caged any longer, but her alarm went off, and Sage returned to the salon to finish her clients.

By the time she pulled up to Ty's with Gypsy in the back of her SUV, it was several minutes past six. She'd texted him when she'd left the salon, and again when she'd left her house, so he knew she wasn't dead on the road somewhere.

In fact, the man came out his front door before Sage had even turned off the ignition. The sight of him in those casual gym shorts and a perfectly normal T-shirt had her fleeing the car and forgetting to get Gypsy out.

He chuckled as he trotted down the steps, and he caught Sage as she barreled into him. "I'm so sorry," she said, though she wasn't sure what she was apologizing for. For... being her? For not being quite ready to have him, but also not wanting to cut him loose?

"Don't," he whispered into her hair. He drove his fingers into her hair and held her head right against his chest. "It's so great to see you. Hold you." He bent down and touched his lips to her forehead, then her ear, then her neck.

Their eyes met in the summer evening light, and he grinned at her. "Dinner's almost here, and Gypsy is not happy you left him in the back."

Sage spun back to her car and vacated Ty's arms. She felt him watching her as she hurried back to her car, and sure enough when she looked his way again, she found his eyes glued to hers. *Sure looks like he likes you*, she thought, not sure where such a thing had come from.

She released Gypsy, and the shaggy dog galloped toward Ty, who laughed and led him up the steps. He opened the front door, and Gypsy went inside his house like he owned the place, leaving Sage to collect her hair-cutting kit by herself.

Armed with that, she approached Ty again. "You've got a beard going on too," she said, smiling at him.

He reached up and rubbed his face. "Yeah, a little bit." He nodded to her kit. "Can you give me a shave too?"

Surprise flitted through Sage. "Yes," she said, because she

did have the equipment to do that. "I haven't done that in a while, so you can't blame me if I nick you."

"I trust you," he said as seriously as ever, and then he took her hand and led her up the steps to his front door too.

"Do you want to do the cut first?" she asked. "Or after dinner?"

"We have about a half-hour," he said. "So now?"

"Sure, now." She followed him into the kitchen, where he turned around a dining chair and sat down. Sage put her head down and got to work, because she wasn't sure if she could just slip into his lap and kiss him. He hadn't kissed her hello, at least not in the way she knew he liked to, and she couldn't quite meet his eyes.

She put the drape around his neck and got out her scissors. "I was busy today, but I hope you got some down time."

"I did," he said. "I watched a movie before I started going crazy, and I went over to Grant's for a bit." He smiled —or at least Sage could hear the smile in his voice. "But they're beach bums, and I didn't want to sit in the sun today."

"Or go to the beach on a Saturday after school's gotten out."

"That either." They laughed together, and it sure felt good.

Sage cleared her throat. "Listen, Ty, thank you for letting me word-vomit on you today."

"Anytime," he said, and it sounded so genuine.

She clipped and pulled his hair through her fingers,

trying to get the lump to go down her throat. She moved to his side, and he turned and looked up at her. Their eyes met, and everything inside Sage wobbled.

Ty was right there, steady and strong and oh-so-capable. He took her onto his lap, scissors and all and said, "Let's pause for a second."

"Pause?" she asked, still trying to find her balance on his thighs.

"Yeah." He looked right at her. "I didn't get to kiss you hello." He matched his mouth to hers, and Sage dropped her hair-cutting scissors so she could get lost in his touch. He kissed her completely, and Sage could not imagine he could do that if he didn't like her.

He pulled away several moments later and leaned his forehead against hers. "Not only do I like you, Sage, I'm falling in love with you."

A tremor of fear moved through her, settling in her heart. "How do you know?" she whispered.

"I've been in love before," he said simply. "I know what it feels like." He opened his eyes and put enough distance between them that he could meet her eyes again. "You loved Jerry, right? You know what it feels like too."

"I thought I did," Sage said. She slid from his lap and retrieved her scissors. She finished his haircut and set about getting her shaving supplies out. With everything lathered up, she looked at him. "It's easier if you can lie down. I'll nick your neck if it's not stretched a little." She turned and looked into his living room. "The recliner?"

"All right," he said easily, and she moved her straight

razor and shaving cream over to the end table. He sat down, fluffed the drape around himself, and leaned back in the recliner. He met her eyes and said, "I trust you," again.

She wasn't sure why that was so sexy, only that it was. Only that it meant a whole lot to her. She lathered up his face, giggling when she got some on his bottom lip and had to wipe it off. He grinned, and then she lifted the razor.

His eyes moved to that, and he swallowed. "Here goes nothing," he said, and Sage grinned as she did the first swipe of the razor against his neck. "Mm, I remember how to do this." She wiped off the cream and the bit of scruff she'd gotten and went back for more.

Two, three, four stripes up his throat, and Sage's heart started beating like a big, steel drum. Ty's eyes never left her, and pure male desire lived there. Sage hadn't seen that burning in a man's gaze in a very, very long time. If ever.

"Ty," she whispered, and she managed to put down the razor before he reached for her and pulled her back onto his lap. Only he was lying down this time, and Sage sank easily into his side. He kissed her and kissed her, even when the doorbell rang announcing the arrival of their dinner.

"Food's here," she whispered against his mouth.

"Sure is." He sighed, and neither of them moved. She could lay in this recliner with him all night, starving, and she'd be happy.

"Why did you never get married?" she asked.

"For a while there," he said. "I didn't try. I was so focused on the agency. Then, when I thought I had a little breathing room, I went out with the wrong women."

"Mm."

"I want to get married," he murmured against her ear, his lips catching there. "If there's anything I've learned in the past few years of watching all my closest friends, it's that I want that. I want to have someone safe to come home to at night. Someone who loves me, forgives me, champions me. But mostly, I just want someone—besides Sherman and Brother—to spend my downtime with."

Sage's stomach growled, and Ty chuckled. "Come on, pretty girl. Let's get dinner off the porch and eat."

"I only shaved half your face."

"I'll fix it up," he said as he gently lowered the footrest so as to not throw Sage onto the floor.

She got to her feet and went around the couch, her goal to get the food. Ty came with her, his hand landing on her hip as she opened the door and bent to get the bags of food. When she turned back, he flicked the door closed but didn't give her any extra room.

"You kiss me like you're falling in love with me too," he whispered. "Tell me I'm wrong."

"You're not wrong."

That seemed to satisfy him, and he backed up a step or two, took one of the food bags, and turned to go into the kitchen. She watched the drape that was still around his neck flutter as he walked, a smile filling her whole soul.

When faced with the question of: *Would you rather eat on your deck alone or here with Ty?* the answer was clear.

Crystal clear.

Now Sage just had to figure out how to get the blasted

lump of fear out of her throat—and then step out of her own way.

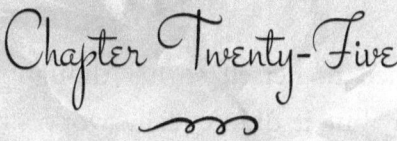

Chapter Twenty-Five

Sage smiled as she threw the butter yellow tablecloth across the table and then started to straighten it. She was hosting Supper Club tonight, and it was the first time she'd have it in her new house. She hadn't thrown Bessie a bridal shower here as she'd wanted to, because Bessie's sister had come into town, and they'd done it at Bessie's house.

But tonight, everyone would be coming, and Sage had been in the kitchen since lunchtime, putting together a fantastic summer menu for her and her friends. Watermelon granita. Potato salad. Corn on the cob. Fried chicken. She even had some red eye gravy to go with, and while she almost always used paper products for Supper Club, tonight she set out her Thanksgiving Day dishes.

Colorful glasses went on the table next, and then Sage started folding napkins. She had some things to talk about tonight, as Bea would be leaving for her National Parks road trip soon, and she wouldn't be at Supper Club in July.

"They'll know what to do," she told herself. She'd invited Thelma too, and her sister had said she'd plan on coming. Wyn had wedding things to do tonight, but Sage had invited her too, and she liked it when Bessie's daughter came.

She hummed to herself so her thoughts wouldn't get away from her, but it didn't really work. She and Ty had found a nice holding pattern for now, but she knew that was all it was. A holding pattern.

He wouldn't stay in it for long, and Sage needed to be able to move faster. If only she knew how.

Her doorbell rang, and she turned away from the table. "Come in," she called, because she didn't get many drop-by visitors. Sure enough, Bessie entered the house, and for the first time in a year, she wasn't carrying copious amounts of bread.

"Hey," Bessie said as she moved into the back of the house. She took in the table and looked at Sage. "I like the yellow."

"It's cheery," Sage said. She turned away from her friend to start setting out the napkins.

"You're not very cheery," Bessie said.

"I'm fine." Sage didn't mean to get her hackles raised, but she also didn't want to be told she wasn't happy. The truth was, she was happier than she'd ever been, so why couldn't anyone see that?

"Did you and Oliver still want Ty and I to come to the movie this weekend?"

"Of course," Bessie said, following Sage's every move.

Thankfully, Bea arrived next, and she brought Lauren and Joy with her.

"Cass is going to be late," she said. "Harry got hurt at work, and she's making sure he's all set at home before she comes."

Sage lifted her head, her eyes growing wide. "Harry got hurt at work?"

"He smashed his thumb with a hammer," Lauren said. "Went to the ER, but he's okay. It's just going to be nasty and bruised for a while."

"That's too bad," Sage said at the same time Bessie did. Joy looked tan and refreshed, and Sage envied her. At the same time, she smiled at her. "You look good, Joy."

"Beach day," she said as she rounded the end of the couch and sat down. "You should've come."

"I was cooking," Sage said. "Maybe next time."

"We're going on Sunday," Bea said. "You and Ty will come, right?" She actually lowered her head and then peered up at Sage through her eyelashes for some reason Sage didn't understand.

"Yeah," she said. "I was counting on it." Since she'd missed the graduation party, she'd been checking and double-checking her calendar every morning. Every night before bed for the next day. "I also have a light Tuesday next week, and I'm thinking of doing some shopping." She turned away from everyone. "Ty's birthday is coming up."

"Ooh, what are you going to get for him?" Lauren asked.

"I think we need to know where she is in her relationship before we can help with a gift," Bea said. With Cass not there, Bea had to say all the irritating things, and Sage threw her a look.

"I'm ready to talk about this," she said. "But not until Cass gets here." She moved into the kitchen. "Come help me warm up the corn." She opened the oven and took out the sheet tray of fried chicken, which she'd been keeping warm there.

It was good served cold or warm, and once that sat on the stovetop, she turned on the burner beneath the red eye gravy to make sure it was piping hot.

"How are you feeling, Lauren?" Bessie asked.

"Good enough," she said as she took a barstool. "Cass has been a life-saver with the nursery."

"I can't wait to see it," Joy said. "I also can't believe June is almost over. Why does summer go so fast?"

"I'm here," Thelma called, and Bessie's pulse perked up for a moment. Her sister entered the kitchen still wearing her work clothes, but she looked really happy.

"Ooh, fried chicken," Thelma said as she took in the activity in the kitchen. "What do you need help with?"

"Nothing," Sage said. "We're almost ready."

"Are you doing the Heritage Festival again this year?" Bea asked Bessie, and she dunked several cobs of corn into the steaming water beside where Sage whisked the gravy.

"I am," Bessie said. "It's not a partnering year, but Oliver pulled some magical strings, and we're sharing a booth space again."

"Yeah, he put down some cash," Joy said with a laugh. "Money can move a lot of strings."

"Yeah." Bessie smiled, but at least she wasn't upset about Oliver paying for things this year. Last year, they'd been at such odds.

"You haven't said anything about your honeymoon," Sage said, giving Bessie a look.

"I'm waiting too," she said with a smile. "I can still barely believe I'm married."

"How's Wyn doing in the house by herself?" Bea asked.

Sage flipped off the burner and bent to get a gravy boat. She poured the gravy into it while Bessie said, "She's doing fine there. When she and Douglas get married, they're going to live there."

"Is your name still on the mortgage?" Bea asked.

"My word," Sage muttered under her breath, but thankfully, Bea didn't hear her. Bessie answered the question, and she didn't seem irritated by it. Sage wasn't sure why she was. She loved her Supper Club friends, but the tension inside her felt like it might snap at any moment.

She put the gravy on the table, then plated the fried chicken and added that to the spread. She was taking the potato salad out of the fridge when Cass called, "I'm here." She came walking into the back of the house wearing an off-white suit that billowed around her arms and legs and looked like it had been hand-sewn for a queen. "I'm so sorry, Sage."

"It's fine." She flashed Cass a smile and stepped over to her. She hugged her as she said, "I'm just barely getting the food out."

Bea put the corn on the table too, and she turned back

for the salt and pepper and butter. Cass said, "He's doing great, but wow, sometimes men are such babies about things. He's sort of acting like he's never done construction before." She sighed as she took a seat at the table.

The others started to gather around too, and Sage got out the watermelon granita and started scraping it one final time with a fork. She then spooned it into some glass cups she usually made individual servings of banana pudding in.

As she put them on the table, Bea's smile lit up. "Sage, look how pretty those are."

"It's non-alcoholic," she said. "Sorry, Cass."

She wiped her hair back out of her face. "I didn't get a ride tonight, so I wouldn't drink much anyway."

Sage put the last glass of granita at her spot and sat down. Everyone looked at her, and she looked back at them. All of her irritation at Bea's questions and Joy's restfulness and Cass's tardiness dried right up.

"It's a summer picnic menu," she said. "And tonight, I want everyone to share one summer secret or summer worry. I'll start, though mine is more like a whole-life-worry." She reached for a piece of fried chicken, but she wouldn't be able to put a bite in her mouth until she'd told her friends what she was worried about.

"I need some advice about Ty," she said. "I...I didn't realize how—" She tossed a look to Thelma on her right. "Stuck in the past I was until I started dating Ty."

No one said anything, and Sage wished someone else would fill in the rest of the story. "Anyway." She cleared her throat. "I thought I could just do things with him and have fun. I even told him when we first started seeing each other again that I just wanted to be his friend. I just wanted to see if I could have a male friend, I guess."

"No," Thelma said quietly. "That's not true, Sage."

All of her frustration came roaring back. "What did I want then, Thelma?"

"You wanted someone to go on adventures with," she said. "So you could start to do things you hadn't done before, but you didn't have to do it alone."

All eyes came back to her, and Sage couldn't argue. So she didn't. "Yeah, that sounds about right."

"But?" Cass prompted, and oh, it was good she was here so Bea didn't have to shoulder all of Sage's ire.

"But we became more than friends really fast," Sage said. "And the newness of adventures wears off even faster." She hung her head and looked around at everyone. The food had moved around the table, and they'd each taken some. But no one had started eating.

"I really like him," Sage said. "Like, I really, really like him. But." She swallowed, the truth right there. "I'm not sure I want to get married again, and he does. Well, for the first time. He wants to get married, and I'm thinking I sure do love this house, and I don't want to move again. I like my independence, and I'm still trying to figure out who I am, what way of life I'm trying to eek out for myself."

"She hasn't let go of Jerry," Thelma said.

"I have," Sage said forcefully. "I'm totally over Jerry."

Bea reached over and covered her hand. "You're not

stuck on Jerry," she said. "You're worried you'll have a marriage like you had with him."

"Yes." Sage cleared her throat. "I'm just not sure I have to be married to be with Ty. People love each other and don't get married all the time."

"Yeah," Joy said with plenty of falseness in her voice. "They do."

Sage didn't like the way the others exchanged glances with one another, so she picked up her chicken and took a bite.

"Do you want advice?" Bessie asked.

Sage nodded, thinking that had been pretty obvious.

"Are you in love with him?" Cass asked.

Sage lifted one shoulder in a half-shrug. That totally meant maybe, because it obviously wasn't yes or no.

Cass made a noise of discontentment, and she looked at Bea. "Say something."

"What should I say?" Bea bickered at her. "She knows intellectually that Ty isn't Jerry. She doesn't need to hear me say it."

"Maybe something about how Ty looks at her like he's in love with her," Joy said. "She'll take it best from you."

"Or Thelma," Bessie said, piling onto the game. "Have Thelma tell her that she doesn't lose anything when she gains a partner. There's only more to experience, because now she doesn't have to do everything herself."

"She wants to do things herself," Sage interjected. Everyone looked at her, and she pushed her hair out of her face. "Sometimes."

Silence filled the house, and Sage didn't like that. She looked around at everyone, wondering how to explain her emotions with words. They didn't seem to exist, and she sighed. "Some days, I don't want to be alone. It's so powerful, I feel...defeated. So lonely. Other days, I can't wait to get home to just Gypsy, and whatever meal I want, and a few hours of peace and quiet. I don't have to ask anyone what movie to watch, and no one makes fun of me because I don't like bacon, and I get to do whatever I want."

"I mean, yes," Cass said. "But it's sure nice to have a date to the movies, and someone to bring you orange juice when you're sick, and someone to worry about you when you don't show up for a party."

Sage pulled in a breath and glared at Cass.

"It was Ty who first noticed you were gone," Cass said. "Ty who was on his phone incessantly, calling you, texting you, calling Thelma, calling the salon. He was so worried, Sage."

"I know," she said quietly. Just like she knew intellectually that she'd like a partner to come home to in the evenings, and her brain knew Ty wasn't anything like Jerry, and she knew Ty had started to fall for her.

Now, she just had to convince her heart about everything.

"Sometimes it just takes time," Bessie said, and Sage really hated that answer. She'd been told that when she'd first filed for divorce too, that it would take time for her to go through the trauma of the loss and then she'd start to heal.

That in a year, or two years, or five years, she'd be in such a different place. She'd feel so differently, so good, so...whole again.

But Sage hadn't been super traumatized by the divorce. Her life had gone on almost as usual—except she didn't have to share a bed with Jerry and she didn't have to worry about what he'd eat for dinner.

So of course it wasn't going to take *her* as much time as it took others.

"Wyn has needed more time," Bessie said, drawing Sage's attention again. She spoke in a quiet voice, and Sage knew a little bit about Wyn's ex-boyfriend, but not as much as Bessie, obviously.

"She needed time to heal all the way. She needed time to make sure she wanted to get all tied up with another man, though Douglas is literally the best there is. He's perfect for her, and everyone who looks at them can see it."

"Sounds like someone else I know," Thelma said.

"Yeah," Sage threw back at her. "Me too." Their eyes locked, but Sage softened quickly. "I didn't mean that."

Thelma reached for her watermelon granita and took a spoonful. "I know. And I've actually started thinking about...calling this guy who asked me out." She swallowed hard. "Maybe."

"I needed time after West died," Cass said. "My girls needed more time than me."

"Oliver needed time," Bessie said.

"I needed time to come to terms with leaving Texas," Joy said. "And that's not even something like what you've gone through, Sage."

"I hate time," Sage complained. She looked around at everyone, feeling more at a loss now than she had before dinner had started. "And why isn't anyone eating? This is Supper Club. We can eat while we talk."

Some of the tension broke, especially when Lauren said, "I wish I had more time right now, because this baby is coming really soon, and I have no idea how to be a mother."

"Oh, you'll be great," Bea assured her, turning to pat her hand. "Is that your summer worry?"

"I think it's more like a whole-life-worry," Lauren said, shooting Sage a knowing, teasing look.

Sage laughed, and that got everyone else to lighten up too. She still didn't have a plan or a blueprint or a list to follow in order to make sure she didn't hurt or lose Ty. Maybe the answer really was time, and Sage determined she better figure out how to use the time she had in the best way possible.

Chapter Twenty-Six

Ty pulled up to Sage's and looked over to the passenger seat. He'd brought flowers, which felt a little cheap in the moment, as he'd never brought her flowers before. But one of her sons had come to visit from Texas, and Ty couldn't help feeling like he better make a good impression on the man.

Sage had told him not to worry about her children, but Harry hadn't had an easy time with Cass's at all. So, sighing, Ty swept the flowers into his hand and got out of the car. Dallen would be here for a week, and that included the upcoming Independence Day celebration on the island.

Ty had been busy this summer, but he always took time off for the Fourth of July. It was one of his favorite holidays, and now that he spent more time with Sage, her friends, and their husbands, he planned to sit with them at the park for the concert and fireworks.

He went to the door and rang the doorbell, then twisted

the knob. It turned easily, and he entered with, "It's me, sweetheart."

"We're outside," Sage called, and that shouldn't have surprised Ty. She'd said her sons were super outdoorsy. They both worked on a farm in the Sweet Water Falls area, but they didn't own anything themselves. Ty knew next to nothing about being a cowboy, but he could see a bonafide one through the glass at the back of Sage's house.

Her son wore a dark maroon shirt with long sleeves, which meant he had to be roasting, a black cowboy hat, and as Ty went from house to deck, he found the young man in jeans. How he wasn't a puddle of sweat, Ty didn't understand.

He put his real estate smile on his face and held up the flowers. "Hey, baby."

Sage grinned and stepped into him. "Hey." She kissed him solidly on the mouth, but he didn't take things too far or deepen anything. She took the flowers and leaned over them. "These are beautiful; thank you."

Instead of heading inside to vase them, she stood at his side and faced her son. "Dallen, baby, this is my boyfriend, Ty."

Dallen got to his cowboy boot-clad feet. His smile spread across his face, and he definitely had Sage's coloring, her nose, and her quick grin. "Oh, howdy. Momma's been tellin' me about you." He stuck out his hand, and Ty shook it.

"Likewise," he said. "It's great to meet you."

Dallen looked from him to his mother and back. "She says you own a real estate agency here on the island."

"That's right," Ty said. "And you work a farm in Sweet Water Falls."

"That's right," Dallen repeated. His smile stayed in place as he sat back down. "It's mighty nice here, though." He took off his hat and wiped his forehead. "Hot, though."

"It's hot in Texas too," Sage said. "I'll go put these in water. Be right back." She did leave him on the deck with Dallen then, and Ty moved over to one of the chairs at the table and sat down facing Dallen on the love seat.

"How old are you?" he asked.

"Twenty-four," Dallen said. "You?"

Ty grinned at him. "Fifty-two. I'm almost fifty-three, though. My birthday's coming up at the end of July."

Dallen hooked his thumb over his shoulder and then checked that way too. Sage stood at the island, arranging the flowers in a vase. "My momma won't say much about you two. Is it serious?"

"Yeah," Ty said, nodding. "I'd say so. We've been dating for about five months. I'm—I'm serious about the relationship, yeah." He smiled at Dallen, who only nodded. He seemed like a serious young man, and perhaps his father had been more like that.

Sage could be serious, but she definitely possessed a carefree, easy-going spirit too. She was flexible, and he wasn't getting that vibe from Dallen at all.

"What about you?" he asked. "Got a sweetheart back in Texas?" He grinned at the boy, who softened considerably. "Oh, I can see you do." He glanced through the sliding glass doors. "And that your momma doesn't know about her."

"It's...well, I can't even say it's new anymore." Dallen sighed and removed his hat completely now. "I've been datin' Jenny for almost a year. That's one of the reasons I came."

"What's a reason you came?" Sage asked as she stepped out onto the deck again. Ty reached for her and pulled her right onto his lap, feeling a little self-conscious about the display of affection in front of her son. Sage had plenty of chairs she could've sat in, but she didn't protest either.

"I came to see you, Momma," he said. "Sweet Water Falls isn't the same without you there."

"Aw, baby." She smiled at him and then Ty. She focused on her son again. "Your daddy still lives there."

"Yeah." Dallen didn't say anything more about his father, and Ty sort of wanted to meet the man for himself. Get a sense of who he was and how he contributed to Dallen —and how he'd affected Sage.

"Another reason is I wanted to talk to you about this woman I'm seeing."

Sage perked up then. "You're seeing someone?"

"For a while now," Dallen said. "Her name's Jenny, and I almost brought her with me, but she couldn't get so much time off work."

"She could've come for a few days," Sage said. "Like over the Fourth."

"Maybe I'll call her and tell her that," Dallen said. He swiped on his phone and turned it toward them. "I'm thinking about marrying her."

Sage took his device and looked at the pretty blonde

woman with Dallen. They both wore smiles made of cotton candy, had shining eyes that spoke of their happiness, and looked like they belonged together. "Wow, Dall." She tilted the phone toward Ty, but he could see it fine. He nodded, and she handed her son's device back to him. "She's beautiful. What does she do?"

"She's a florist," he said, his expression turning lovesick as he looked at the picture himself. Ty wondered what his face looked like when he saw Sage or a picture of her. Like that?

Probably, he told himself. He hadn't been fighting his feelings, and he hadn't been holding them back. He was too old for such games, and it wasn't like he was trying to get Sage to go out with him on a first date.

"What's holding you back?" Sage asked, and wow, that was the question of the year. Did she hear herself? Ty glanced at her, but she simply studied her son.

"I'm not sure," Dallen said. "Maybe the fact that I don't have a house for us to live in. Or a job that can support us." He sighed. "I've been thinkin' of getting my own farm, Momma."

Her eyebrows practically flew off her face. Ty didn't know what was so major about that, but obviously something. "You are? How are you going to do that?"

"I dunno," Dallen said. "There are a few things up for sale right now. Do you think...?" He shook his head. "I can't afford it."

"That's why there are loans," Sage said. She slipped from Ty's lap and joined her burly, broad-shouldered son on the love seat. "Baby, if you want to get something of your own, then do it."

"You think I can?" Dallen looked at his momma with open vulnerability on his face, and Ty loved the maternal love pouring from Sage.

She cradled her son's face in one hand, and said, "Of course you can." She smiled at him. "And does Jenny love you?"

Dallen smiled, his face turning a light shade of red. "Yeah, Momma. I think she does."

"You think?" Sage spoke a bit harshly, and Ty watched her. "Son, you have to *know*."

"She loves me," Dallen said. "I love her."

Sage nodded and glanced over to Ty. He smiled at her, and time seemed to slow for a moment. He could see her sitting there in her peach-colored tank top and those sage green shorts. She didn't wear shoes, and somewhere behind him, Gypsy barked.

Her son, with his dark hair that curled on the ends, sat beside her, the windows framing them both. But it sure felt like it was just her and Ty in that moment, and to him, he felt himself slipping further in love with her.

She got up, and the moment broke. She came over to the table and pulled out another chair. "I ordered pizza for dinner tonight," she said. "It should be here soon."

Ty took her hand in his and squeezed, hoping that simple gesture told her that he sure liked being here with her and her son.

"So how do you become a cowboy?" he asked Dallen,

and the young man brightened. Ty could see so much of himself in Dallen, because he'd wanted to be a real estate agent at that age, and he'd worked for it.

As he listened to him talk about the jobs he'd had over the years, and when he'd known he wanted to be a cowboy as a profession, Ty realized something else too. He'd worked for what he had, and he could do the same with Sage.

He wouldn't give up on her, especially after hearing that her son had been dating someone for almost a year and they weren't engaged or married.

Maybe his friends had just been moving faster than him. *No maybe about that*, he thought as he considered Bessie and Oliver, who had started dating, fallen in love, gone through their engagement, and gotten married all within a twelve-month timeframe.

He didn't have to do that. He didn't have to be them.

He and Sage were on their own path, and he'd sure been enjoying the adventure.

"I CAN'T BELIEVE YOU GOT ALL THREE OF THOSE dogs in the back," Dallen drawled as Ty turned into the parking lot at the park. "Or that I haven't been slobbered on yet." He chuckled, but he had a point. Getting Sherman, Brother, and Gypsy in the back of Ty's SUV had been no small feat.

They had a rolling cooler and camp chairs with them too, but those rode in the backseat with Dallen.

"Right there on the left," Sage said, and Ty eased the vehicle that way. He took the parking space she'd found, and while they had to walk a bit, they'd have to do that no matter where he found to park.

"Everyone out," he said. "Dallen, can you get the chairs for us?"

"Yes, sir," he said, and Ty liked the young man a whole lot. He'd been here for a week, and he was going home on Saturday. Ty had spent his free time with Sage and Dallen for the past several days, and he was looking forward to being alone with Sage again.

Not that he minded her son being here. Of course not. He just wanted to kiss her without an audience or without sneaking her out onto her own front porch and then pulling back before he'd really sunk in.

"I'll get the cooler," Sage said.

That left the trio of dogs for Ty, and he moved to the back of the SUV and pressed the button to lift it. "Stay," he said, holding his hand out as the liftgate rose. "Wait." He picked up the leashes and started linking them to collars. Only when he had all three of them done did he said, "Okay. You can get down."

Gypsy and Brother did and then stayed close, but Sherman leapt down like a deer and started to run off. Ty had to hold the leash tight and tell him, "No," to get him to calm down. "You walk right by me, bud."

He closed the liftgate and joined Sage and Dallen. They started the trek to the path that led through the park to the concert area, and Sage said, "Lauren and Blake have a spot staked out for us."

"Don't you guys sit in the same place every year?" Ty asked.

"I guess so," Sage said. "I'm never the first one here, so I don't know."

Ty liked having someone else be in charge at things like this, and he was more than content to go along. They found their group easily, as they sat just off the path near the clearing so they could enjoy the shade until darkness fell, and then move out into the open area to see the fireworks beyond the tree limbs.

"Ty, hey," Blake said as they arrived. "Wow, you brought all the dogs."

They all panted already, and Ty grinned at them. "They'll just lay right on down. Won't you, guys?"

"Let me help you with the chairs," Grant said, ever the people-person. "I'm Grant."

"Oh, this is my son," Sage said. "Dallen. Dallen, that's Grant. His wife is my friend, Bea. Remember her?"

Bea got to her feet, her grin absolutely huge and infectious. "Look how old you are, Dallen."

"Ma'am." He chuckled as he stepped into her for a hug.

"I met you when you were ten years old," Bea said, and Ty couldn't imagine having that kind of history with someone.

"Cass," Sage said, indicating her as she lined up to hug Dallen. "She married Harry."

"Howdy," Harry said, and Ty noticed his thumb had a far smaller bandage on it than before.

Introductions continued to go around, and all of the women knew Dallen, of course. He and Sage weren't the last to arrive, and Bessie and Oliver took some of the spotlight from them when they got there.

Ty set up his chair on the end next to Scott, who'd brought Ghost to the park that evening. The three canines with him knew Ghost but smelled him anyway, and then they all found a spot on the grass to lie down.

Sage sat beside him, and Dallen next to her. The sky held a shade of blue that could only be produced in July, and Ty sighed into the evening breeze. "This is nice," he said.

"I love this park," Sage said.

Ty leaned closer to her, glad when she edged toward him, dipping her head so his mouth lingered right at her ear. "I'm falling in love with you." He lifted her hand to his lips and pressed a kiss there while she giggled and ducked her head the way he'd seen her son do.

"Thank you, Ty," she whispered, and he settled in for an amazing night of music, food, and fireworks.

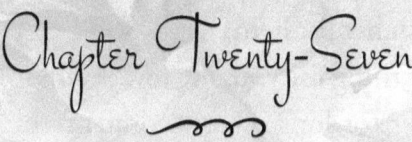

Chapter Twenty-Seven

Bea watched her husband reach up and press the button to close the back of their SUV. "Ready?" he asked and she could only smile.

"Ready."

Shelby already sat in the back seat, and she'd put her backpack up there with her, along with a blanket and a pillow, as they were settling in for several hours of driving today.

"Congaree National Park or bust." Grant wrapped her in his arms, causing Bea to stumble. She laughed as he did, and she sure did love this man.

"Thank you," she said as they sobered. "I know this is a big deal for you, leaving your management company for this long." She knew he was doing it for her too, as she'd once put *Visit 10 National Parks* on her love list.

She still hadn't crossed that one off, though she'd been

to seven now. With Shelby moving away to college in just a couple of months, Grant had come up with this idea of the three of them going on "the most epic road trip ever," and that had included the remaining National Parks that Bea needed to finish her list item.

"I'd do anything for you, my love." Grant kissed her, but he didn't linger for long. "Now come on, or we might lose Shelby before we get out of the driveway." He grinned at Bea and led her around to the passenger seat.

"Dad," Shelby said. "Can we stop for drinks and snacks before we get going?"

"That's a given, sugar," he said as Bea sat down. Grant closed her door and went to get behind the wheel.

"I want some boiled peanuts," Bea said.

"I'm gonna load up on candy," Shelby said, and that made Bea laugh again.

"Just as long as neither of us gets sick." She nodded like she could keep viruses and bacteria out with that simple gesture. She and Grant had worked hard to be able to take the next three and a half weeks off from the management company Grant owned and Bea organized. He'd brought in someone six weeks ago to train them, and Bea's stomach swooped as he pulled out of the driveway.

Their trip had officially begun.

"All right," Grant said, his voice a little too loud. When he got excited about something, it was hard to rein him in. "First stop, the gas station for drinks and treats." He looked at his daughter in his rearview mirror. "Second stop, Aunt Julie's for some of the best on-the-road food."

"What's she making this time?" Shelby asked. "Bea, one time when my dad was taking me back to my mom's, Aunt Julie made these pimento cheese swirls. I've never tasted anything so good."

Bea grinned as Grant picked up speed on the main highway that led off the island. "I hope it's that, then."

"Oh, no," Grant said with a laugh. "Julie never makes the same thing twice." He scoffed like the idea was absolutely ridiculous. He glanced over to her, and Bea leaned back and simply smiled at him. He'd introduced so much joy into her life, after such a rainy season. "I told her we were doing a National Park trip, and we'd need some *good sustenance* for the outdoor adventures we're about to have. She'll make the exact right thing, I'm sure."

"Dad usually gives her a theme," Shelby said.

Grant pulled over and into a spot, and they all piled out of the car. Bea went her own way inside, because she wanted one of those Glacier Cherry Gatorades and plenty of red licorice. "Oh, and those peach-O's," she muttered to herself. She located all of her candy, passing Shelby a couple of times as her hands got fuller and fuller.

"Oh, baby." She found Grant over by the doughnuts. "I want some of those boiled peanuts." She looked down at her full hands too. "Can you get them for me?"

He looked at her wares too, his grin growing. "Well, we're certainly not going to starve."

Bea grinned, giggled, and gathered her stuff with all of the things Grant and Shelby had gotten. Once they'd checked out, Grant got going again. Bea started to play games on her phone, as Shelby had put her earbuds in once she'd had her truckload of candy and Grant had commanded the radio and currently had it on a station that played only music from the nineties.

Bea didn't care what she listened to, because she could solve puzzles to anything. She could remain present, and after only ten minutes of driving, Grant said, "Blake said they might name the baby Daisy."

"Oh, that's cute." Bea looked up. "I'm so excited Lauren's having a girl."

"Girls are the best," Grant agreed, his smile appearing quickly. "Did you decide what you wanted to do first when we get to Congaree?"

"I thought we were doing the Boardwalk Loop Trail," she said. "Isn't that still the plan?"

"Yeah, sure," Grant said, his voice pitching up.

"Oh, boy," she said, grinning at him, her games forgotten. "I know that tone of voice."

"No," he said. "There was no tone of voice."

"There so was." Bea watched him, and he kept his eyes on the road like he'd never driven it before. "What did you look up on the internet?"

"I just think it might be fun to do some fishing, that's all."

Bea grinned. "Fishing? Grant, baby, have you ever been fishing?"

"Of course I have," he said. "Just because I haven't been *lately* doesn't mean I've never been."

"What are we going to do with fish?" They'd be staying

for two nights in Congaree, and they'd be there all day tomorrow. Bea had specifically not wanted to make plans, because Grant thrived with spontaneity—thus the fishing.

"You just throw them back, Bea," he said with a laugh. "We're not going to keep them and then fry them up around a campfire or anything."

Bea didn't mind the teasing, and she shook her head as she looked back at her phone. "I don't even know how to hold a fishing pole."

"Maybe you should've put something else on your love list," he said.

"Hey." Bea reached over and swatted his shoulder.

"What?" He laughed. "You realize National Parks are outdoors, right? You hike and camp and *fish*."

Bea shook her hair over her shoulders, but it was barely long enough to do that, though she'd been growing it out. She'd done it her whole life, and old habits were hard to break. "When I went with my friends, we just drove to lookouts."

Grant burst out laughing. "I'm not surprised by that at all, sweetheart."

"Don't make fun of me and my friends," Bea said.

"I would never," Grant said. "I just know none of you ladies are doing hard hiking."

"The boardwalk sounds nice, though, doesn't it?" she asked.

"I can't wait," Grant said, and when he said it with so much enthusiasm, Bea believed him.

"Okay, look," he added several minutes later. "No one is

getting out of the car at Julie's, okay?" He looked in the rearview mirror. "Shelby? You hear me? We're not getting out at Aunt Julie's."

"Why can't we get out?" Bea asked.

"Because then we'll get stuck there for an hour," Grant said. "We just need to get the food and go." He nodded. "Yep, we're just there to get the food and go."

"It sounds like you're using your twin sister," Bea said.

"Yes, it does," Grant said. "Because I am." He grinned and kept driving, and before Bea knew it, they'd arrived at his sister's house.

"Don't honk," Bea said.

Grant gave her a withering look. "Come on. I'm not going to honk." He put the car in park and reached for his phone. "I'm going to text her." He did that, and only a moment later, Julie opened her front door and came out carrying a platter—yes, a platter—of food.

"My goodness," Bea said. "You guys weren't kidding."

Shelby opened the door, and Grant said, "No, no, no, no. Don't get out."

"I'm just going to hug her," Shelby said. "She made us road trip food, Dad. You don't have to be rude."

"She's too Southern," Grant muttered as his daughter closed the door. He sighed and unbuckled. "Here we go."

Bea grinned as she got out too, and Julie radiated happiness to see them all. "National Park treats," she said. "I've got the most amazing beef jerky bites you'll ever taste. Hello, sweetie." She kissed Shelby's cheek and gave her a side-hug.

"I also made pizza pinwheels," Julie said. "My brother loves those."

"I certainly do," Grant said. "I was hoping for something pizzarrific."

"Dad, don't say stuff like that." Shelby rolled her eyes, but Bea grinned. Telling Grant not to use weird words or tell Dad-jokes was like trying to get the sun to stay down in the morning.

"Hey, Julie," Bea said as she rounded the hood.

"There's my favorite sister-in-law." Julie grinned at Bea, passed the platter to her brother, and embraced her. Since she was Grant's only other sibling, Bea would be her *only* sister-in-law. She still hugged her back and grinned at her when they separated.

"Thanks for the food, Julie," she said.

"Yes," Grant said. "Thank you, Julie." He kissed her cheek and started packing the pizza pinwheels into a plastic container Bea hadn't even known he'd brought. She should've known he'd be prepared, because Grant always had everything they needed, whether it was for a beach day or for a new guest coming to one of the properties.

She could still remember how he'd shown up at the beach house she'd rented when she'd come to Hilton Head Island for the first time with the ice cream she loved most.

"Back in the car," Grant boomed. "Let's load up, people. We have a National Park to get to!" He met Bea's eyes, his smile only growing. "Thanks, Julie." He opened the door as Bea rounded back to her side of the car.

Once they were all back in the car and buckled, Grant glanced over to her. "Ready, sweetheart?"

She nodded and leaned toward him. "Ready, baby."

He kissed her quickly, and then they got back on the road toward their first National Park. This was going to be an epic road trip, and she couldn't wait to get to Congaree.

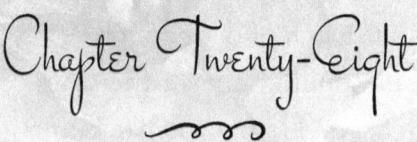

Chapter Twenty-Eight

"It's gorgeous," Bessie said as she stepped back from the cake. She looked at Sage, who couldn't look away from the birthday cake she and her best friend had been working on for the past couple of hours.

Tears filled Sage's eyes, and she turned into Bessie. "Thank you," she whispered.

"He's going to love it." Bessie was the best at reassuring Sage. She nodded against her friend's shoulder and then pulled back.

"I hope so. I'm not the baker you are." She also felt sticky from head to toe. "I couldn't have ever made it look like this either. Those instructional videos make everything look so easy." She grinned at Bessie, because they'd complained about this before. "It's so not."

"Definitely easier when you have the right tools," Bessie said. "You're heading to his place now?"

"Mm, yeah. I'm going to get a bunch of balloons on the

way. Tie those around. Put the cake on the counter. Take in my gifts." She turned to follow Bessie over to the sink in her bread kitchen. Hillie, the woman who baked with Bessie every morning, continued to hum at another counter where she worked with a batch of dark dough.

"You're really pulling out all the stops for this." Bessie glanced over to Sage. "I know you like him, Sage."

She got her hands wet in the semi-warm stream. "Of course I like him, Bess." She smiled as the stickiness ran off her skin. "I know what you want to know." She met her friend's eyes. "I don't know. I don't know if I love him. I don't know how to trust those feelings."

She soaped up with a sigh. "It's frustrating to be fifty years old and not be able to trust yourself."

Bessie didn't say anything. Bea or Cass would've told her that of course she could trust herself. Thelma's mantra was to let go of the past so she could move into the future. Lauren and Joy tended to watch Sage with almost beady eyes, and Bessie usually had something kind, tender, and reassuring to say.

Unassuming, like she didn't dare think she knew more about Sage than Sage knew about herself. She'd always appreciated that about Bessie.

"You know, I didn't come here to find someone to fall in love with," she said.

"Neither did I," Bessie said. "I wanted the bread bakery. It was my only focus."

Sage nodded, because Bessie had that. She and her daughter had made their dreams come true. "Maybe it's because I don't have any dreams," she said. "Or that my dreams aren't business-focused." Maybe she needed something to work toward that wasn't *Enjoy the slow summer nights on your deck.*

"What do you mean?" Bessie asked, handing her a towel.

Sage didn't know how to explain it. "I just...You and Wyn moved here with a purpose. A goal. The bread bakery. I moved here with Thelma to outrun her abusive boyfriend and to keep the Supper Club together. I have no purpose."

"Of course you have purpose," Bessie said, sounding like Bea now. "You had dreams to get that house, and you got it. You're living your waterfront way. You can't diminish that just because you didn't open your own marketing firm."

"Or a bread bakery," Sage said as she stared at the terrycloth. "Or an interior design business. Or...whatever." Bea and Joy hadn't started their own businesses here on Hilton Head either.

Sage sighed in frustration when she didn't want to be frustrated today. "It's too much to add an outside entrance to that office. So I could have people go through the house, but I don't know. It doesn't feel like what I want."

"You want that house to be a sanctuary," Bessie said. "Without the outside entrance, Sage."

"Yeah," she said. She drew in a breath. "Okay, it's Ty's birthday, and I'm not going to let anything drag me down today." She hung the towel on the hook beside the sink and drew Bessie into a hug. "Thank you so much for helping me with the cake. It's beautiful."

"Anytime, my friend." Bessie squeezed her, and then

Sage returned to the three-tier, bright-blue-frosted birthday cake. Bessie had done swirls of rainbow-dyed frosting around each tier, and Sage would put those big chunky number candles it the top right before she sang a solo of *Happy Birthday* to him.

After getting the balloons, Sage pulled up to Ty's pink house knowing he wasn't home. His pups would be, and she hoped Sherman would behave and let her tie the balloons to the backs of chairs. Maybe a lamp or two. She'd have to keep her eye on the black lab in the kitchen too, because he loved sweets, and she had that birthday cake riding shotgun.

She got out and collected it from the passenger side, then went up the steps to the front door. No dice. She hadn't truly expected Ty to leave his front door open, and she turned toward the garage.

Tapping in a four-digit code and then pressing the pound sign sounded easy enough. But Sage held a three-tier cake in her arms, and the buttons on his keypad didn't seem to depress. It took her four tries, and she was just about to hurl the cake on the concrete, burst into tears, and drive back to Texas when the door finally rumbled upward.

Relief streamed through her, and she took a deep breath to calm her emotions. She'd taken today off of work so she could dedicate the whole day to Ty, and she'd already spent the morning assembling everything to make his birthday absolutely amazing.

Sage knew she was good at this type of thing. She'd made birthday cakes, hosted parties for friends or just family, for each of her children growing up. Year after year. Jerry too. Her children had since told her that she'd always made them feel special on their birthdays, and she worked hard to do so.

With her confidence high, Sage entered the house and called, "Hey, puppies. It's just me," to the dogs. Barking ensued, but it took several long seconds for Sherman and Brother to get off Ty's bed and navigate their way into the kitchen. By then, Sage had the cake safely on the counter.

She grinned at the dogs as she bent down to pat them and say hello. "Yes, you know me, don't you?" They did, and as she rose again, she looked at the cake. Then Sherman. "I don't trust you. Come on, let's go out while I bring in everything."

Every time she got home, no matter the time of day, she opened the door for Gypsy. Her dog expected it, and Ty's did too. So Sage opened the sliding glass door for them, and both Brother and Sherman went right out, no balking. They went down the steps to the yard, and Sage watched them for a moment, smiling, before she went back outside to bring in the ballons and the gifts.

She'd ordered dinner from Ty's favorite restaurant that night, and she'd asked him to keep in touch with her throughout the afternoon. She planned to arrive back at his house about the same time as him, with dinner, and they'd walk in together, she'd shout, "Surprise!" and they'd spend the evening together, celebrating him.

Everything went exactly right in her head, and Sage had his house set and ready to go in only a few minutes. After all, it didn't take long to tie helium balloons to chairs and lamps, nor to hang a banner across the entryway, nor to set out the two gifts she'd gotten for him.

One was a tie of the month club. The man wore a shirt and tie six days a week, and Sage had gotten the subscription that would allow Ty to pick from five ties the one he wanted every month.

The other was a key, and Sage paused as she looked at the tiny box next to the festive envelope she'd put his tie of the month club subscription paperwork in. Hesitation and indecision raged through her. If she gave him a key to her house, what would he think?

That she wanted him to move in with her? That she didn't want to marry him? That he could simply come and go at her place whenever he wanted? He sort of already did that, no key required.

To her, it meant she wanted him. But getting into nittier and grittier details became muddy for her. Ty was a smart man, and he'd have questions. She pictured him holding up the key, his eyebrows raised, those dreamy eyes filled with *What's this for?*

She picked up the box. "It's a key to my house," she said to the empty kitchen. "So you can..."

What? So he could what, exactly?

Still outside, Sherman barked, and Sage jumped. She slid the box in her shorts pocket and went to let the dogs back in. "Sorry, guys," she said to them. "But come on. You get to hang out with me this afternoon instead of moping on your dad's bed." She grinned at his dogs, and a few hours later, when Ty said he'd be home in about an hour, Sage left his house.

She collected Gypsy from her house, then dinner from The Santiago Grill, and she arrived back at Ty's before him. "Perfect," she said.

After herding Gypsy inside and the doggy reunion that followed, Sage laid out dinner on his countertop. She'd just turned to get down plates when the garage door opened. She heard him pull in, and the anticipation and adrenaline racing through her made her throat narrow and her breathing quicken.

He'd know she'd entered his house without him here. Surely he'd checked her car and hadn't seen her.

The door opened, and her handsome boyfriend walked in. He carried his sexy briefcase bag, and he wore dark slacks, a light blue button-up, and a paisley tie in gold, brown, and navy around his throat.

"Hey, sweetheart," she said, and his whole face transformed from surprise to joy. She *saw* it, and it slammed into her chest a moment later, making her *feel* it too.

He tossed his bag to the side as he said, "What's this?"

"Happy birthday." She swept her arm toward the food, then where all three dogs sat waiting on the cusp of the kitchen. He'd trained his to sit at a line they wouldn't cross, and Gypsy knew how to get a bite of human food too.

Sage barely had time to look back at Ty to judge his reaction before he took her into his arms. "Wow, Sage, this is amazing."

She wrapped her arms around him too, the whole world

swaying as she let herself experience the warmth of his body. The happiness seething between them. The tenderness of this moment, where she'd done something for him he really appreciated.

He pulled back and looked at her. "How I love coming home to you." He kissed her, his mouth hungry at first, but softening in intensity only a couple of strokes later. Sage kissed him back, the world around her falling away.

She fell and fell and fell, until Ty pulled away and she managed to say, "Happy birthday, baby," one more time.

He didn't say the words *I love you*, but Sage felt them lingering in the air. She wondered if they came from him or her, but she didn't say anything either. Fear trapped how she really felt, and she swallowed against it as she moved over to the counter and told him what she'd ordered for his birthday feast.

"And," she said. "I hope this present isn't too lame." She picked up the envelope with brightly colored gifts and party hats printed on it and handed it to him.

He took it without looking at it, those hazel eyes lasered in on her. "I'm sure it won't be lame." He lifted the flap and took out the paperwork. It took him a few moments to read it, and then he laughed. "A tie of the month. That's great." He swooped her into his arms again and held her tightly.

"This is all so great, Sage," he murmured. "Thank you."

She couldn't remember Jerry ever reacting this way when she'd set up birthday meals, cake, and gifts for him. He'd smile, sure. He'd say thank you, but it had never held this level of...intimacy. Of genuine gratitude.

As she stood in Ty's arms, the two of them breathing together and their three dogs patiently waiting for the eating to begin, Sage felt herself take one more giant step away from what had gone on in Texas and toward Ty.

Getting closer, she thought, and then she stepped out of Ty's arms and said, "Go sit down. I'll bring you your birthday meal."

"This cake is amazing," he said without moving to go sit down.

"Bessie helped me with it," she admitted.

He slid his hand along her waist. "Maybe I can have a little of you for dessert too." He hummed, took the plate from her that she'd just picked up, and turned her toward him. "Starting right now." He kissed her again, and Sage had no complaints about that.

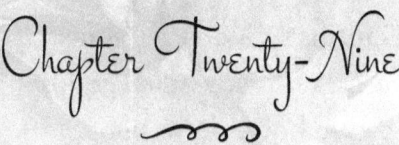

Chapter Twenty-Nine

Ty pulled up to Elite Lending, his heartbeat pounding in the back of his throat. He'd closed seventeen deals this summer alone—and it was only mid-August—but for some reason, he'd stopped by Gourmet Goods for a bread-basket for this signing extravaganza.

That was what he called the hour-long process of clients signing a mound of paperwork to make the house they'd bought theirs. He told them it was a celebration, because they got their keys afterward and could go enjoy their new place.

Everyone liked getting their new house; they just didn't like everything that came with it. He aimed to make the process as smooth as possible, and he usually got the selling agent to let him into the house during the signing extravaganza, where he'd leave a little welcome-home gift for his clients.

But this morning's client was Katherine Tallison, and

thus, Ty reached for the breadbasket and headed inside the lender.

He'd told Bessie last week that he'd preorder breadbaskets for his clients if she had them available. He'd taken her and Sage to Gourmet Goods to show her the different shaped and sized baskets with baked goods in them, caramel pretzel rods, and even home décor signs.

She'd been interested, but wary, and Ty supposed he could appreciate a businesswoman who considered all of her options before diving in. Right now, she couldn't really dive into anything new anyway, as the Heritage Festival sat only three weeks away.

Ty's pulse now bounced in his jugular for a whole new reason. He and Sage had first gone out at the Heritage Festival, and while it hadn't been a stellar first date and the second hadn't happened for six more months, Ty wanted to take her back there. He wanted to come full circle. He wanted to see if things were different this year.

"Of course they're different," he muttered to himself as he pulled open the glass door. Since she'd come to cut his hair near the beginning of June, things between them had been just amazing. He kissed her every time he saw her. She didn't forget the things they'd set up to do together. She let him come lounge with her on her deck, and she came to his place plenty too.

They hung out with their friends—the number of beach days Ty had attended this year outstripped any he'd done in the past five years combined.

And his birthday?

Ty had fallen completely in love with Sage Grady on his birthday.

He could admit it inside his mind, but he had not told her yet. He wasn't sure when he would, and somehow, the Heritage Festival held all the answers for him.

"Katherine Tallison?" he asked the woman at the front desk. "Or Peter Klein."

"Mister Klein is setting up in Harbor Bay," she said, indicating the hallway to his right. "Straight down and in the corner."

"The corner," Ty repeated. Nice touch for a client as big as Katherine. Ty stood to make almost fifty grand from the sale of this one home, and suddenly, the breadbasket felt too small and insignificant.

He found Peter in the room and set the basket down on the credenza just inside the door. "Good morning, Pete."

"Ah, the man of the hour," Peter said as he turned from setting down a third pen on the oval conference room table. It only held six people, because people didn't usually bring their entire clan to an hour's worth of signing papers.

Nautical art hung on the wall across from the table, and the corner two walls bore big windows. "Great room," he said.

"That's such a real estate thing to say." Pete chuckled and shook Ty's hand. "I don't normally see you at these."

"Yeah, I know," he said, reaching to button his suit coat. "It's Katherine. I showed her two dozen houses to get here, so."

"So you're telling me I better have my A-game on."

"A-plus," Ty said with a grin. He settled into a chair and pulled out his phone, because he had a full morning of showings after this, then he was meeting another client for another round of walking through houses. The number of texts he could send in one day boggled the mind, and he checked for confirmations for that morning and sent reminders for the afternoon.

When Katherine walked in, she wore a ball gown—a legit ball gown—in red and feathers, and Ty jumped to his feet, his phone forgotten. "Good morning," he said, moving to embrace her and kiss both cheeks. "You ready for this?"

She smiled at him and took the offered seat. "Yes," she said. "I can't wait to move into this house."

Everyone in the room knew Katherine wouldn't do any of it, but she did have to put her John Hancock on every paper to make it all legal. When it was done, Ty presented her with the breadbasket, laughed with her, and walked her out to her car.

As she drove away, his adrenaline buzzed through him. His high-profile clients stressed him out, but already, he couldn't wait to find another one.

Feeling brave and confident, he strode toward his luxury SUV too. Behind the wheel, he stared straight ahead, his heart in some sort of freefall-jackhammering beat.

He couldn't even believe what he was considering, and yet, the thought to go find Sage a diamond ring would not leave his mind. He put his car in gear and backed out of the spot. He drove down the road, making turns until he found himself heading south to the shopping and lighthouse district. His showings were down here too, but he had forty-five minutes to spare.

"You can't find the perfect ring in forty-five minutes," he said to himself. He pulled into the mall parking lot. He'd been here plenty of times before. He knew where to park to get over to Steiner's quickly.

He'd purchased two diamond rings from the shop already. He knew the master jeweler there; had sold him a house a couple of years ago. He made beautiful, custom pieces—and he accepted returns if the woman said no.

Ty's heart squeezed painfully in his chest, causing him to gasp for air. He wasn't sure what shape a human heart was, but his suddenly felt like it had morphed into a cube only two inches big.

"You're not doing this," he told himself. He even locked the doors, as if that alone would keep him in the vehicle. He and Sage had not spoken about marriage again, not since June. She hadn't told him she loved him; she'd given him no indication—other than the way she melted into his embrace, kissed him hello and good-bye, spent all her spare time with him—that she'd say yes if he showed up on two knees wielding a diamond.

He'd been here before; he would not do this again. He would not go into a situation where he didn't know if the woman he was proposing to would say yes or not.

"She'll say yes." His whispered words sounded like a manifestation, not a fact. They sounded like the desires of his heart, not something he knew intellectually.

With indecision raging through his whole body, he

turned off the vehicle. Got out. Walked to Steiner's in a matter of minutes.

"Ah, hello, Mister Parker," a woman said with a bright smile. She wore a straight dress in all-black, with black heels, and minimal jewelry around her neck, at her ears, or on her hands. She'd have perfectly manicured fingernails, though, and he smiled at Rose.

"Good morning, Rose." His eyes moved to the case in front of him; his pulse danced as if he'd dropped it onto a hot tin roof and told it to survive. "I'm—" His voice broke. "I'm looking for something...simple. Elegant. Something that makes a statement without being obnoxious."

Plenty of people in Hilton Head had money, and plenty didn't. At Steiner's, they had something for everyone, or so they claimed, and Ty followed Rose toward the back of the store as she asked, "Is this an engagement ring, Mister Parker? Or something for your sister's birthday?"

He smiled, but it felt plastic and brittle, like it might break off his face if he let it linger too long. "Well, I don't have a sister, Rose, so I'm going to go with an engagement ring."

She looked at him with knowing and compassion in her eyes. "I understand, Mister Parker. Let me show you something new Gentry has been working on."

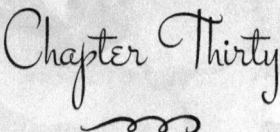

Chapter Thirty

Sage held Ty's hand as they wandered along the line of booths at the Heritage Festival. She loved things like this, and she'd already been back to the car once to deposit the tea towels, the facial scrub, and the water bottle she'd purchased.

She marveled that every booth here belonged to someone local, a business who served the population of Hilton Head all summer, and year-round too. The Salon Mionic had gotten a booth this year when Sage had mentioned to Barb, her boss, that she'd seen others in the beauty industry at the festival last year.

Ah, last year's festival.

Sage had helped Bessie set up and take down her booth. She'd wandered around with friends. She'd met Ty for the concert in the park—exactly what they were doing this year too. He'd told her he went every year, and he'd understand if she didn't want to go with him.

She'd laughed and said, "I didn't have a bad time on that date, Ty. I just...wasn't sure about you." She'd been flirty and fun, and she'd almost expected him to ask her if she was sure about him now.

He hadn't.

He didn't know the band this year, and they'd come far earlier so they could walk around the booths, then get dinner, then watch the concert. He'd brought the same camp chairs they'd sat on over the Fourth of July, and Sage felt more her age than she had last year.

She felt more like herself.

"Look at these," she said, taking Ty over to a booth with cast iron everything in it. "You need something like this for those Dutch pancakes you were trying to make last weekend."

"*Trying* to make?" he asked. "I *did* make those just fine."

She smiled at him, because he wasn't annoyed or upset, and picked up a tiny little pan that would make a pancake that would just fill a dinner plate. "Look at this. It's adorable."

"They crisp everything up better than anything," a man in the booth said. "Hey, Ty."

"Stanley." Ty shook the man's hand. "How's it been going this year?"

"Just great," Stanley said. He looked at Sage, his smile big and round. "This—"

"This is Sage Grady," Ty interrupted. "We're seeing each other."

"Oh, great," Stanley said. "He definitely needs to make you pancakes with this pan."

"I agree," Sage said, already moving to get out her thread wallet. "I'll take that little one."

"Sage." Ty wore a suppressed smile in his voice, but Sage didn't stop getting out her card. "You're going to have to carry that around."

She hesitated then, because it was getting close to dinnertime. "I can take it back to the car before the concert." She handed Stanley her card and took the tiny cast iron pan that had been bagged for her.

As they left the booth, Ty leaned down and murmured, "I only make those pancakes once a year."

Sage's next step landed a little woodenly. "For your daddy's birthday." They hadn't gone to Charleston to see his parents. He said it was too hard in the summer, but that he usually went in late October or November, when everything slowed down and cooled off.

"Right."

"Then they'll be absolutely amazing next year," she said. "And I can season the pan for you in the meantime."

"So it'll go back and forth between your house and mine?" he asked.

It almost sounded like he was asking something else, and Sage heard precisely what. Would he continue to go back and forth between her house and his? Would she? Would they ever live together?

She hadn't given him the key to her house on his birthday. It still sat in the wrapped box, and she'd hidden it away in her nightstand drawer. Ty had no reason to be in her bedroom, digging through her personal things. They hadn't merged their lives like that yet.

When Sage realized she'd thought the word *yet*, her steps slowed. Ty paused with her. "You see something, baby?"

She looked at *him*, and she saw *him*.

She saw herself with him. "Ty, I—"

"Ty," someone in the crowd crowed. He turned away from Sage, laughter spilling from his mouth only a moment later. He released Sage's hand to step into the man who'd interrupted her from spilling the contents of her heart in the park at the Heritage Festival.

Sage should be grateful to Harold Burl, and she was as she shook his hand. "He's an old friend of mine from the early days of the agency," Ty said, positively beaming. "What are you doing on the island? Last I heard, you were in...Miami?"

"Miami, yep." Harold wandered along with them for several minutes while he caught up with Ty, and then he peeled off to go find his family.

"Too bad about his dad," Sage said, because Harold had come back for his father's funeral.

"Yeah," Ty said, frowning. "I hadn't even heard that."

"Summer's busy for you," she said. "I'm gonna take this pan to the car, and then we can get dinner, okay?"

"Yeah, okay."

She left him standing in the shade, his phone already out when she walked away. She didn't mind how much time he spent on the phone. She knew he conducted a large part of his business from his device—and she did too.

Sage also knew she practically ran away from him, and she was jogging by the time she reached his SUV. She started it remotely, then got in the driver's seat and put the cast iron baby skillet behind her seat with the rest of her stuff.

The AC blew, calming her. Drying the tears that had started to manifest themselves. Everything inside her felt shaky and strange, and Sage struggled to figure out why.

All at once, she knew why.

She was in love with Tyler Parker.

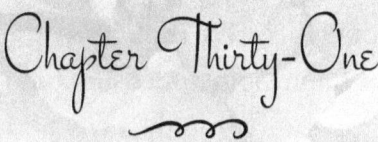

Chapter Thirty-One

Lauren sat cross-legged on the floor, trying to make her back as straight as possible. She'd finished her work for the day, for the weekend too. With her baby due on Tuesday next week, Lauren had been trying to tie up all loose ends for her marketing clients for the past couple of weeks.

She would still be able to do a few things, as she worked out of a home office, but she didn't have any meetings scheduled, no major campaigns launching, and no new clients getting onboarded. Everything was humming along, and now Lauren needed to find her center.

She liked the way the fan blew through her office, because it drowned out other sounds that might have distracted her. She continually pulled her concentration back to her breathing whenever her mind started to wander.

After she did her meditation, Lauren would move to her desk to do her journaling. She knew her thoughts about becoming a mother were irrational and unfounded. It didn't stop them from coming, and when they piled up, Lauren felt like drowning.

She'd been seeing a cognitive behavior counselor, and she'd learned about negative thought patterns and how to get herself out of them. Sometimes she could get herself back to a place of better sanity in only a few minutes, and sometimes she wrote for pages and pages.

With her baby girl due in only three days, the nursery sat ready for a new human being. She and Blake had arranged their careers so they could devote themselves to each other and their baby. Everything she'd been able to prepare, she'd prepared.

Except herself.

With another deep breath in, she pulled her focus back to the air moving through her nose. She held it there for a count of five, then slowly released it. When her music of pond sounds ended, Lauren opened her eyes and gave herself a moment to come back to the present.

With her nine-month-big baby belly, Lauren used a chair to help herself get back to her feet. She stretched her arms high above her head and pulled up her right side, then the left. She hadn't been sleeping well for the past month, but the infant she carried was worth it.

Her feet hurt almost all the time, because they'd swollen in the last couple of weeks, and even when Blake rubbed them, she didn't find much relief. The only thing that would bring her true relief was having this baby, and truth be told, Lauren couldn't wait to meet her daughter.

She had dark hair and eyes, but Blake was a bit lighter than her, especially in skin tone. She wondered if their baby would have her olive coloring or his lighter complexion. She felt sure she'd have the dark brown hair and eyes, but she wasn't sure how deep.

Would she have hair? Be bald? Would she be fussy or fiery or perfectly pleasant? Would she know Lauren's voice?

Lauren couldn't wait to find out.

A pain radiated down her spine and moved forward through her pelvis. She released her stretch, and that relieved some of the sting flowing through her. Lauren had gotten used to strange, never-felt-before pains in the past nine months. She'd never been pregnant before, and she'd never gone into labor.

She had read plenty on the subject, because when Lauren didn't know what to do, she researched. When she didn't know something, she learned about it. She didn't have a mother she could call on for help, but Blake's mother had been to the house several times in the past month, helping Lauren get the nursery set up, going over how to clean a bottle, and just talking about having her children.

She'd spoken to her friends too, all of whom had children. "I'm ready," she told herself as she went over to the desk. Her therapy journal sat open, her entry from the last time she'd needed to iron flat her thoughts, shining up from the page.

A sigh slipped from her lips as she sat, and she rolled her head to stretch her neck. "I need a nap," she said out loud, and in fact, she wrote that line first for today's entry. She knew being tired could influence her thoughts, and she hadn't slept well last night.

Her belly tightened as her pen scratched, and Lauren groaned as she pressed her free hand against it. The baby pushed back, which actually caused Lauren to smile. "You getting ready, baby?" she asked her daughter. "Your time in there is coming to a close."

She finished her therapy in only a few minutes today, and when she picked up her phone, she saw she'd missed quite a few texts on the Supper Club thread. She loved her friends so much, as they'd been at Lauren's side for such a long time. Through so many of her major life events.

Sometimes she said something to upset one or more of them. Sometimes they irritated her. But no matter what, she could count on them for anything. Today's conversation revolved around Bessie's survival of another Heritage Festival, more pictures from Bea's road trip, and the menu for this month's Supper Club, which Joy was hosting.

Will you be there, Lauren? Joy had asked, though Lauren had told them all she wasn't sure how the baby would impact her ability to come to Supper Club. Bea had missed in July, but other than that, the six of them were always there. Even when half of them had lived in another state, they'd done video calls and participated.

Joy wanted to serve some new Chinese recipes she'd gotten from another teacher at the school where she worked, and Lauren wasn't going to tell her no. *I'm due in four days,* she said. *Supper Club isn't for another two more weeks. If I'm still pregnant then, someone better do something outrageous.*

She smiled at her own text and scooted away from her desk to go start dinner. Blake would be home from work soon, and Tommy had had enough time on his computer. She stood, and a hot flash of wetness saturated her yoga pants.

"Oh," she said, freezing her feet to the floor. She reached for the desk and pressed one palm against it as the baby seemed to stretch her whole body out, including into places she had not moved before.

"Tommy," she called, because the teen's computer sat out in the kitchen, where Blake and Lauren could monitor it. "Tommy!" He wore headphones a lot of the time, and Lauren couldn't recall right now if she could move now that her water had broken.

"Of course you can," she told herself. Women didn't turn into lumps of ice when they went into labor. They had to get to the hospital somehow, and Lauren fumbled for her phone still on her desk.

She tapped to call Blake, her panic rising as the phone took precious seconds to connect. Her abdomen tightened, and Lauren groaned as the pressure reached a level she'd never felt before. She felt like she might pop, and she pressed her eyes closed.

"Hey, honey," Blake chirped. "I just left the office. Do you want me to pick something up for dinner, or are you in the nesting mode already?"

"I'm in labor," Lauren said. She gasped as the pain started to recede. Things connected in her mind—finally—and she added, "I just had a contraction, and my water broke."

"I'm ten minutes away," Blake said, all chirpiness gone. "Have Tommy help you get your bag and get you out in the driveway. I'll be there as fast as I can."

"Can you stay on the line?" Lauren asked, tears coming to her eyes. Her nose ran, and she tried to pull everything tight again. It didn't quite work, and a sniffle and a whimper escaped.

"Yes," Blake said. "Lauren, baby, it's okay. Take a deep breath with me, okay?"

She nodded rapidly. "Okay." He breathed in, and Lauren tried to copy him, but air seemed like the wrong thing to put in her lungs.

"Now," Blake said. "Go out into the living room and get Tommy."

"Okay." Lauren lifted her palm from the desk and straightened. Her legs didn't buckle, and her baby didn't kick or push, and she managed to take the required steps to her office door. She opened it and called, "Tommy," again.

He turned from his computer this time, swiping his headphones off. "Yeah? What's up?" He was sixteen, but he wasn't stupid, and he got to his feet a moment later. "What's wrong?"

"I'm having the baby," she said. "Your dad's on the line, and I need you to go grab my baby bag."

"Good job, hon," Blake said in support. "Tell him I'll be there soon."

"I'm on it," Tommy said, and he hurried by her and into

the master suite. He returned only a few seconds later. "What now?"

"Can you help me outside?" Lauren reached for him just as a slicing, horrible pain moved through her from sternum to pelvis. She cried out, and Tommy braced himself against her.

"Lauren," he said. "I'm scared."

"It's okay," Blake shouted through the phone. "Put me on speaker, Lauren."

Instead of doing that, she handed the phone to Tommy. He fumbled it with the bag, trying to support Lauren, and he dropped the device. He swore and bent to get it.

"Dad," he said as he swiped the call to speaker. "She's... in a lot of pain."

"I'm having a contraction," Lauren said. "It's...I'm okay." It was new. It hurt. She didn't know how to deal with the sharp pain, nor the radiating remnant of it as it faded away. "I can move now."

"Tommy, son, take her outside between contractions. I'm almost there, and we'll get her to the hospital."

"Should I call Mom?" he asked as Lauren took the first step. Tommy stayed right at her side as they went down the hall. He opened the door, letting in the afternoon sunlight, and they stepped out into it.

"If you want," Blake said. "But you can be home alone for a bit without someone with you, Tommy."

"I'll call her when you and Lauren go."

Lauren clutched his arm as they navigated the steps

down to the sidewalk, and she watched the street as she neared the driveway.

"I'm coming around the corner," he said. "Everyone okay?"

"Yes," Lauren and Tommy said at the same time. A few seconds later, Blake's dark SUV came into view, and he roared into the driveway. He leapt from the vehicle almost before it came to a stop, and more relief struck through Lauren like lightning.

Blake was here, and now she'd be okay. "Come on, Lauren," he said. "Let's get you in the car."

She took one step before another contraction tore through her. She yelped, froze, and Blaze pressed his hand against her lower back. That actually seemed to help, but every muscle from her scalp to her pinky toe had turned to concrete and wouldn't move.

"Put the bag in the back, son," Blake said. "Move when you can, Lauren."

She suddenly thought of something she'd read. "Shouldn't we be timing these?"

"Hon, your water broke. They're going to admit you."

The pain subsided, and Lauren moved around the vehicle to the passenger seat. Blake got behind the wheel, and he looked at her, pure nervous energy radiating from him. "We're having the baby."

"*I'm* having our baby," she said with a wry smile. "Can you please get me to the hospital so I don't have her in your car?"

Chapter Thirty-Two

*A*re you going to be okay away from Baby Daisy for the weekend? Ty teased in his text to Sage.

It'll be touch and go, she sent back. *But I'm headed home to pack. You can come over for dinner if you want. I don't think I have time to go out and pack for our amazing weekend together.*

Ty smiled to himself and looked at the open weekender bag on his bed. He'd already packed for an afternoon departure tomorrow. He and Sage were staying in the South Charleston Hotel, using the voucher he'd gotten her for her birthday.

Nerves ran up and down his spine, because he and Sage would be sharing a room. It had two queen beds, and he had no idea if they'd use both of them or not. He'd brought up the idea of this trip to go see his parents in Charleston, and she'd suggested they use the hotel voucher, go on the food tour, and make a whole weekend of it.

All the things he'd given her for her birthday that she hadn't used yet, except for the pass to Hunting Island State Park, which was in the opposite direction from Charleston. She'd then called to book the two nights at the hotel, as well as the food tour, which was on Sunday morning.

He'd called his parents to set up a time to bring Sage to meet them, and they were all going to dinner on Saturday night. The whole trip had taken form in only a couple of hours, and Ty had never been more excited for a weekend trip to Charleston to see his parents.

He turned and looked at the little black velvet box sitting on his dresser. Should he pack the engagement ring? September had turned into October, and the housing market had slowed a little.

Sage had taken time off from the salon, and Ty felt like everything rode on this weekend. He'd thought that about the Heritage Festival too, and that had been an absolute magical Saturday afternoon, evening, and night. He and Sage had been dating for almost eight months now, and Ty picked up the ring box.

"I love her," he said aloud to his mostly-packed bag and his two dogs. He turned and looked at the canines on his bed. "Do you think she'll say yes?"

Neither of them answered, and Ty tucked the box into his bag. He might as well take it, right?

His cell chimed again, and he sank onto the bed beside his dogs to see what Sage had said. She'd sent a picture of her and Lauren's baby, Daisy, who was now two weeks old.

She's so perfect came in next, and Ty loved the light of happiness in his girlfriend's eyes. *I miss my grandbaby.*

Maybe we should go to Santa Fe for our next weekend trip together, he said. *I'd love to meet your daughter and your other son.*

That would be amazing, Sage said, though it would probably take them another eight months to leave Hilton Head again.

He stood up and walked into the kitchen with long strides, trying to reason through how tomorrow, Saturday, and Sunday would go. How they *should* go. How they could go.

He wanted to ask her to marry him, but he should probably have a conversation with her about his feelings first. Or at least find out if she would ever get married again. Ty felt like he'd entered this endless loop, and one wrong step or one errant question would send him off the path he wanted to be on.

I'm going to get sandwiches and bring the dogs over to run, he sent to her. *Okay?*

See you soon, Sage said, and Ty paced back to his bedroom to get his hounds. "Come on, guys," he said. "Let's go see Gypsy, okay?"

He cast his packed bag one more glance, didn't remove the ring, and headed to his girlfriend's house.

Ty gripped the steering wheel as the skyline of Charleston came into view. "Did you know that they don't build skyscrapers in Charleston?" he asked, his nerves bubbling near the top of his eyeballs.

"Is that right?" Sage asked. "Why's that?"

"Probably lots of city zoning laws and whatever, but the rumor is that no building can be taller than the church steeple at St. Philip's Church." He smiled over to her, the questions and conversation he really wanted to have nowhere near this one.

He wasn't sure how much more he could take. Every nerve felt like snapping, and Ty wanted to yell out his tension and pound the steering wheel. "Sage," he said, and her name came out with too much force.

She turned toward him, surprise on her face. "Yeah?"

"I need to know what tonight looks like."

"Tonight?"

The inclination to yell didn't diminish. "Yes, tonight." He nodded. "We have one room, sweetheart. Let me be plain. Are we sleeping together or in separate beds? I don't care either way. Well, I do, but I'm fine either way. I just need to know."

Sage remained silent for several heartbeats, because he'd just laid a lot out there. Now that his tongue had started to wag, words like *I love you*, and *Do you think you'll ever want to get married again?* ran through his mind and up his throat.

He coughed to shove everything back down, wondering how long it would stay there.

"I thought we'd use both beds," Sage said, her voice on the hoarse side.

"Okay." Ty could finally release his breath. "This...don't you think this feels like a big step for us, Sage?" He glanced over to her. "We're spending the weekend together in a hotel. I'm taking you to meet my parents."

"It's a big step," she admitted.

More relief filled him. "Okay, I just want to add a few more things to this conversation." He took a deep breath. "I don't want to ruin the weekend, so if at any point, you don't like what I'm saying, just hold up your hand."

"Ty." She shook her head, her beautiful smile appearing. "We can talk about anything."

Oh, how he wanted that to be true. "Sage, I'm in love with you."

She stared at him, and Ty wanted to press on the accelerator and ram the SUV into the back of the car in front of him.

"You don't have to say it back," he said. "I fell in love with you on my birthday, and I'm tired of keeping it to myself." He looked over to her, his smile growing as hers did too. She was *smiling*.

"Do you believe me?" he asked.

"Do I believe that you love me?"

"Yeah."

She took his hand and squeezed it tight, tight. "I wish you weren't driving, so I could kiss you."

"Would that kiss tell me that yes, you believe I love you?"

"Yes," she whispered. "I believe you."

"Great." His lungs finally operated normally, and his grip relaxed on the steering wheel. He drove into downtown, the streets tight and narrow and crowded. "Sage, I just have to know one more thing."

"You don't need to ask." She stroked her thumb across the side of his. "You want to know about marriage."

He thought of the diamond ring he bought almost two months ago. The one he'd packed and brought along on this trip. "It's been on my mind, yes."

Sage looked out the windshield. "I'm..." She sighed. "Ty, I love you."

He chuckled before he realized what she'd said—and that she meant it. "I really wish I wasn't driving right now." He spotted a parking lot ahead that went to the beach, and he flipped on his blinker.

After pulling in and parking, he reached for her, and kissed her. "I'm a little shocked," he murmured.

"Join the club." She matched her mouth to his again, and Ty simply basked in the moment, trying to commit it to memory. She wasn't his first girlfriend, but he definitely thought Sage was the first woman to truly love him.

She ducked her head and let her breath wash over his collarbone. "Is this real?" she whispered.

"I love you," he said again.

Sage looked up at him, her eyes wide and wonderful. "I love you, Ty," she said. "Can we table the topic of marriage so we can enjoy this weekend?"

Ty saw her nerves plainly. He honestly wasn't sure what

he'd do if she told him she just couldn't get married. But he nodded. "I think I can wait one more weekend."

She nodded too, and they both looked out the windshield. Since he wasn't fifteen, and he didn't need to sit in the beach parking lot to make-out with his girlfriend, he put the car in gear and navigated them to the historic hotel where they'd be staying.

TY WOKE THE NEXT MORNING, THE FIRST THING HE saw the white wall of the hotel room where he'd slept last night. Sage slept in the next bed over, and it had been awkward for a few minutes last night as he'd settled down to go to sleep. It had taken longer than usual, but he'd managed.

He rolled over and found her still asleep, her beauty only enhanced by the softness in her face and the golden morning light. He got up and took some clothes into the bathroom, feeling like he was back in college and traveling with a group of friends.

Except he was thirty years older now, and he wasn't with a friend. He was with the woman he loved. Yeah, it was awkward all around.

He got dressed in the steamy bathroom, then left for long enough to grab his wallet. He looked at Sage, still snoozing in her bed, and he stepped over to her. He leaned down and kissed her cheek. "Baby, I'm going to go find us some breakfast."

"Mm." Her eyelids fluttered, and then she opened them sleepily.

Ty smiled at her. "I'll be back in a bit."

"Okay."

He touched his lips to hers in a chaste kiss and left the room. They'd planned to do whatever struck their fancy today—maybe the beach, maybe a walking tour of the historic downtown area of Charleston, maybe a museum visit—and then go visit his parents tonight.

He exited the hotel to the fall morning and straightened his shoulders. This weekend was going just fine. Better than he'd even thought it would. "You're not going to ask her to marry you, though," he told himself.

Part of him still wanted to, but the other, louder part absolutely could not risk being down on both knees and getting a no—for the third time.

As he picked up bagels and cream cheese, orange juice, and coffee, he told himself to be patient for a little longer. Sage had asked for the weekend, and he'd said he'd give it to her. Not only that, he could wait and see what his parents thought of her.

Okay, so the last one was just him trying to convince himself not to propose the moment he walked in the hotel room with breakfast. And he coached himself to simply enjoy the weekend, no proposal, with every step he took back to their room.

Chapter Thirty-Three

~~~

S age straightened her skirt, her anxiety flowing freely through her. She reminded herself that she met a lot of people because of her job. Ty's parents were just two more people. A man and a woman.

"Ready?" he asked as he killed the ignition. He'd parked in the driveway of what looked like a normal house in a suburb of Charleston.

"Is this where you grew up?" she asked, eyeing the dark blue house with white shutters.

"Yes," he said simply, also watching the house.

Sage felt like she'd been taped to the passenger seat, taped to an unmovable fragment of land, taped and trapped, so she couldn't move forward. She felt like someone had pressed pause on her life, but she was still living.

She took a deep breath. "Okay," she said. "We better go in, so they don't think we don't want to be here."

"They're great," Ty assured her again. He'd told her the

same thing before. He hadn't run from home because he was unhappy. He returned to visit his parents when he could, and he loved them. He got out of the car, and Sage joined him at the hood.

He took her hand as they entered the house, and he called, "Momma? We're here."

Sage committed herself to entering the house, and she hated how weak she felt at Ty's side. She told herself that he loved her, that his parents would too.

Then, there they stood. Both of them, the pair, framed against the light coming in the back windows and spilling through the arched doorway that probably led into the kitchen.

"You're home," his momma said as she broke ranks and left his father standing on the cusp of the other room.

The house definitely had history, and old bones, and so many secrets to tell. It also held charm, and charisma, and a spirit of liveliness that really called to Sage. She stepped back as his mother embraced him, both of them talking over the other.

Ty then retreated to her side, beaming with that golden light he'd always possessed. "Sage, this is my momma, Savannah. Momma, this is Sage Grady, the woman I'm in love with."

"Oh, my." His momma clutched at her non-existent pearls as she took in Ty's face and then looked at Sage. "It's so wonderful to meet you." She spoke with a heavy Carolina accent, and Sage loved her instantly.

"You too." She hugged his momma, sinking into the older woman's arms for only a moment.

"Kenneth, get over here." Savannah gestured her husband forward, and she made the introduction to Sage this time. "Did you hear, Kenny? Ty says this is the woman he's going to marry."

Ty gave a light laugh that carried a nervous undercurrent. "Momma, that's not what I said." He exchanged a glance with Sage, and she merely smiled at him. "I said I loved her."

"That's wonderful," Kenneth said as he shook her hand. "Do you love him too, Sage?"

"Daddy, I swear." Ty shook his head. "You two promised you'd be on your best behavior."

"This is my best behavior," his daddy said with a twinkle in those light green eyes. His momma had darker hair and eyes, and Ty sat right in the middle of them. The best of both of them.

"Come in, come in." Savannah herded them back into the kitchen. "Dinner is ready, and I can't wait to hear all about Sage."

"Oh, boy," she said with a laugh. "Those stories aren't very interesting."

"Ty says you have three kids?" His momma bustled around the kitchen, bringing dishes over to the table, which was already set.

"Yes," Sage said. "Two boys and a girl. None of them live here, though."

"We'll probably be headed to Texas for a wedding in the New Year," Ty said. "Don't you think, sweetheart?"

"If Dallen and Jenny ever set a date, yes." He'd asked her to marry him. She'd said yes. As far as Sage knew, wedding plans were being made. But no date had been set. She wasn't sure if that was how young people did things these days or what, but she needed to call Dallen and press him for a date she could put on her calendar.

"This house is beautiful," she said. "I love how these older homes are more segmented. It gives each room purpose, I think." She smiled as she accepted the bowl of soup his father had ladled for her.

It looked like Savannah had prepared a five-course dinner, and Sage's stomach growled. Maybe she wouldn't make a fool of herself in front of these people.

"This is chicken gumbo soup," Savannah drawled. "It's an old family recipe."

"My grandmother's," Ty said.

"Did you teach Ty to cook?" Sage asked, finding such a thing very charming.

"Only a little," Savannah said with a laugh. "That boy didn't have the patience for much."

"That's why I'm good at meals that take thirty minutes or less." He grinned at his momma and poured her a glass of wine.

Dinner progressed, and his mother could have definitely won a multitude of cooking awards. By the time Sage put the last bite of chocolate mousse cake in her mouth, she felt like her dress would burst off of her.

"This was *so* delicious," she said, still licking the chocolate from the spoon. "I'm never going to eat this well again." She smiled around at everyone. The conversation had been easy, and she thought his parents had minded their manners just fine.

They didn't press either of them about their relationship. No questions were asked. No stray or sly glances. At least Sage now knew why Ty approached things the way he did.

"Ty, I want to show you something," his daddy said, and the two of them got up together.

"I'll help you clean up." Sage got to her feet too, and she and Savannah started to clear the table. The old kitchen had endured some modern updates, one of which was a big, deep farmhouse sink.

"I love this," Sage said, running her hand along the countertop that went over it. "It holds so much." In fact, it looked like every bowl, pot, or pan Savannah had used to make their meal of pork roast and mashed potatoes still sat in the sink.

"It's wonderful," Savannah agreed. "I do a lot of cooking, and I didn't realize how much the sink couldn't hold until we got that one." She started loading the dishwasher, and Sage attacked the bigger items in the sink.

"You're a stylist," Savannah said, straightening. "What do you think of my hair?"

Sage was not going to go down this road. "I think it's lovely," she said with a smile.

"I want to color it, but Kenneth thinks it might make me look like I'm trying too hard."

Sage looked over to her. Her hair had definitely turned gray, but it could be shined up into a healthy silver and she'd be happier. At least Sage thought she would be. She had soft bangs that hid her tall forehead—always a good move—and her hair fell to her shoulders in even, very age-appropriate layers.

"Trying too hard to do what?" she asked.

"I don't know." She shook her head. "Look younger, I suppose."

"What don't you like about your hair?" Sage finished scrubbing the pot that had boiled the potatoes and laid it to dry in a dish rack.

"I think it's...well, it's really dry and brittle," she said. "So I don't think it looks very healthy. It has no...oomph."

Sage smiled to the pan as she rinsed the gravy remains out of it. "If you came to me, Miss Parker, I'd simply highlight your grays. They're so pretty on women your age—on women any age—and it would give it shine. Sparkle."

"That's what I need," she said. "Do you dye your hair, Sage? It's so beautiful."

Sage gave her a look out of the corner of her eye. "I'm going to tell you something I haven't told anyone. Not Ty. Not my Supper Club friends, who are my best friends in the whole world." She stopped scrubbing and Savannah stopped rinsing and loading.

Their eyes met, and Sage felt a little dangerous. A little

naughty. Like she might just be about to take off on a long flight and wouldn't be able to make it back.

"Yes," she said. "I color my hair, but—" She laughed. "I've told all my friends for years that I don't."

Savannah's smile grew into something wild and beautiful. "That's so interesting," she said. "Why not just tell them?"

"I don't know." Sage shrugged as she went back to work on the pots and pans. "One of them made *such* a big deal out of it once, and I denied it so strongly...I can't go back now." She giggled and finished up with another pan. "I don't do it all the time. Mostly when I want to look my best—like for my son's wedding. I'll give it a little *oomph* a few weeks before I go to that."

"Would you do mine, Sage?" she asked, and she looked eager and apprehensive at the same time.

"I so would, Savannah."

His mother leaned into her, and Sage did the same to her, almost like they were sisters or long-lost friends.

"Ty loves you so much," his mother said next. "I've never seen him like this with anyone. Of course, he's only ever brought home that awful Gloria, and it was—" She cut off when she caught Sage looking at her openly.

"Well, anyone could tell they weren't right for each other."

"And us?" Sage asked. "You think we're right for each other?"

Savannah ducked her head as she put a handful of silverware in the dishwasher. Sage wasn't going anywhere though, and she really wanted to know what his mother thought.

"Yes," Savannah said boldly. "There's something... magical about you two. I think you belong together, and I'm thrilled my son has finally found someone to love the way he's always wanted."

"Yeah," Sage said almost absently. "The way he's always wanted."

"And I don't need to ask if you love him. I can see you do. I can feel it." She smiled and nodded like that was that, and they finished up the dishes a few minutes later.

Sage dried her hands as Ty and his father re-entered the kitchen. "Coffee's ready," Kenneth said, and Sage looked around to find it. She hadn't noticed him come into the kitchen to make it, nor could she smell anything remotely related to coffee.

"Momma," Ty said as he came to Sage's side and claimed her by pulling her against him. "Did you know Daddy has a hand-built coffee maker in the garage?"

"Oh, that thing," his momma said with a wave of her hand. "It barely works."

"It works just fine," Ty assured her, his smile only growing. "I'm just worried he's going to burn down the house, starting with the garage."

"Come on, come on," Kenneth said, now the one to herd them out of the kitchen instead of into it. "We've got everything we need out here."

Sure enough, a coffee bar had been set up in the living room, and Sage could only mull over Savannah's words as Ty fixed her a cup and brought it to her. His daddy did the same for his momma, and they raised their mugs to one another in a silent toast.

Sage wasn't sure what she was saying to Savannah, but she felt certain his momma was saying, *Welcome to my family.*

Now she just had to decide what that meant. A wedding? Or not?

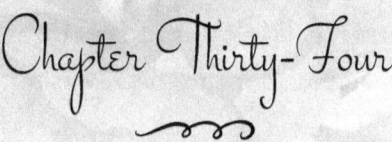

Chapter Thirty-Four

Ty sipped his after-dinner coffee, surprised that his father's homemade contraption could brew something this rich and delicious. They'd settled in the front living room, and Ty used to love to sit here with his father while they watched sailing or football or the news.

His mother had taken very good care of them tonight, and as Sage leaned into his side even more, he said, "Thank you for dinner, Momma. Sage was right—we won't eat that good for a while."

"Until we come visit you again, I'm sure," Sage said.

He looked at her, the hope that had been blooming inside him since the drive here yesterday expanding again. It grew and grew, accelerating as he watched her smile prettily at his mother.

Ty put his arm around her and kissed her hairline. She smelled like dish soap and cotton, and he wished they were back in the hotel room again. Or maybe not. That place wasn't exactly romantic, and they danced around one another there.

He didn't want to ask her to marry him there. He didn't want to do it in the car, though they'd had some of their best discussions there. He didn't want to get down on both knees in public, so a restaurant or the beach was out.

Truth be told, he wished they were back at her house, on the back deck, with the dogs running in the side yard or splashing in the water, dinner just over, and just the two of them watching the sun paint pictures over the water.

He shifted, the diamond ring he'd brought along to show to his parents like a boulder in his pants pocket. He hadn't shown it to his momma or his daddy, because there hadn't been an appropriate time. Sage had not left the room at all yet, not even to use the restroom.

He glanced at her as the conversation shifted to what his father had done for a living. "Machine repair," he said.

"Ah, the homemade coffee maker makes so much more sense now," Sage teased.

"Daddy's very handy," Ty said. "I didn't get that skill from him."

"Oh, come on, now," Sage said. "You've fixed a few things around the houses you sell. I know you have."

"A few things," he said. "Like straightening a piece of art or screwing in a light bulb." He chuckled, because no, he wasn't handy and he'd stopped worrying about it a long time ago.

The conversation paused again, and Ty wondered how

many more times it would have to do that before he found his bravery, tugged on it, and proposed to Sage.

No, the weekend wasn't over. They still had the food tour in the morning, as well as the drive back to Hilton Head.

If she tells you no...

Wow, what an awkward night and day tomorrow he'd have.

But if she says yes...

Well, things tonight and tomorrow would be radically different then, wouldn't they?

You said you'd give her the weekend.

Ty had said that, but he also suspected that Sage already knew what she wanted. She just needed to take the step.

"I'm going to use the restroom," she said, and Ty watched as she stood, got directions from his momma, and left the room.

With his heartbeat crashing like cymbals, he quickly pulled the diamond engagement ring out of his pocket. "Momma," he hissed. "Daddy. Help me propose to her." He held up the gem so the lamplight caught it, and Momma sucked in a breath.

"Oh, my, Ty."

Daddy grinned and grinned. "Do I need to delay her? What's your plan?"

"How will you delay her in the bathroom?" Ty shook his head, his thoughts scattering with the movement. "No, it's fine. I just need..." He looked around the living room. "Can we move this chair? That way, when she comes back, I can be right there, front and center."

His throat felt like someone had forced him to drink a bottle of white glue. But he and Daddy moved the chair, and Ty let his momma look at the ring while he wiped his sweaty palms down the front of his slacks.

Down the hall, he heard the door open. "Momma," he hissed again, and she handed him the ring. He dropped to both knees, making more noise than he'd anticipated. Didn't matter. He couldn't hear anything above the booming of his heart.

"That soap in there smells—" Sage cut off when she crossed from hallway to living room and saw Ty.

"Sage," he said, his voice as strong as he'd ever heard it. "I'm so in love with you. I believe in the institution of marriage, and I want to pledge myself to you. I want you to be mine, and I want the world to know it." He held up the ring, praying with everything inside him that it would be something she liked. He figured it would be, as it was a simple, white-gold band that was obviously circular, but not smooth.

It had bumps in it, and swirls, and while it matched up, it was a crooked circle. The diamond on it wasn't ostentatious, as she had to wear gloves at work while she colored hair, and be able to move her fingers through someone's hair as she cut it.

"I chose this ring," he said, his courage coming in strong now. "Because it's not a perfect circle. It's wavy, and it has some potholes in it, and sometimes it goes a little off-course.

That's how my life has been, and I know that's how your life has been."

She sniffled, the light catching on the glassy tears in her eyes.

"But it's still a circle," he said. "The two ends still meet up. It's still whole, and beautiful, and it still represents the endless way we could love each other. The infinite way we could be together."

He swallowed, the most dangerous words in the English language about to come out of his mouth.

"Sage, will you marry me?"

Chapter Thirty-Five

꩜

S age sent the picture of herself and Ty to her Supper
Club friends. She added a caption, then did the same
for the group thread with her three children on it.

She couldn't stop smiling as the picture went through,
the caption right behind it. In the photograph, she looked
radiant and happy, tucked right against Ty's side, who
laughed in the picture, pure joy flowing from him and going
out into the world for anyone who saw the photo.

I said yes.

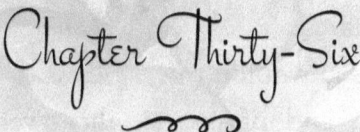

Chapter Thirty-Six

ix months later:

S Sage worried her newly manicured nails in her teeth, sure everything that was about to happen that day would be a mistake.

Including three big dogs in a wedding took some real guts, after all.

So did moving in with another person.

And saying I do.

Sage wasn't sure she could do any of it, and she wasn't the one moving everything she owned into someone else's house.

No, she told herself. *It's not your house. It's his too. It's* our *house.*

She'd told Ty that right out loud, and she needed to start thinking it and saying it. He'd sold his wonderful, pink house by the sea and had started moving over boxes last week. She loved him all the more for agreeing to live her waterfront way of life, and she fell for him all over again every time he said, "I *want* to do it, Sage. I want to be in that house with you."

"Sage," Cass said as she came into the master suite. "Why aren't you dressed?"

"I told you she wouldn't be," Bea said. She entered hot on Cass's heels, and of course, they were both dressed already.

Joy came next, and she paused and shook her head. "You've got to stop chewing your nails." She kindly lowered Sage's hand from her mouth as she knelt in front of her. "You're zoned out. Is this really how you want to be today?"

"I—no." She met Joy's blue-eyed stare and got to her feet. "Cass."

"Right here, Sage." She held her wedding dress so Sage could simply step into it, which she did.

"I have the shoes," Bessie said.

"I brought the entertainment." Lauren cooed at her seven-month-old, and Sage couldn't stop herself from smiling at Daisy too.

"Let's button her, ladies." Cass pulled the dress tight along Sage's chest, and then she stepped around to the back, where seventy-four cloth buttons needed to be done up.

Sage held still while five pairs of hands fastened the buttons, and then she turned into her friends. Arms went around one another, and Sage sniffled in the middle of them all. She could, because she hadn't done her makeup yet.

Her hair, yes, but she could cry and not ruin anything.

"I love you guys," she said tearfully. "Thank you for being here with me today."

"Of course," Bea murmured, and it was like she spoke for the group.

"We're so happy for you," Bessie said. "You've—you're so amazing, Sage." She peered at her, her dark eyes earnest and kind. "I hardly recognize you right now. I didn't realize how unhappy you were."

"I didn't either," Sage said as the huddle broke up. She wiped her eyes and patted her hair. "Plus, I dyed my hair, so it looks amazing of course."

Stunned silence filled the bedroom, and Sage grinned as she looked around at her friends.

"I knew it," Lauren crowed, her smile filling her face. "Did you guys hear that? She dyes her hair!"

"Just for her wedding," Joy said. "Right, Sage?"

She shook her head. "No, I've been dying it for a while now. Whenever I want it to be more even, be shiny." She'd done her soon-to-be mother-in-law's last week too, and she'd never seen a person radiate so much shine after they'd been to the salon.

"You snake," Bea said with a smile and a gentle push to Sage's shoulder. She'd opted for a dress with sleeves, because she was over fifty and had upper arms to consider. She wanted her photos to be perfect, and if she cared about any part of her body looking good, it was her upper arms.

"You need to be outside in ten minutes," Cass said. "Get over here and let's get your makeup done."

"I'll lay out the jewelry," Lauren said.

"I still have the shoes." Bessie stayed out of the way as she played with Daisy, and ten minutes later, Sage finished putting on her earrings and she stepped into her shoes.

"So?" She spread her arms wide and did a full turn. "How do I look?"

"Like the most amazing bride in the world," Cass said. "He is so lucky."

Sage's heart and stomach did a synchronized somersault. "He loves me," she whispered. "I know he loves me."

"Yes," Bea said as she linked her arm through Sage's. "He sure does, so let's not keep him waiting."

TY STOOD OUTSIDE, THE MORNING NEARLY noonday sun beating down on him. Okay, only kind of. It beat down on the tent he stood under. Sage had wanted to get married in her backyard, on her little beach, and he wasn't going to tell her no.

He just wanted her to show up and say I do, so they could start the rest of their lives together. He didn't care when, or where, or how. He'd left all of that to Sage, and when she asked him for help, he gave it. He'd offered his opinion, and sometimes she took it and sometimes she didn't.

He shifted his feet in the rocky sand, his eyes glued to the back of her house. All of the guests had arrived. Almost every seat in the tent had been taken. The front row on his left held all of his groomsmen—his best friends: Grant, Harry, Blake, Scott, and Oliver.

The row on his right sat empty save his momma and daddy. The five chairs there were for Sage's Supper Club ladies. They were all walking her down the aisle today, and he twitched again in anticipation of them making their entrance.

He'd already led all three dogs down the aisle behind his groomsmen. He'd kissed his momma and hugged his daddy and passed the canines to Thelma. She sat in the second row with Sage's children, and it seemed like everyone was looking toward the house now.

His eye caught Grant's, and his friend's eyebrows went up. Ty shook his head. Sage was going to come out. He didn't need Grant to go check on her.

His pulse accelerated until he felt sure it would bust through a vein and skim across the water.

Then the door opened.

Cass stepped out first, and she wore a muted peach-colored dress. She moved to the side to let Bea out, then Joy, then Lauren, and then Bessie. The five of them all looked at the door, and finally, finally, his Sage emerged from her house.

A shade had been set up over the deck, and she had to cross it and go down the steps before she'd enter the tent. She waited, the most radiant smile on her face, as the crowd stood and turned toward her.

Only then did she link her arm with Bessie on the right and Lauren on the left. Then the six of them came forward, one delicate step in high heels at a time. By the time they reached him, and Bea said, "All right, Sage. Go fly with your eagle," he was ravenous for her.

Her dress had a scalloped bust, with sleeves that went almost to her elbows. The bodice was fitted, with plenty of sequin action happening. The skirt flared at her hips but didn't get huge like some dresses he'd seen. It fit Sage like a glove and accentuated all the best parts of her.

He took her into his arms, leaned down, and kissed her hello, the way he had many, many times before. How he hoped he'd be able to many, many more times. This was not a quick hello. Not a peck. He didn't want that in a month, or six months, or a year. He wanted to be as excited and passionate about seeing her then as he was now.

Only when one of his groomsmen cleared his throat did Ty remember he stood in front of a whole host of friends and family. He pulled back, heat squirreling up his neck and settling in his face. "Sorry," he murmured to her, to the pastor, to everyone.

They turned to the pastor, and he smiled at them. "There's nothing like being in love, is there?"

"No, sir," Sage murmured, and he looked at her. She didn't seem nervous or scared to be standing here, at his side, at an altar. She nudged him, and he turned back to the pastor, who'd started speaking.

Ty wanted to listen; he really did. He simply couldn't make himself focus, because the woman next to him smelled like peaches and cream, and her hand in his was silk, and he couldn't wait to be hers and for her to be his.

He perked up when the pastor said, "Sage Marie Grady, do you take this man, Tyler Benton Parker unto yourself, to be his lawfully wedded wife, to love and to cherish, as long as you both shall live?"

"I do," she said in a loud, clear, perfectly angelic voice.

He waited for his turn, his smile made of pure gold. And when he said, "I do," the first round of cheers went up from his front row of groomsmen. They caused such a ruckus that Ty could barely hear the pastor say, "I now pronounce you husband and wife."

But he did hear it, and he heard the cheers and whistles and applause of many others as he dipped closer to Sage and whispered, "I love you."

"I love you more," she whispered back, and then he kissed her, this woman who had just become his wife.

Want to know what the small Texas town of Sweet Water Falls was like for these Supper Club friends? I have TWO other series set here! **Keep reading for a sneak peek at CROSS COWBOY, the first book in a grumpy cowboy family saga romance series.**

Scan the QR code below to read CROSS COWBOY, the next book in the series.

Sneak Peek! Cross Cowboy
Chapter 1

~~~

Travis Cooper whistled through his teeth, his irritation spiking. "Get up!" he yelled, though the dairy cows he herded only lowed in return. Some of them gave him the stink-eye, though he supposed he'd started the somewhat volatile relationship with the cattle by muscling them around, telling them not to stop in doorways, and perhaps even calling them a name or two when they disobeyed.

People thought the big black-and-white dairy cows were "just so cute" on social media, but to Travis, they were nothing but trouble. They loved to break down fences to get to the grasses and other tasty vittles in fields they weren't supposed to be in. They made a huge mess of their pastures, day in and day out. Diseases spread like wildfire, and they never waited nicely in line for their turn to be milked.

"Come on, Bertha," he said, shoving his shoulder against one of the huge beasts. Every dairy cow was named Bertha to Travis, and he actually smiled at his private joke. "To the right, girl," he said, digging in with his boots and *pushing*. See? Stubborn things, cows were.

He got Bertha #1 in the chute, and by some miracle, the girls after her followed suit—at least for a few cows. He and the veterinarian had been playing this game of chutes and udders for four days, and Travis was so done with it.

But the cows had to be checked every so often, and it was up to Travis to get that job done around Sweet Water Falls Farm. His older brother, Lee, took care of so many other things that Travis had gladly accepted the health of the herd as his responsibility. He just wished it came with less mud and less lowing.

Sometimes his ears heard the sound cows made when he was all alone, and that noise followed him into his dreams too.

He finally got the last Bertha into the chute, and she lumbered along until she reached Finley Rappont, the veterinarian who came out to the farm to check eyes, ears, tongues, and udders. He made a report for Travis, though he'd have separated any cows that had a problem.

Today, there were none, and Travis thanked his lucky stars above for that. Five or six of their newest milkers had shown sores, and Finn had pulled them. That hadn't been a good day for Travis, and the conversation around the family dinner table at the farmhouse had contained a lot of rolled eyes and pointed questions.

The energy between Travis and his brothers always ran high, and he blamed all the redheaded genes in the family. Lee could go from grinning to gunning in less time than it took to breathe, and the worst part was that Travis never knew what would set him off.

Truth be told, he never really knew what would set himself off either. Sometimes, he just couldn't carry one more thing, and something simple like a broken fence—something he'd dealt with countless times over the years he'd worked the farm—would irritate him to the point of snapping.

Not that it really mattered. He didn't rant to anyone but Daddy, Lee, or Will. He treated his cowboys well. He didn't have a girlfriend to speak of, and even when he did, those relationships barely made it out of the dugout. He might get to first base, but he might not, as he hadn't had a girlfriend who'd lasted longer than two months in at least a decade.

"Lookin' good?" he asked Finn.

"Yeah, today was easy." He glanced up from his clipboard, which had a tablet attached to it. He tapped and swiped, and then he added, "All sent. You'll get the report in your email."

"Thanks." Travis shook his hand, and they started toward the milkshed, where the small, dirt parking lot held their trucks. He had no idea what Finn got to go do now, but Travis had to get over a thousand cows into and then out of milking stalls in the next couple of hours. The work at Cooper & Company, the milking side of their family farm, could consume a man, as Travis had seen with his very own eyes.

Lee had been married and divorced, and while his ex-wife had never said their marriage had dissolved because of

Lee's dedication to bottles, Berthas, and milk. Travis had a suspicion it did. All of the women he'd dated over the years had said some form of the same thing to Travis—he worked too much. He was never available when they wanted to go to dinner. Sometimes he had to text during their dates.

Blah, blah, *blah*. He'd heard it all, and he'd decided Lee had things figured out now—he didn't date at all, ever. After Travis's last attempt at a relationship had ended after only a few dates, he'd put himself on a female-free diet too.

He bid farewell to Finn and turned to enter the milkshed, where the brothers kept the administrative office for Cooper & Co. The moment he did, shouting met his ears. Oh, boy. Lee wasn't happy this morning.

"...that just won't work," he said.

"Why are you yelling at me?" Will fired back, and he was definitely the grumpiest of the trio of brothers. "I *know* it won't work. That's why I came to talk to you about it."

Travis strode the few steps to the office and found Lee sitting at the desk while Will hovered near the window. There were no clenched fists or red faces. The brothers just had loud voices, growly barks, and short fuses.

"What won't work?" he asked, and both Lee and Will looked at him. Will was the lightest of the gingers, with almost blond hair, and eyes between blue and green. He was the middle brother, and his eyes definitely came half from Mama and half from Daddy. When he grew out his beard, the red really came in then.

Lee was the darkest of the brothers, in attitude and physical appearance. His hair shone like red gold, a deep auburn that matched their oldest sister's. Cherry didn't live on the farm, but she and Lee could've been twins with their auburn hair. His green-black eyes only glinted with darkness when he was angry, as he was right now.

Travis sat somewhere in the middle of the two of them, with tons of the typical red hair people pictured when someone said, "he's the redhead." His eyes came straight from Mama, as did his hair, and they glinted like emeralds when he laughed. Or so Mama said.

He was the youngest son, and he was very close to his mother. He didn't deny it when everyone in the family told him he was a mama's boy. He was, and he wasn't embarrassed about it.

Lee stood. "What are you doing?"

"Milking three," Travis said, glancing at Will. "Why?"

"We've got a shipment of essential parts coming for the threshers," he said. "And Leonard can't get them to us until next week."

Travis didn't work much on the agriculture side of the farm, but he knew so much of the nutrition of the dairy cows relied on the grain they grew over there. "That won't work," Travis said. "Why can't he deliver it?"

"I don't know," Lee said, sighing as he sat back down, that permanent frown etched between his eyebrows. "Will?"

"He's got one guy who broke his leg or something, and another one quit. Bottom line, he's behind on deliveries, and we're so far out that he won't come until Wednesday."

Lee shuffled some papers. "I could maybe send Chris."

ELANA JOHNSON

"Yeah, and I'll hear about it for months," Will said. "He'll want every Sunday off to make a trip to town."

"It's a trip to town," Travis said, not getting the problem. "We'll just go pick up the parts ourselves." Sure, the farm sat about thirty minutes from the town of Sweet Water Falls, but it was a half-hour, not a half-day. They went once a month for groceries and to run errands, and Travis himself definitely left the farm more than his brothers. He could go. In fact, an afternoon off the ranch suddenly held great possibilities for him.

"If we send Brad, we won't see him until evening," Lee mused.

"I'll go," Travis said, looking from Lee to Will. "Send Brad over to help with the milking, and I'll go right now." He dug in his pocket for his truck keys.

Lee looked up from his papers. "While you're there, you'll have to load up the fertilizer too."

Travis almost backed out. No wonder they weren't happy about not getting the delivery. No one wanted to load up the fertilizer, as they bought it from the farm supply store, and it was all-natural and organic. That made their milk organic, which meant they could make more money for the dairy products. It also came with a certain...smell.

"So I can't drive my own truck," Travis said.

"You'd take the dump truck." Lee looked up, his eyes filled with questions.

Travis didn't really want to drive the dump truck. It had no radio, and while he didn't usually mind the silence, right

378

now, it had a way of screaming the truth at him. And the truth hurt at the moment.

"Please?" Will asked. "If you go, I'll take care of all the milking today and tomorrow."

"Tomorrow too?" Travis couldn't remember the last time he'd had a day off. They all paid for it when men took full days off on the farm.

"Yes," Will said. "We need those parts, and the fertilizer is just on the way."

Travis didn't really need to think too hard about it. He'd get off the farm today and he'd get to sleep in tomorrow. "Fine," he said, folding his arms. "I'll go."

Will grinned, his face lighting up from within. "Thanks, Trav." He looked at Lee. "Let's call Leonard right now."

"I'll get the receipt printed for the fertilizer too," Lee said. "Thanks, Travis. This is really going to help us."

"We're okay for me to be gone for the rest of today and tomorrow?" he asked.

Lee frowned again. "We'll see about tomorrow. We're on the last harvest here, Trav."

"As if I didn't know," Travis said sarcastically, smiling at his older brother. Lee didn't return the gesture, and Travis wondered what it would take to get him to loosen up a little. Probably a miracle from the Lord above.

From there, things happened quickly, and the next thing he knew, he climbed into the dump truck and started her moving down the dirt road from the equipment shed to the highway. Everything bounced in the old truck, and Travis had loved riding in it as a child. He hadn't had the opportunity very often, but when he did, it was just him and Daddy. He got to go to town with Daddy, and they always got ice cream in Sweet Water Falls before they returned to the farm.

They were good times, and Travis felt some of the tension he carried everywhere with him finally start to seep away.

The drive to town passed in a blink, and Travis wasn't even sure what he'd thought about. He pulled around to the back of the farm supply store, and he showed the attendant there his receipt for the fertilizer.

The man handed Travis a pair of gloves and put on a pair too. Travis pulled around to the fertilizer bin, the scent of it permeating the inside of the dump truck already. It had been mighty hot in Texas lately.

"Oh, boy," Travis said, noting the attendant had put a bandana around his nose and mouth. He handed Travis a shovel, and they faced the dark brown stuff spilling from the bin. Neither of them moved.

"Let's dig in," Travis finally said. "It's not going to shovel itself." He took the first shovel full, and the other man got to work too. Dislodging the fertilizer only made the smell intensify, and it was impossible to stay clean. Travis swore the fertilizer—which contained manure and bat guano that had been baking in the sun—covered him from head to toe by the time they got the truck filled.

"Thanks," he said to the attendant, who waved to him as he pulled back up to the loading dock. Someone brought out the mechanical parts they needed, and Travis signed the invoice and accepted the receipt.

It had a flyer stapled to it, announcing the Fall Ball, which the farm supply store was sponsoring that year. They often sponsored events and happenings around the town of Sweet Water Falls. Looking at the cartoon rendition of a man and a woman, both dressed in their finest clothes, dancing under the stars, Travis's heart bumped out a couple of short, stilted beats.

He wanted to go to this ball. He loved dancing, and he hadn't been in a while.

"Nope," he told himself, tossing the invoice and attached flyer onto the seat beside him. "That would not be a female-free date." Plus, he probably didn't have time anyway.

He backed away from the dock and got the truck moving toward the exit. He slowed as a large F-350 appeared, slowing to obviously turn into the back lot behind the farm supply store. The truck had a sleek, sophisticated logo on the side that said *Sweetspot*, with the silhouette of a hiker hanging off the long end of the P.

His heart tapped strangely again, because he knew this company. And he knew the woman behind the big truck now turning toward him. Shayla Nelson.

He'd picked her up on the side of the road a few months ago, and he hadn't exactly been nice to her. His mouth had a way of running away from him, and he only seemed to be able to realize it after the fact.

She made the left turn, but he hadn't stopped the truck, and he'd crowded the entrance. When she realized it, he clearly saw the displeasure on her face. Her disgusted and frustrated look screamed at him through two windshields, but he couldn't move.

She really was pretty, and his mind started thinking about what Shayla Nelson would look like in a ball gown... all that dark hair piled on her head in some elegant updo...

She honked her horn and gestured for him to back up, and Travis jumped into action to do just that. He eased the truck backward, giving her room to get into the lot, which she did.

His phone chimed, and he pushed on the brake to check it, as that was Daddy's specific sound. *Lee says you're in town. Can you stop and get Mama's medicine at the pharmacy?*

Sure thing, Travis said, his heart heavy in his chest now. He thought of his mother and the constant medications she needed. He pressed his eyes closed and said a prayer for her health, and that if she had to suffer, maybe the Lord could just take her home already.

His eyes jerked open when someone rapped on his window with sharp knuckles.

He flinched away from the sound, his gaze locking onto Shayla's through the glass to his left. Adrenaline ran from his toes to his scalp in half a second, and his heart dropped to his stomach, rebounding back to its rightful spot a moment later.

He reached to roll down his window. "What the devil are you doing? You scared me."

She'd climbed right up on the runners of the dump truck, and she didn't look happy. Snaps, crackles, and pops filled the air between them, and Travis wondered if he was the only one who could feel them.

"What the devil am *I* doing? You're blocking everyone coming in and out of the parking lot." Her eyes narrowed, and she pinched her fingers over her nose. "And you stink."

He looked in his rearview mirror, and sure enough, three or four other people waited behind him so they could get out too.

"I'll move," he said, releasing the brake pedal where his foot sat. The truck started backward, and Shayla yelped.

"I'm on the truck," she said. "Stop. Stop it!"

He jammed on the brake again, and Shayla grunted and groaned as if he'd been going fifty miles per hour and had slammed on the brakes. She glared at him. "My goodness, Travis Cooper. What is wrong with you?" She peered at him as if she was really trying to figure him out. Could she feel that electricity now zinging from the ends of his fingertips? Or was that all him?

"Well, get off the runner," he said, not looking away from her. "I need to move."

Sneak Peek! Cross Cowboy Chapter 2

S hayla Nelson thanked every star in the universe that she had a good grip on the metal arms holding the rearview mirror out to the side of Travis Cooper's stinky dump truck. The man himself smelled like he'd rolled in manure and then old, wet grass. But those eyes...

She drew in a breath and hopped to the ground, repeating her prayer of thanksgiving for the trail boots she wore. She'd just introduced these boots into the market, and they were selling really well. Better than even she'd expected, despite the marketing money she'd put behind their launch.

Travis's truck groaned and the brakes released as he put the behemoth in park. At least he'd moved it out of the way, and Shayla turned as a truck towing a horse trailer with three equines in the back of it edged around her and the truck. She had to press pretty close to the big vehicle, and that only made everything smell worse than before.

The stunningly handsome cowboy got out of the truck, and Shayla tried not to scan him from those delicious cowboy boots up to that delectable cowboy hat. Tried, and failed.

Wow, he was good-looking. And boy, did he know it, if the dark glint in his eye said anything. He lasered that gaze on her and said, "Sorry about that."

Surprise filled her from head to toe, rendering her mute. He wore a baby blue T-shirt with the outline of Texas on it in faded white, with big, blocky letters through the state that said STRONG.

Mm hm, he was Texas strong, if the way his shirtsleeves clung to his biceps was any indication. She'd found him downright mouthwatering a few months ago when he'd happened past her on the highway out by his farm. He'd been right gentlemanly by helping her with Sweetie, her dog, and giving her a ride all the way back to town.

It was just the conversation that had been terrible. He'd accused her of stealing Sweetspot from her former partner, Kylie, which so wasn't true. Shayla pushed against the memories of what had really happened between her and her once-best friend. They still caused bitterness to surge in her throat and her stomach to tighten.

She hadn't explained anything to Travis, and while she'd thought she'd like to get his number when he'd first picked her up, that thought had fled pretty fast. Now, though, faced with him in the blazing hot September sun, with those long legs clad in jeans... She could admit she'd like the man's phone number, if only to text him all the funny horse videos she saw on her social media.

He owns a dairy farm, she told herself as another truck went past them and left the parking lot. *And you should say something instead of staring at him silently.*

"Thank you," she said, not even sure what she was thanking him for.

His brow furrowed in an adorably sexy way, and he was obviously wondering the same thing. "For what?" he asked, his voice stuck somewhere in the back of his throat.

She waved toward the pickup going by them now. "For moving." She wanted to press her eyes closed and disappear. Teleporting to another location sounded amazing about now, but when she opened her eyes again, she still stood six feet from Travis Cooper. Her heart still boomed strangely in her chest when she thought about holding his hand. Her mind still went a bit blank when talking to him.

"It was like you didn't know there were other people in the world," she said. "I realize you probably don't get off the farm much, but still."

"You're right," he said, folding his arms and cocking a hip, which was a fairly challenging stance. "I don't get off the farm much." He didn't say why he'd been taking up the whole driveway, and Shayla wasn't going to ask. She just needed to get her feed and get back to the showroom.

"The traffic is cleared out," she said.

"You don't work here," he said, glancing toward the farm supply store. "In fact, what are you doing here?" He looked at her again, his eyes traveling down the length of her body.

Shayla felt every inch of that look, and she was glad she'd put on the lightweight trail shorts to go with her new boots. She ran the trails in the morning, and she'd simply put on a fresh pair of shorts and the matching tank once she'd gotten to the showroom floor. She had the complete trail running package on that day, and the way Travis licked his lips made a current run through her veins.

"I don't have to tell you why I'm at the farm supply store," she said dryly, glad her wit had returned. "It's none of your business." She turned away from him to go get her wallet and then the chicken feed she needed for her hens. Everyone in Sweet Water Falls had chickens now, as it was the trendy thing to do. Travis would likely make fun of her for it, and she really didn't need the cowboy's attitude today.

Shayla bore the weight of Travis's gaze on her back as she walked away from him, and she checked discreetly over her shoulder as she opened her truck door. Yes, he was still watching her, that frown frozen between his eyes. She collected her wallet and went in the back door of the supply store, running through ways she could get his number.

You don't want his number, she told herself as she grabbed a flatbed cart and started for the outdoor animals section. A shade had been erected over this part of the store, as it was outside, and she found the chicken feed without incident. Her hens seemed to be going through quite a lot of it, and she found someone wearing the bright green vest, and asked them about it.

"They should be getting out too," the man said. "To root for bugs and the like. Do you let them out into the yard?"

"Well, sort of," Shayla said, thinking of her coop. "I don't have a farm or anything. They're backyard hens."

The man smiled, and it felt a little placating to Shayla. "They still need to be out in the grass or weeds. A garden even."

"I've got a garden," she said, brightening. "I can put them in that."

"Try that," he said. "Then they won't eat as much feed. You'll probably get better egg production too."

"Thanks," she said. She paid for the feed, tossed the flyer about the Fall Ball into the trashcan, and drew a deep breath as she headed toward the exit. Her breath whooshed out of her body the moment she stepped into the parking lot.

Travis's dump truck was gone. That was that, though her heart wailed at her to make *that* into something else.

She lowered the tailgate of her truck—a huge, white vehicle she'd bought with business money since she hauled so many boxes to and from festivals and shows. Not only that, but she spent as much time outdoors as she possibly could, and she loved throwing a tent and a backpack in the bed of the truck and heading into the wilds of Texas.

She returned the flatbed cart to the store and hurried back to the truck. One couldn't abide this heat for long, and she muttered, "It would be nice if it could cool off a little," under her breath.

She reached for her door handle at the same time she saw

the paper stuck to her window. Her hand froze halfway there, as the handwriting looked sloppy and like it had been hastily scrawled.

Did you get a receipt?

She read the sentence again, not sure she'd gotten it right the first time. "What?" she asked herself. Below that nonsensical question, he'd written *Trav*—and his phone number.

Shayla pulled the note from the window, the edge of it ripping from where it had been stuck between the window and the metal on the truck. She sucked in a breath as the bottom of the eight on the last digit of his phone number tore off, quickly glancing around to see if anyone had seen or heard her.

Everyone seemed to be going about their business as usual, and Shayla told herself she better do the same. She'd left her assistant, Elaine, and her junior partner, Jadyn, alone in the showroom, and it could be a lot to handle if more than a few customers came in.

Shayla told herself that they didn't get extremely busy in the afternoon on Wednesdays, and she didn't go a mile over the speed limit on the way back to the showroom. She needed the extra space and time to think about Travis's note. Or rather, *Trav's* note.

"Trav," she said, rolling the single-syllable name around in her mouth. "Sure, Trav," she added. "I'd love to go out with you. Have you been to The Bluebell Café?" Of course he wouldn't have been there. It was total frou-frou food, and a man with muscles like that ate red meat for every meal. Probably *raw* red meat.

She made the turn to get on Main Street, as Sweetspot had just secured a prime, downtown location for their new showroom. Their foot traffic had increased over three hundred percent since they'd moved into the light, airy storefront three weeks ago. All the spots out front had cars in them, and Shayla navigated around to the back.

The feed could stay in the truck, and she leapt from it and jogged inside to make sure Elaine and Jadyn were okay. Several people milled about in the store, and sure enough, when Elaine turned and saw her, the entire story spilled from her eyes. She didn't have to say a word, because Shayla had been working with her long enough to communicate telepathically.

The blonde nodded toward a couple perusing the lightweight jackets, and Shayla put on her game face. "Can I help you two find something?" she asked, adopting her professional voice. She could gush about Trav later and ask Jadyn and Elaine how she was supposed to answer such a weird question.

Right now, she wanted to sell one of these jackets, and as she looked from the man to the woman, she thought she could probably get two sales out of this couple.

SHAYLA PEERED AT THE COMPUTER SCREEN, wondering when things had become so hard to see. She squinted at the comment on social media, trying to make sense of it so she could answer it. She personally manned their social media accounts, posting pictures of herself using their equipment, or collecting photos from her customers that she then reposted or shared to their main account.

Sweetspot had quite the following, and their online sales had ticked up another five percent last quarter.

Her eyes hurt, and she answered the question and then leaned away from the computer, pressing her palms to her eye sockets. Maybe she needed glasses, but they were a pain in the neck. She didn't want to deal with contact lenses while camping, or glasses sliding down her nose while rock-climbing. Fine, she wasn't that into rock-climbing, but she did like hiking, picnicking, hammocking, and camping. Her favorite part was a campfire, with a tin foil dinner or a charred hot dog, cooked right over hot coals.

"Shayla," Elaine said, and Shayla opened her eyes. Elaine blurred along the edges, but that was because of the bright, flashing lights in Shayla's vision.

"Is it time?" She got to her feet. Her hours in the office could pass with the snap of a finger, and she always had something more to do.

Elaine approached with a couple of folders. "The new accounts for Wiseman's and Mountain Top Outfitters."

"Oh, great," Shayla said, taking the folders and putting them on her desk. Elaine did all the paperwork. She made sure all the contracts got signed. She made sure payments got sent on time and that their accounts payable kept the company thriving. She'd started at Sweetspot as an accountant, but she oversaw that entire department now. They had another woman running all the money in the company, and

Shayla met with her team every other week to make sure everyone was happy, that things were operating the way they should be, and that the communication stayed open.

If they'd have done that from the beginning, maybe Kylie would still be with them. Maybe Shayla wouldn't have such a hollow feeling every time she thought of the woman she'd known since childhood—and that she hadn't spoken to in over four years now.

"We have a conference call with Alexander Huffman on Monday at seven-thirty in the morning."

"My goodness," Shayla said, locking eyes with Elaine. She had bright blue eyes to go with her blonde hair, and Shayla couldn't remember a time when she'd seen her assistant wear anything but skirts, blouses, and heels. While Shayla opted to wear the clothing they sold, Elaine was a professional through and through. "Why so early?"

"He's in London," Elaine said. "It'll be two-thirty for him there, and it was the only slot he had."

"All right." Shayla pulled out her phone and made an alarm for the call. "Here? Or can I do it from home?"

"We can all call in from home, if you'd like," Elaine said, clicking her pen into operation mode. That *click-click* triggered something in Shayla, because it was the sound of Elaine about to get stuff done. "Just let me know, so I can set up the online meeting."

"Let's do it from home," Shayla said. "Then I won't have to be showered and here so early." By that time, she'd barely be back from running.

"Okay." Elaine made a note on the clipboard she carried.

As she finished up, she cocked her head, which meant their saleswoman was likely talking to her.

She reached up and pressed the button on the wire coming down from her ear. "I'll let her know." She looked at Shayla. "You've got a customer asking specifically for you."

Time to do business. Shayla felt her mask sliding into place, and she actually cracked her neck left and right, as if she were going into a battle. Elaine turned and left the office, with Shayla right behind her.

They went down the hall together, Elaine telling her about the supplier meeting on Tuesday, and the price comparison sheet she'd put together for the nylon they needed to make their tents. Their agreement was expiring soon, and Shayla needed to lock in a price for the next couple of years. But the prices had gone up over fifty percent, and since she ordered so much, she wanted a better deal than that.

In truth, she'd sign the contract with the higher prices, because finding a new nylon supplier would be a nightmare. Her customers expected a certain quality of product, and she actually had all of the tents Sweetspot sold custom sewn. She didn't skimp on anything, which was why Sweetspot had grown so fast and still did so well.

"I'll be right there." Elaine paused and turned back the way they'd come. "There's a delivery coming to the warehouse," she said. "I want to see if it's those sweat bands."

"I hope so," Shayla said with a smile. "You've been sweating about those for a week." She giggled at her own lame joke, glad when Elaine did too.

The two women parted, and Shayla went out into the showroom, wondering who was asking about her. She'd sold outdoor equipment to a lot of people—companies, suppliers, retail stores, as well as the common man taking a biking trip with his family.

She glanced around, the world narrowing to a single man standing in the camping section—Travis Cooper.

"Campers unite," Shayla murmured as a form of swearing. The man stood out like a sore thumb in the store, because he was the only one wearing a cowboy hat.

She'd never texted or called him to answer his question. In truth, she hadn't known how. Every time she'd thought about it, she just felt stupid texting him a yes or no answer. Not to mention the last couple of days had been extraordinarily busy. She hadn't forgotten about Travis Cooper. Such a thing seemed impossible, and he lifted his head as if he could feel her watching him.

Their eyes met, and lightning cracked right through the roof. He grinned at her and walked toward her, every ounce of confidence in the world in those shoulders.

"Hey," he said.

"What are you doing here?" she asked.

"Thinkin' about goin' camping," he said, indicating the gear on the shelves.

She blinked, her long eyelashes almost sticking together, and she realized she'd been pressing her palms to her eyes. Had she mashed her false eyelashes? Surely Elaine would've told her if she had.

Still, she reached up and brushed her fingertips along her lashes. "Why does that sound so false?" she asked.

Travis chuckled, and that sound could make a woman swoon. "Guilty, I suppose." He ducked his head, barely lifting it enough to peer up at her from underneath the brim of that big, brown hat. "I was wondering if you got my note. The one I left on your truck at the farm supply store a few days ago?"

Shayla's chest crackled with heat and sparks. "Yeah," she said slowly. "It was confusing."

His expression darkened as he ticked his head up even more. "It was?"

"Did I get a receipt? I don't get it. Why did you want to know that?" She had programmed his number in her phone, but she hadn't used it. Yet.

"Did you get one?"

"Yes," she said.

"It had that flyer for the Fall Ball on it," he said, immediately clearing his throat.

Shayla could only stare at him. "Okay."

Travis laughed lightly, though his feet shifted along the painted concrete floor. "Gonna make me work for it, I see."

"Work for what?" she asked, genuinely confused.

His face turned blank, and Shayla glanced around to see if anyone was watching them. Didn't seem to be. Then Travis blinked, and that familiar fire entered those pretty, emerald-green eyes.

"I was wondering if maybe you'd like to go with me," he said, lowering his chin again. "To the Fall Ball."

Shayla's mouth dropped open, and she quickly snapped it shut. Her brain whirred, taking a long time to come to a three-letter or a two-letter answer. In fact, she still hadn't landed on what to say, and the seconds ticked by, each one like a silent bomb landing in only her ears.

Scan the QR code below to read CROSS COWBOY, the next book in the series.

Books in the Hilton Head Romance series

The Love List (Hilton Head Romance, Book 1): Bea turns to her lists when things get confusing and her love list morphs once again... Can she add *fall in love at age 45* to the list and check it off?

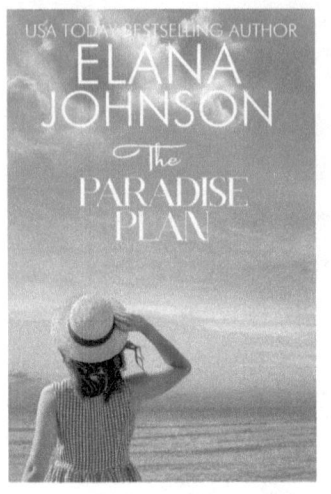

The Paradise Plan (Hilton Head Romance, Book 2): When Harrison keeps showing up unannounced at her construction site, sometimes with her favorite pastries, Cass starts to wonder if she should add him to her daily routine... If she does, will her perfectly laid out plans fall short of paradise? Or could she find her new life *and* a new love, all without any plans at all?

The Seaside Strategy (Hilton Head Romance, Book 3): Lauren doesn't want to work for Blake, especially not in strategic investments. She's had enough of the high-profile, corporate life. Can she strategically insert herself into Blake's life without compromising her seaside strategy and finally get what she really wants...love and a lasting relationship?

The Beach Blueprint (Hilton Head Romance, Book 4): Joy Bartlett needs a blueprint before she takes a single step in any direction. She loves seeing what she's getting into before committing, and moving 1200 miles from Texas to South Carolina just because half of her Supper Club has doesn't mean she's going to start packing boxes. Can she figure out how to arrange all of the pieces in her life in a way that makes sense? Or will she find herself cut off from everyone who's ever been important to her?

The Tropical Ticket (Hilton Head Romance, Book 5): Bessie Clifton adores baking. With her daughter Wynona by her side, she's turned her passion for the perfect loaf of bread into a dream for a bakery. They move to Hilton Head Island and work to get their shop open with the help of Bessie's five best friends.

It's not just a relocation.

It's a reinvention.

Will Bessie's journey to self-discovery lead her to the love she's always craved?

The Waterfront Way (Hilton Head Romance, Book 6): Sage Grady is a master of transformation. She's a seasoned hairstylist who's perfected the art of change, one cut and color at a time. Yet, her own life has started to feel somewhat monotonous, almost like she's stuck in someone else's style–and she needs to shake things up.

It's not a mid-life crisis.

It's a new way of thinking, of living.

Will she find that the path to true love doesn't always follow the path most trod, but might just be discovered through...the waterfront way?

Books in the Sweet Water Falls Farm Romance series

Cross Cowboy, Book 1: He's been accused of being far too blunt. Like that time he accused her of stealing her company from her best friend... Can Travis and Shayla overcome their differences and find a happily-ever-after together?

Grumpy Cowboy

Grumpy Cowboy, Book 2: He can find the negative in any situation. Like that time he got upset with the woman who brought him a free chocolate-and-caramel-covered apple because it had melted in his truck... Can William and Gretchen start over and make a healthy relationship after it's started to wilt?

Surly Cowboy, Book 3: He's got a reputation to uphold and he's not all that amused the way regular people are. Like that time he stood there straight-faced and silent while every-one else in the audience cheered and clapped for that educational demo... Can Lee and Rosalie let bygones be bygones and make a family filled with joy?

Salty Cowboy, Book 4: The last Cooper sibling is looking for love...she just wishes it wouldn't be in her hometown, or with the saltiest cowboy on the planet. But something about Jed Forrester has Cherry all a-flutter, and he'll be darned if he's going to let her get away. But Jed may have met his match when it comes to his quick tongue and salty attitude...

About Elana

Elana Johnson is the USA Today bestselling and Kindle All-Star author of dozens of clean and wholesome contemporary romance novels. She lives in Utah, where she mothers two fur babies, works with her husband full-time, and eats a lot of veggies while writing. Find her on her website at feelgoodfictionbooks.com.